It was there one chance to escape, but there could be a traitor in their midst...

"That's the Churn," Aya said. "The turbines that churn the water to make power. They're very dangerous and well-guarded. The water and the steep cliffs along the river are the most dangerous for us, though. That's why they call it No Man's Land because few people have survived out there. If you fall off the cliffs and into the water—"

"I know the path," said a voice behind them in the depths of the stairwell. "If you will follow me, I will lead you."

They all turned, but saw nothing on the dark stairs.

"Who said that?" demanded Aya. "Show yourself!"

Slowly, a shadowy form crossed the shaft of light coming from a crack in the door. Everyone shrank away as it passed down the stairs, clinging to the rail for support.

"You poor creature," Aya said. "How long have you lived in the Flyover?"

The nearly translucent form shook his head. "I've lost track of time. Months, no, years. Now, let me lead the way past the Churn and to the bridge. If I perish, at least it will be outside this awful place."

"We are going to Trezarium," said Riga. "Can you show us the way? We will share what little nutrition we have with you if you will."

"Surely," the form replied. "But I ask nothing. Keep the nutrition for the young ones. I am beyond that."

"We'll see about that," said Aya firmly. "Now, open the door, Riga, and let us smell the fresh air."

Riga pulled the heavy door back and everyone gasped. The roar from the Churn became so intense, little Annabeth and the droll child put their fingers in their ears. Everyone had the same thought—somewhere be-yond the clouds of steam and spray blocking their view was No Man's Land and, if they survived that, freedom.

The form plunged forward into the clouds and they followed, holding each other's hands. Riga stowed his lazorizer weapon in its sling on his back and grasped Miri's hand. She, in turn, held Qin's hand, and Blu carried Annabeth and the droll. Aya, with surprising energy, and, as if she knew the way, walked briskly behind their dark leader.

None of them gave another thought to Borg Guard 80047.

Aya's family has to move. The Triumvirate have picked up their sound and, even now, are sending the Borgs on patrol, sweeping the sewers for signs of anyone breathing the oxygen so vital to human survival. One by one, Aya has rescued a collection of human children from the Re-cycling Dumpster, as well as a mutant reject and an old robot named Blu. Raising them in the old sewers below Megacity on cabbage, water cress, fish, and frogs, she preserves the history of human kind by telling them sto-ries about The Time Before when their kind ruled the earth.

But now, they must move like rats through the sewers under the city to the fabled place called Trezarium where they can see the sky and breathe the air. Aya remembers the way back from her parents who survived the purge, only to be recycled by the Triumvirate. Those tales kept her company when she was orphaned, warm through cold nights, and fed her when she was hungry. Now she would have this small band of wanderers do the same, salvaging the history of humans.

KUDOS for *Flight to Trezarium*

In *Flight to Trezarium* by Trisha O'Keefe, a group of refugees, living in the sewers of the city in some distant future, try to escape and make it to Trezarium, a wilderness outside the influence of the "powers that be." Their adventure and the civil war that follows is a fascinating journey. Aya and her small family of three young human girls, a young human boy, a rejected mutant, and an antique robot abandon their meager existence in the sewers for the unknown outside of the city. But what if Trezarium is only a myth, as Aya fears, and there is no refuge? An intriguing adventure, filled with wonderful and zany characters, fantastic creatures, and a well-thought-out plot make this a delightful read. I highly recommend it. ~ *Taylor Jones, The Review Team of Taylor Jones & Regan Murphy*

Flight to Trezarium by Trisha O'Keefe is the story of political corruption in a city were humans are considered the dregs of society and scheduled for termination. Mutants, robots, and cyborgs are the upper echelon in a city that keeps its citizens peaceful by addicting them to drugs and "Happy Pills." In this dystopic landscape, a group of humans, with one rejected mutant and an antique robot, survive in the sewers. All they want is for their little family to be left in peace, but if the borg guards catch them, they will be sent to the Dumpster and "recycled." So they flee the city and head for the wilderness of Trezarium where they can live free. Or can they? *Flight to Trezarium* is a bit zany, clever, and fun, while still being a fast-paced page-turner. If you like fun interesting books you can't put down, you'll love this one. ~ *Regan Murphy, The Review Team of Taylor Jones & Regan Murphy*

Trisha O'Keefe

A Black Opal Books Publication

GENRE: SCIENCE FICTION/THRILLER/DARK FANTASY

This is a work of fiction. Names, places, characters and incidents are either the product of the author's imagination or are used fictitiously, and any resemblance to any actual persons, living or dead, businesses, organizations, events or locales is entirely coincidental. All trademarks, service marks, registered trademarks, and registered service marks are the property of their respective owners and are used herein for identification purposes only. The publisher does not have any control over or assume any responsibility for author or third-party websites or their contents.

FLIGHT TO TREZARIUM
Copyright © 2017 by Trisha O'Keefe
Cover Design by Jackson Cover Designs
All cover art copyright © 2017
All Rights Reserved
Print ISBN: 978-1-626947-97-9

First Publication: NOVEMBER 2017

All rights reserved under the International and Pan-American Copyright Conventions. No part of this book may be reproduced or transmitted in any form or by any means, electronic or mechanical, including photocopying, recording, or by any information storage and retrieval system, without permission in writing from the publisher.

WARNING: The unauthorized reproduction or distribution of this copyrighted work is illegal. Criminal copyright infringement, including infringement without monetary gain, is investigated by the FBI and is punishable by up to 5 years in federal prison and a fine of $250,000. Anyone pirating our ebooks will be prosecuted to the fullest extent of the law and may be liable for each individual download resulting therefrom.

ABOUT THE PRINT VERSION: If you purchased a print version of this book without a cover, you should be aware that the book is stolen property. It was reported as "unsold and destroyed" to the publisher, and neither the author nor the publisher has received any payment for this "stripped book."

IF YOU FIND AN EBOOK OR PRINT VERSION OF THIS BOOK BEING SOLD OR SHARED ILLEGALLY, PLEASE REPORT IT TO: lpn@blackopalbooks.com

Published by Black Opal Books **http://www.blackopalbooks.com**

DEDICATION

To my mother, Jeanne.
Her love and devotion will never be forgotten.

PROLOGUE

THE ESCAPE

In the years following the Lost Times, humans had nearly erased their own species from Planet Earth. A new and powerful society emerged from the darkness that engulfed the world. It was called The Triumvirate.

❧❦☙

After humans began to count time once again, they found that the mutants—those who were crossed with another species—outnumbered them almost two to one. The humans thought this was because the mutants had survived by any means possible the calamity that had almost erased them and their entire civilization from Earth. The mutants, on the other hand, thought their survival was due to their superior traits. They blamed the humans for nearly destroying the planet and considered them an inferior race.

In spite of their differences, both races—mutants and humans—began to reconstruct the skeleton of civilization. They agreed to establish their capitol city on the ruins of a once sprawling metropolis. The new capitol

Megacity was to be ruled by a high council or ubercouncil, made up of representatives of each group. On the human side, there were the Noble Warriors—clans with a well-established system of government. Also representing the human side were the scientists, and the artists who hoped to bring human traditions and culture back to the new society.

On the mutants' side, there were various drummans, who had mechanical extensions; droids; cyborgs; and chimeras—animals with human qualities.

Since every great civilization has its shady side, that was represented by the Grays. Like wolves, the legendary animal they were named after, the Grays lurked at the fringes of civilization. They made a profit selling contraband—scarce commodities like food, fuel, and human slaves which they kidnapped and sold to the mutants. They also did a brisk business in making imitation Happy Pills and Swaug, a drink that made everything beautiful—except work. Since the Grays were involved in everything that was illegal, they might as well be included in any policy decisions.

The ubercouncil directed the policies of the Triumvirate, the executive branch of the government. It was composed of one representative from each group, except the Grays. As time went on, though, humans were considered greatly inferior to those mutants who were more than seventy-five- per cent Other species—drummans, droids, cyborgs, and pure robots. Humans without robotic adaptations were not only considered physically inferior, but disloyal as well, always ready to rebel at the slightest provocation.

At a secret meeting. the mutants decided to engineer that provocation. "If they want to rebel, let us give them ample cause to start a war. That will finish the Neanderthals once and for all." That was Ubercouncilman Riksbury. He was a drumman, a mutant with wheels for legs. A nasty sort, mean as a snake. Of course, I have never seen a snake, but legend has it they have a reputation for being mean.

Who am I? Oh, I forgot to introduce myself. My serial number is BUZ323, but call me Blu. Everyone does. Buz doesn't sound very dignified, sort of like a demented bee or something. Besides, Aya called me Blu the night she found me beside the Dumpster where that ungrateful son-of-a-shovel left me because I couldn't dig ditches fast enough. He said I wasn't worth the money he paid for an old piece of junk like me. The idiot mutie didn't know I was programmed by a scientist to record important data, for pity's sake, not to do manual labor. Good grief, even robots can't do everything!

In case you haven't guessed, I'm a robot, but that doesn't mean I don't have feelings. Aya has taught me those, you see. Who's Aya? Keep your armor on, Shorty! I'll get to that part. Let me finish with all this history first, will you? Good grief, you little humans get bored easily!

As I was saying, the Triumvirate didn't have to wait long for the rebellion to take place. When the Noble Warriors lost control over the meager resources the ubercouncil had allotted to them, they rebelled. Led by the powerful Lombardi clan, all the tribes left Megacity, to become nomads once again in the vast unknown lands beyond the river. They were determined to create another city where humans could live in peace.

But the Borg Guard, the military arm of the Triumvirate, had orders to not let anyone escape. The Borgs set out in pursuit of the rebels, and the two sides finally clashed at Sumi where the Warriors had set up camp.

At the Battle of Sumi, the Thane of Galen was killed, bless him, and the rest of the tribes escaped across the Sumi River to the Trezarium, taking his body with them.

They laid him to rest in an unknown place, but legends say a chestnut tree marks the spot, the chestnut being the sacred symbol of the Galen Clan.

The Trezarium was an experimental forest started by Doctor Edward Spencer, a former member of the Ubercouncil, to house a collection of plants and animals considered extinct after the Lost Times. Even the Borg Guard dared not follow the humans into the vast sprawl of plant and animal life. They were programmed for the cement streets of Megacity, not where strange things sprang out from behind rocks, and tree roots tripped up the unwary stranger. The tribes of humans escaped and some made themselves at home in the Trezarium while the others made their way into The Land Beyond and disappeared somewhere into tomorrow.

The mutants gradually tightened their grip on Megacity. Anything considered to inferior, obsolete, or useless to the Triumvirate was condemned to be recycled by the Brain, a giant computer system which controlled every aspect of Megacity. According to the caste system set up by the ubercouncil, humans fit all three categories and were termed Rejects. If they were designated useful by the Scanner, a function of the Brain, - though usually only the young and strong, they were made slaves and sent to work in factories making parts for mutants and robots.

If the Scanner found that they fit all three categories or designated to be dangerous, they were to be recycled. A few Rejects escaped and went underground where they hid in the old sewer system beneath the ruined city.

That was where Aya assembled her family—four children, one mutant marked dangerous by the ubercouncil, and an old robot. That was me, Blu. Aya raised the children on love as well as on a diet of fish, frogs, and sewer cabbage—not me! I don't eat that stuff. Give me a good can of oil any day. I'm an easy keeper. Except that, in the sewers, cans of oil don't come down the drain very often. So what did dear Aya do? Gave me fish oil instead. Yuck!

With my help, she taught them how to read, write, and cooperate with each other. You can press any button on me, and I will recite any history or any book in three languages.

But the time grew near when Aya knew we must leave the safety of the underground for the peril of the unknown. The Borg Guard were sending patrols with sensors that detected any human presence, even the heat of their bodies and the smell of their cooking. It was time to leave, but where would we go? Here's the story. If you sit still long enough, you may find out!

CHAPTER 1

THE SEWER RATS

Quiet, they're coming!"

The little group froze, mouths opened to ask questions, eyes wide with fear, but they knew better than to speak or move. Aya's whispered command was law in their underground world. They looked upward, as if they could see through the layers of cement that separated them from their enemy. The Borgs' sound detectors could zero in on the rustle of a rat through the old sewers below the city.

At Aya's signal, they all held their breath except for Blu. Being an old robot, his control panel made a whirring noise which the Borgs could detect. Thur had to press the button to put him on power-saving mode, which made his mismatched eyes roll in opposite directions. He looked so funny, Miri and Qin stifled giggles as the Borg sensors approached, making their high-pitched, hissing sound. Then, just as the Borgs were right overhead, little Annabeth sneezed.

And before anyone could stop her, she sneezed again.

The high-pitched whine stopped, and they could hear the sensor come down through the iron bars of the grate.

It sounded like rats' feet over broken glass and looked like a big glass eye. The sensor turned around slowly, scanning the long tunnels of the sewer. For one horrible second, it seemed to look squarely at them, and then it rotated away like the eye of a cyclops looking for its prey.

While the sensor was turned in the opposite direction, at a signal from Aya, the Reject family began to move along the sewer walls. With Aya and Riga leading the way, they crept back up the passage in the direction the Borgs had come just from.

Miri kept her hand over Annabeth's mouth in case she sneezed again.

"Whew, that was close!" Even though the Borgs had long passed them, Aya kept her voice to a whisper. They always whispered, not daring to raise their voices.

The sewers echoed, magnifying any little sound by ten times. That way, the sensors could catch it a mile away. But Riga always led them out of range, tossing a stone far down the sewers or banging on the pipes overhead to make it sound like someone was running down the endless labyrinth of tunnels.

At last, Riga gave the signal to stop, and they all dropped against the sewer walls, exhausted by fear and hunger. Their supply of cabbages was nearly gone and their supply of frogs, fish, and rats was running out. There had been some little frogs and minnows swimming in the sewer water, but even those were gone, probably eaten by the voracious rats.

"Can you read us the story now, Aya?" Annabeth asked. She was sucking her thumb again, a sign she was hungry and frightened. Even Aya didn't have the heart to correct her. "The one about the little boy who asked for more food and the bad people wouldn't give him any."

Aya looked at Riga, and the mutant nodded his

agreement. "Well, just a little bit, Annabeth, while we're resting," Aya replied, taking a battered, mildewed volume of Oliver Twist out of her knapsack. Everybody knew the story of how, as a child, she had discovered the book floating down the sewers, probably abandoned by someone fleeing the Borgs. Even when she had fished it out of the water, the book was very old. In fact, older than Aya herself, she said. Since they had never seen anyone older than Aya, they all thought the book was ancient. The outside was covered in scraps of faded cloth concealing the title and author's name. The pages had come loose, and been sewn back into the spine by loving fingers with colorful string.

The story of the little boy who had lost his mother when he was born, but had triumphed over every obstacle, soothed fears and hunger pangs every time they heard it, which was usually once a day. The older children could even read the book themselves, having been taught to read by Aya. A whole world of learning had been built around that single volume.

The old woman had just begun the story when Thur, who had been covering their retreat, dropped down beside her. He signaled for Miri to take over reading. "You don't look well, Aya," he said. "And we have to move on in a little while. We have to find a place to hunt for food. A safe place where we all can hide. You have told me of such a place a long time ago." He put his weapon gently down against the damp wall, not too far away in case he needed it. "Trezarium, you called it. I remember it well. All about the trees and the blue sky. And birds, you said. Little animals with wings that fly. Whatever they are, they were part of it, too."

Aya touched his crisp, dark curls, which should have been soft, but the city's dirty air had caked them almost stiff with soot. As a result of being raised underground where baths were rare, Qin's copper hair and Miri's honey-colored waves matched Thur's so that they looked like dark-haired triplets.

But in reality, Thur was older by several years. As Aya had roamed the dark streets of Megacity, she had found Riga, a warrior in training at the Academy. He was sheltering from the constant black rain in the wreck of an overturned Robocar with a small boy he called Thur. He told her he had been cast out of the Academy when they discovered he had a human ancestor. With Riga's help, she had found the robot Blu beside the Dumpster where someone, who was too lazy to get a recycle permit or too busy or too poor, had left him. The three girls she had found on the dark streets where they were scrounging for food. Slowly Aya had assembled her little family in the old sewers below the old city. Now they all were in danger of being discovered.

Riga was their defense, using his mutant powers and his warrior training to keep them safe so far. He had trained Thur to be a warrior like himself and even taught the girls some warrior moves. Under Riga's watchful eye, Miri and Thur would spar together but Qin preferred to teach little Annabeth to read and write from their battered copy of Oliver Twist.

"That's right, my boy. Trezarium they called it, but you will certainly die trying to get there so I will not tell you where it is. Let me rest a bit and we will find a new place to plant our cabbages, there's a good boy." Aya leaned back and closed her eyes. "Let me sleep a bit now."

Coming back from leading the sensors away, Riga saw Aya slumped down against the wall. He immediately squatted before the old woman, looking intently into her face. Thur knew he was scanning her to detect her life force with his mutant powers. Then his eyelids dropped down over his pale eyes, as though what he saw wasn't good.

Opening her eyes, Aya didn't miss his expression of sorrow. "I don't have long, do I, Riga?" She made an attempt at laughing, but it was a strange croaking sound. "That's all right. I have lived too long in this place, anyway."

"That's exactly the trouble, Aya. We've got to get you out of here." Riga got to his feet with a slight shake of his head. "We'd better move on now. Blu and I will take turns carrying her," he said to Thur. "You carry Annabeth. We must be gone before the Borg Guard passes again."

Miri had been listening to their conversation. "Did you say the Guard? If they even suspect we're here, they'll vaporize the whole tunnel." Turning to the old woman, she said, "Aya, please tell us where we can find Trezarium. There's no life for us here, that's for certain. The Guard are going to come down here to search us out. Before they find us and send us to the Dumpster, please let us try and escape this place. The Triumvirate get rid of humans and Rejects like Riga and Blu. You, above all, know that, Aya. You said they destroyed everyone dear to you. Aya, please, please tell us now before it's too late."

"Sweet child, you'll just die trying." Aya began to slump, crumple like a snail retreating into its shell. "I want to spare you that. I've seen so many of our kind perish."

"I don't care, we'll all perish anyway, don't you see that?" Miri looked away, wiping off tears of fear and frustration.

"Yeah," said Qin, "They don't have any use for Rejects like us. 'Obsolete mistakes,' they call our kind, and the Triumvirate hides hide all their mistakes in the

Dumpster. If it weren't for you rescuing us, that's where we'd be. Is that what you saved us for, Aya. I don't think so."

"Hush, Qin," Mira cautioned her out-spoken sister. She's just trying to keep us safe."

"I feel about as safe as a rat in a trap with a hungry cat nearby."

"What's a cat?" Annabeth asked, taking her thumb out of her mouth long enough to ask the question.

"Ask Aya," Qin snapped. "She has all the answers."

Pretending to ignore them, Aya sensed their hopeful glances in her direction. She had known that hope once. Years ago, when the Triumvirate had abruptly ruled that all humans were to be reduced to slave status, her father, a prominent scientist, had arranged for her to escape capture and hide underneath the city with many other families. She had never seen her parents again, although she had searched every night for years.

"No more talk!" The order came from Riga. His signal for quiet was immediately obeyed by the huddled little group. It meant the Guard was coming their way again. The Borgs knew they were on to something, having picked up Annabeth's sneezes. They had programs for everything—even reading finger prints carelessly left on railings or doorways, a sure sign that human Rejects were hiding below.

The group began to move as one body, staying low, creeping from shadow to shadow. Their eyes grew wide with amazement as Riga led the way up flights of what had been the subway stairs. This was higher than they had ever been before, but Riga was motioning them with his gloved hand to go even higher.

It was obvious Riga had a plan, but right now, he wasn't sharing with anyone, not even Thur. A little disgruntled at being left out of Riga's confidence, Thur followed close behind his mentor, his adl-adl drawn and ready. Blu carried Aya in his powerful arms, as though she were made of glass, his round eyes moving back and forth in different directions like scanners.

Though of obsolete design, Blu had many built-in custom features that modern robots didn't include. His hands were padded with water-resistant fabric so he wouldn't scratch things he carried. These pads kept moisture out of the computerized joints of his fingers so he could easily pluck a fish from the sewer water. A matching pad on his head protected his central controls. To complete the ensemble, Aya had made Blu slippers from an old scrap of carpet to keep his feet from clanking on the cement floors of the sewers.

The coverings were made of shaggy fabric in light and dark shades of brown and gray. The whole effect, though no one had the heart to mention it, made Blu look like a giant, spotted puppy.

Miri grasped Qin by the arm and led little Annabeth with the other hand. At a signal from Riga, they suddenly froze like statues of old caught in the middle of a gesture. One flight below them, a troop of Borgs passed by with their scanner, their suctioned boots making the distinct hissing noise the Rejects had heard only minutes before. They all knew what had brought the Borgs back.

The little girl looked up at Miri and smiled. "I fooled them," she whispered. The hissing stopped. The sensors had picked up the sound of human voices.

Immediately, Riga motioned them to move up to the next level and, as one, they obeyed. Thur rapidly descended the stairs until he was behind Miri and the girls, bringing up the rear. Trying to make as little noise as possible, they ran up the stairs behind Riga

But a noise suddenly rang out far down the sewers and, being programmed to investigate any sign of life, the

Guard went in search of it, double-time. Riga kept them climbing up and up until they reached the level below the street. There they all crouched in darkness and looked up through the grate.

For a moment, they saw nothing, heard nothing, except the sound of softly falling rain.

And then Annabeth pointed one finger at the grate. "I see one," she whispered to Miri. "I see a star."

Even Thur looked at the direction her finger was pointing and nodded. His eyes met Miri's and, embarrassed by the feeling that welled up in her, she looked away. He took that as a rejection and told himself what Riga had told him a million times before—that he was a warrior like his father before him. The Dark Warrior, Riga called him, a name they had called his father. Riga had lectured him since he was little that, someday, he would be a leader of warriors like his father. He could not go looking at girls now—perhaps never.

Hidden and raised here in the bowels of the earth, most of her Reject family thought of Aya as their mother, except Blu, the robot, of course, and Riga, the mutant. Most of her little band had never seen the sun or even the sky, although Thur had ventured up to the grates, where he had seen the night sky through the iron bars.

"Leave me here and go on, all of you," said Aya. "You'll never make it with me holding you up. I'm wheezing like an old horse about to drop in its tracks. Leave me, I say."

"What's a—" Annabeth started to ask but Qin stuck the child's thumb back in her mouth.

Thur looked at Miri and then at Riga, who just shook his head, warning them not to argue with the old woman. Everybody knew it was useless. Aya would only remain fixed on death. It was her way of preparing them to become independent.

"That's right, Aya." The mutant's face glowed faintly blue beneath the light filtering down through the grate. "That's why we have to leave, so you can be well again."

"Oh, hush, Riga!" Aya said harshly, straightening up in Blu's arms. "Let's get on with this fiasco." Suddenly, she straightened up and sniffed. "I smell rain. It's been so long since I've smelled rain. I always loved that smell. Put me down, you walking tin can!" she said to Blu. "You're making me seasick!"

Once on her feet, Aya looked around. "Now where are we headed? Across the Flyover, I presume. That's the only way out, isn't it, Riga?" She looked around, wheezing hoarsely. "Dressed as Rejects in tatters and rags, we'll never make it."

"We'll just have to dodge the patrols, unless you have some magic spell to make us invisible." Thur looked impatient, tapping his adl-adl against his palm. He longed to hit something else besides sewer rats with it. Even in his dreams, he pictured braining some Borg with lightening accuracy and how his father would glow with pride. "The sooner we get started, the better. The daylight is coming, not that it makes much difference. As usual, the smog is so thick and dark, you can't see your hand in front of your face."

"What's a Flyover? And what's daylight?" Annabeth questions were whispered, but impossible to ignore. She would only keep asking until someone answered.

Thur hunkered down beside the little girl. "Daylight is when the sun comes out. It lights up everything so we can see. But we can also be seen, so it's a good thing and a bad thing. And the Flyover? We'll find out together, how's that? I've never been there, see."

"What's a sun?" Annabeth asked, cupping her small hand around Thur's chin. "And underneath the dirt, you are still dark. And why have you got soft hair on your face and Miri doesn't?"

"You just gave me an idea," Riga interrupted to Thur's relief. "Here, Thur, take my lazorizer. It's rusty, I know, but it still works. You keep answering all Annabeth's questions and I'll be back in fifteen minutes. If I don't come back within that time, move on. Don't wait longer than fifteen minutes, understand? But I plan to be back," he added, looking at Miri.

"I'm coming with you, Riga. You're not armed," Miri said. "I'm trained as a fighter. I know I'm not warrior class, but just the same, you trained me yourself."

"No, someone has to stay here in case…well, just in case." But everyone knew what he meant—in case the Borg Patrol spotted them. "Thur has the only weapon and he'll use it."

"Don't forget I have my adl-adl," she said, holding up her version of a slingshot. "I've been practicing on frogs and fish ever since you showed me how to use it. I can even beat Thur at close range."

"Always bragging, Miri," Thur muttered. "I'll take a good lazorizer over an adl-adl any time."

The mutant regarded Thur sternly. "Arms led to the downfall of your kind. Lazorizers didn't help the Noble Warriors at the Battle of Sumi, not when the Borgs have lazor cannons. There are other ways of accomplishing things without arms. Miri, mark what I say, even if Concrete Brain won't let it soak in."

Thur bristled at being called Concrete Brain, a term Riga used when Thur didn't catch on to something right away. "I'd like to know what's wrong with vaporizing Borgies. It's either them or us."

But Riga just gave his half-sad, half-twisted blue smile. "Remember, fifteen minutes."

Miri turned to Thur. "You shouldn't have let him go

alone. If they find him, they'll only trash him, you know that. He's a Reject."

"What's a Reject?" Little Annabeth looked from one tense face to the other, wondering what was wrong with her usually good-humored companions.

They were all brought down to reality by her question. Their perilous situation loomed even greater in their minds when they were forced to put it into words.

"Someone who doesn't meet the Triumvirate's standards for the categories," said Miri trying to plait the little girl's unruly hair into braids using her fingers as a brush. "Or they might be defective in some way."

"Or a mutant military machine like Riga," said Thur, still smarting from Riga's jibe.

"Or just a human, like us," Qin said.

"I beg your pardon." Everyone looked Blu, as though they had forgotten he was there. They usually did. "Speak for yourselves. I am a fully papered robot. Both my parents were robots, and I am practically put together from their old parts."

"Which is exactly why I found you in the Dumpster." Aya seemed to be revived by the air coming through the grate. "Your parts were rusted, and you creaked so loud you sounded like a rusty gate."

"Well, at least I can be recycled," answered Blu. Everyone looked at him sympathetically. "Except for my fur. They don't do fur."

Aya never let them think their differences made them superior to anyone else. "We're all part of a family, and that allows everybody to be themselves yet we all stick together. That what a family does."

"What's a family?" The question hung there in the thick, humid air, daring any of the group to grab it with an answer. Little Annabeth looked from one to the other. "Well, I'm waiting," she said, looking at Thur.

"It's where everyone is related, I guess," he said, looking to Miri for help.

"What's 'elated' mean?"

"Not elated, related," Aya corrected. "Sometimes families are put together by experiences and stick together out of love. Now, hush the talk. The Guard aren't that far away."

Riga was back in fourteen minutes, just under his original estimate. "That will give you one minute to change," he said. "To your new identity."

"What's a—"

Annabeth was silenced by Miri pulling something down over her face. "Hush," Miri said, "we have to hurry."

She suppressed an explosive giggle when she saw Annabeth. She was dressed as a monkey which suited her petite frame and frisky movements perfectly.

Qin was struggling into an acrobat's costume, and Aya was a happy clown. Thur was a lion tamer, although his whip was a piece of string tied to a stick, and Miri a pretty tightrope walker with black tights and a short ruffled skirt. Riga climbed into another clown's suit and shoes with wheels on his feet. On his back was a large sack full of what appeared to be pink spun sugar cones. Blu was dressed as himself carrying Annabeth on his shoulders, but she soon climbed up to sit in Aya's lap. Between his fur mittens, the robot grasped an accordion as if it would explode any moment.

"It plays a tune, Blu. Here let me show you." Riga took the squeezebox and played a few notes. "Think you can do that?"

Blu rolled his mismatched eyes in different directions, which meant he was thinking. "After a search of my programs, I think I can play Bach's Fugue but I'm a bit rusty, I'm afraid."

"Oh, swell," Qin muttered. "That will liven things up."

When the Borg Patrol passed, they hardly glanced at the strange collection of Rejects. Street entertainers were a common sight in Megacity. Usually, they were composed of Reject mutants, but, occasionally, a human slipped among them unnoticed. In any case, they were periodically swept up by the street cleaning machines along with any trash to be recycled. In between cleanings, the entertainers were tolerated if they had a permit to perform. Which is what Guard 80047 stopped to ask them.

"Permit, please. Take your time," he said politely in his robotic voice. "You lot go on ahead," 80047 said to the rest of the Patrol. "Keep an eye out for the humans. They must be around here somewhere. Well?" He turned his attention back to the little group. "Who's in charge here? Hurry up, please, I am off duty in twenty minutes."

"In that case, we invite you to our show," Thur said, bowing from the waist. "You'll be our honored guest." He hoped Riga approved of his diplomacy, even though it was killing him to be polite.

Guard 80047 scowled behind his Borg mask. These Rejects were a tricky bunch. Likely they were up to something, like stealing a keg of Swaug, a few Plasticles, or worse yet, homemade Happy Pills. "Are there any humans in your troupe? We don't allow humans to perform, you know. Only drummans, droids, and mutants of the right percentage, or if they are in charge of a chimera."

"We're all mutants except for one tin box as you can see," replied Thur.

"I resent being called a tin box," said Blu. "I'll have you know my parts are all certified interchangeable."

"Shut up," said 80047. "You're only allowed to speak when spoken to. Someone should have programmed you for better manners. Even though you are the oddest-looking piece of equipment I've ever seen, you'll pass as robotic."

"Well, I never—" started Blu before he received a jab in the fuse box from Qin.

"Mutant," the Guard said to Riga, "do you have a permit to perform in a public place? Only mutants with the class rating of seventy-five percent Other are allowed to perform."

"We are all of that class," replied Riga, regarding the Borg with a steady gaze.

"Then prepare to produce it when you get where you're going. Where are you holding this show, anyway?"

That's when Miri stepped forward. "The Flyover at eight sharp. Be there or be square."

Suddenly, Guard 80047 couldn't get his brain to work. It seemed have jammed up, shut down, and otherwise, refused to work correctly. He tried to speak several times but all that came out were a series of squeaks. She—and she was a definitely she, even mutants of a certain class were divided into she-mutants or he-mutants—was wearing, among other things he tried not to notice, a large pair of bat wings or bird wings. He hadn't seen either animal except on the Learning Screen. Remnants of the Human Age, he realized. But what he hadn't realized was how beautiful, how perfectly charming they could look on a she-mutant.

"See you there, Borgie," she said and smiled, her lips curving under her bat mask.

"Hrrumph," was the only sound 80047 could make, and it was ugly in his ears.

CHAPTER 2

THE FLYOVER

As the Borg Guards marched away, Riga waved the group into a huddle. "Well done, aside from Miri calling that robot Borgie," he said. "Now, if you can carry off the performance, we'll get the chance to make it to Trezarium. But there's a lot that can go wrong. If we're discovered, then we'll just have to make a run for it."

"What's Trezarium? Is that where Oliver lives?"

Qin rolled her eyes and groaned. "Not now, Annabeth. We're in a hurry."

"Didn't you tell her, Aya?" Behind her black mask, Miri's eyes were accusing. "How could you keep the best part from her?"

"Because I didn't want to get her hopes up," replied the weary voice behind the clown mask with its eternal smile. "I didn't want to risk her life, trying to get there. I couldn't bear to lose any of you that way. I lost so much in my lifetime."

"Everyone has to have a dream," said Thur. "It's like the stars up there, hidden by the clouds. Always reach higher than you can, even if your dreams are out of reach, isn't that what you've always told us?"

"And like our dreams, the stars are fading while we are wasting time talking," interjected Riga. "Now listen. We have to pull this off or end up as fertilizer. Here's what each of you are going to do."

At eight, on the hour, a hush fell over the east end of the Flyover. All eyes were fixed on the top of the stairs where a tower of comical figures stood atop Blu's shoulders. The effect made the usual Flyover inhabitants—Swaug drunks, Happiness Pills addicts, and Rejects awake from their stupors, thinking they were hallucinating.

Then the monkey figure opened a striped umbrella, floated down to the outstretched hand of a robot, and started playing a little squeezebox. The pretty bat lifted off the shoulder of a sad clown while the smiling clown balanced on the other shoulder. Suddenly, the sad clown went flying slowly across the Flyover while the bat flapped her wings. The ring master, holding the acrobat by one foot, went soaring across the room on a zip line, held in place by a powerful magnet. The robot then followed slowly with measured steps with the monkey back on his shoulder.

Borg Guard 80047 followed the noise to the first room of the Flyover and stopped short in amazement. The addicts and the Rejects were on their feet, clapping their food pans together and showing the first signs of life, which alarmed their suppliers who had thought they were wasting away.

The Grays instantly buzzed the ear implants in the ears of their droids on the Flyover to light up and advertise their varieties of Happiness pills, Swaug, and all twenty-one flavors of Plasticles. The powerful crime syndicate supported the Triumvirate by putting any sign of rebellion put down fast. They made a fortune off of distributing bootleg Swaug, fake Happiness Pills, to the addicts who might cause trouble. But they hadn't counted on a bunch of street performers to bring the inhabitants of the Flyover to life.

The Borgs, on the other hand, expressed their pleasure by clapping their lazorizers on their arms and making an "Uggah" noise, which served as laughter.

"That was fun! Let's fly to the other side again!" Luckily, the Borgs clamor drowned out Annabeth's voice.

"No," Riga said. "We must cross another room and another and one more before we get to the bridge." His blue lips twisted in what passed for a smile, white teeth showing sharply against his blue skin. "You did well, little miss. Everyone did well." His eyes rested on Miri who was talking excitedly to Qin. "It is lucky there was an antique costume shop nearby the entrance to the sewers."

While the Guard was still changing patrol, the Rejects, waiting to be recycled, huddled around the machines dispensing Happiness Pills and Swaug. Taking advantage of their preoccupation, Riga herded the little group into the next room. The second room was another step closer to the Dumpsters and annihilation. It had an atmosphere of death and despair that was mirrored in the thin figures scattered around its interior.

The second room in the Flyover was smaller than the first, full of sinister-looking Guards in charge of the skeletally-thin addicts. While they were looking for a spot to perform, Thur whispered, "What I don't get, though, is where you got those little motors under the umbrella and your jet pack."

"The same antiquities shop where I got the costumes," Riga said over his shoulder. "Old stuff like astronaut suits and jet packs are all the rage. Even the Borgs and droids have costume parties. They dress up like humans. I learned that at the Academy."

"Just a minute, you lot," growled a voice behind them. "Where do you think you're going?"

"We're The Flying Clowns." Riga turned around to face a huge furry droll who towered over the little band like a storm cloud. "We've been invited by the Triumvirate to perform in honor of the big celebration."

"You have? What celebration is that?" The droll scratched his bald, dome-like head. "I didn't hear about any celebration."

"Don't tell me you don't read the Mother Boards! I wouldn't say that out loud, if I were you." Miri flexed her bat wings as she faced the giant. "If you don't read the Mother Boards, you're in big trouble!"

Coming up behind the little group, 80047 marveled at her courage—her light voice carried authority that clearly confused the troglodyte.

"Well…well," the droll mumbled, looking around to make sure no one else was listening. "I can't read. Nobody can read all that stuff they put up there. Move on, then. Move along."

They had all drawn a relieved breath and started forward into the room when an authoritative voice said, "Just a minute, please, clown troupe."

They froze in mid-step, afraid to turn and face someone that obviously had more brains than the droll and had figured them for what they were—human remnants and Rejects. Borg Guard 80047 advanced to face Riga. "Take off your mask, Clown. I like to know whom I'm addressing."

"This isn't a mask," Riga replied calmly. "It's my face, 80047." He was so insulted he didn't even add "sir" but the Guard didn't seem to notice.

"Sorry, mutant. I overheard you say you were personally invited by the Triumvirate to perform here. The

Guard looked from one strange figure to another. "Is that correct?"

"It is."

If Riga thought he could bluff his way to freedom, he was wrong. That was obvious by the way Guard 80047 folded his arms, as though forbidding them from moving farther into the room.

"In that case, you must have a permit. May I see it, Clown?"

Riga hesitated, looking desperately at Aya. "Well, you see—"

"Will this do?" Aya limped forward with a paper in her hand. "The date is not correct, but the official stamp is there. See, right at the bottom, left hand side."

Guard 80047 started to ask the bizarre crumpled figure with the comic smiling face to take off the mask, but then thought better of it. "This is official, all right, although this permit has expired."

"But you can update it, right?" The long-legged bat stepped in front of the little smiling clown. What was it about her lilting voice that filled him with such confusion? Guard 80047 wasn't accustomed to being confused about anything, and it was a strange experience. *Like drinking the strongest Swaug ever made*, he thought.

"Yes," he answered, without knowing why. "Yes, it is possible I can do that, seeing as how the Guards want to see you perform again. And these scum—" he said, looking around to indicate the listless inhabitants of the second room, "—are doomed to go to Recycle and it makes no difference to them. So go ahead."

"Good," said Miri, "then that's settled. Get ready, everyone! Places!"

"Just a minute, I haven't said 'yes' yet!" said Guard 80047.

"Oh, but you have," Qin said, on her way up to Blu's shoulder. "You just don't know it yet."

Their performance had the same electrifying effect on the dreary residents of Room Two as it had in the previous room. They got to their feet and tottered forward, banging their Swaug cups together, as the bat and fellow performers flew across the room to the other side. Having given up food and all sustenance, except Happiness Pills and Swaug, the residents had no use for plates. Instead, they made a feeble effort to clap their hands.

Just then, Annabeth dropped a handful of coins she had collected from the Guards in the Flyover. At first, the residents didn't know what to do with them. Then with a rush that caught Guard 80047 squarely in the middle, they fell on the coins.

"Food," became the chant. "Food, food, food!"

They were so preoccupied with getting to the Flyover where the Happiness Pills were being passed out, they didn't notice the performers escape into the third room.

Except for Guard 80047, who was fighting his way through the crowd. Through the face-guard of his helmet, he saw everything he had only imagined was true disappearing into an abyss of blackness and danger.

Guard 80047 had to follow.

CHAPTER 3

THE THIRD ROOM

Even Riga was daunted by what awaited them in the third room.

Thur strained his eyes to pierce the darkness. "Phew, what is that smell?"

"We are only one step away from the first Dumpster," Aya whispered.

"Where they recycle everything, including humans with big mouths." Riga's voice was a growl in the dark. "I remind you, therefore, to keep your voice down to a whisper, or better yet, don't talk at all."

"Well, that really makes a change," Qin muttered. "When did we ever say anything above a whisper?"

"The Brain has very powerful sensors everywhere, especially here at this end of the Flyover." Riga's voice came out of the shadows.

"What does this Flyover fly to, by the way? Isn't a Flyover supposed to fly over something?" Qin squinted into the darkness. "Doesn't look as though it's going to fly anywhere."

Stacks of small cubicles climbed the dank walls of the third room. In each tiny compartment lay a motionless figure.

"Are they all dead?" asked Annabeth.

"Just about," said Aya, gripping the child's hand more tightly. "If they are our kind, the Swaug has done its job, replacing their desire for food. Now, let's get it over with."

Guard 80047 appeared in the doorway. "Wait!"

"Not him again," Qin said. "The Snoop Patrol."

The Guard came up to the little group gathered just inside the doorway. "You have to show your permit to the Brain in here. Performers are not normally permitted in Room Three, you know."

"I can see why," said Riga. "But would it really matter if we did our show for them? They seem pretty lifeless."

"Look , if you don't keep your voice down…" Guard 80047 stopped in horror as the floor underneath them began to move. The door slammed shut behind him with such force that 80047 jumped into their midst. "Now, look what you've done!" he yelled. "You've started the conveyor belt moving to the first Dumpster."

"What?" Thur grabbed Annabeth up in his arms. "You did that, Borgie! You trapped us! That was your game all along."

"We're all doomed to go to the Dumpster." Aya sighed. "I told you not to try to escape. It would have been better to die in the sewers than go to the Dumpster!"

One by one, the stacks of compartments with their motionless forms moved forward in an assembly line, passing in front of a large screen, as they followed a conveyor belt track into the darkness. Once the screen appeared, a number followed by a beep, acknowledged a bar code registered for that body.

Aya found her voice first. "Just do the same act, but I will stand in front of Blu instead of climbing on his shoulders. That way I will pass in front of the screen. It will only record my number. Guard, you will take my place on Blu's shoulders. Annabeth, you will hold on to the jet umbrella and fly to Riga, understood? Hurry up, now."

"I certainly will not," 80047 protested. "I will go first."

"It's perfectly all right with me if he goes to the Dumpster instead of me," Blu said.

As they took their places, Riga revved his jet pack. "Get ready to start out when I get the line fastened on the other wall. If I get it well above the sensor, it won't register any of our numbers."

Just as Miri was getting ready to climb to the top of the pyramid, she felt a tug of her hand. "Please take Tookie with you. Please, pretty human."

Miri looked down to see a large pair of eyes, a turned-up nose, and a wide smiling mouth. It was a small droll, a child about Annabeth's age. Grime coated her fur so she looked like a small, black bear.

"Are you scared of flying?" Miri said.

"Tookie not scared of anything, except the Dumpster," said the child. "Try me."

"Don't take him, he's only a little droll." Guard 80047 looked at the rapidly approaching assembly line. He scrambled up on Blu's shoulders. "Let's go."

Blu rolled his eyes separately. "I don't transport Borgs, you know. It's not in my programming."

"I order you to carry me through that Scanner unless you want to end up in spare parts!" said 80047, beginning to sweat inside his helmet.

"I'll tell you what, Mr. Guard." Miri held up the droll child. "You hold on to this little droll here, and we'll let you come, won't we, Blu?"

"All aboard," Blu said. "Even rude Borg Guards, if I have to make an exception."

CHAPTER 4

NO MAN'S LAND

As they rode down the assembly line toward the Scanner, Riga flew into the air and fastened the magnetic line to the far wall. Qin and Miri flew through the air, hooked to the zip line, while Annabeth held on to the jet umbrella and landed in Riga's arms. Blu came next holding the Guard, who had the droll child in his lap, and Aya aloft.

As they approached, the Scanner let out a loud screech and the assembly line ground to a halt. "Negative bar code." said the Scanner. "Overdue for recycle."

"Not me," said Blu. "I'm in my prime, I am."

Then Guard 80047 took a small object out of his pocket. He pointed it toward the Brain's screen and clicked. "Malfunction. Redirecting. Malfunction. Redirecting," the Scanner squawked. The Borg Guard got down, put the droll child on the floor, and lifted Aya down beside him. "Now hurry and join the others," he said.

"What about me?" Blu's eyes were orbiting in opposite directions. "Aren't you going to take me?" Just then Thur and Riga rushed over and lifted the old robot down. "Well, I never! Here, I made an exception for that Guard, and he was going to send me to the Recycler."

All around them, dark forms were slipping out of their compartments and crossing in front of the stalled Scanner. When they were all on the other side of the room, the Scanner announced, "Malfunction cleared."

Slowly, with a screech that made the girls put their fingers in their ears, the conveyor belt started up again.

Immediately, Guard 80047 took charge. "This way," he said, opening a door leading to a flight of stairs.

"Wait!" said Riga. "He's a Borg. How do we know it isn't a trap?"

"Because you, for some reason, are a human Reject who survived getting thrown into the Dumpster—twice, as a matter of fact," retorted the Guard. "But I don't expect thanks from the likes of you. Now get going. I've got to report in, or they'll be looking for me."

"We all thank you," said Miri, hesitating at the top of the stairs. "Don't mind Riga. He's very over-protective, sometimes."

"I would be, too," replied 80047 in a gentler voice. "And no thanks are necessary."

"He's one of you," said the droll child.

But in the noise of the assembly line, no one heard her.

Miri led the way down the narrow spiral stairs until they all reached a landing and another door.

"Just a minute," Aya called, but Riga lunged ahead of her, shoving Miri out of the way.

They could hear a mighty, thundering roar as if some giant machine were right outside the door.

Miri rubbed her shoulder where he had pushed her. "Riga, don't be so rude! You don't have to be so bossy all the time, you know."

But Riga held up his hand. "You don't know what's on the other side of this door, Miri! That Guard could have led us straight to the Dumpsters, for all we know."

"I know what's on the other side of the door, you blockhead! Let me through! Let me down there." One by one, Aya crept down the stairs until she was on the landing. No one had ever seen her move so fast or so spritely.

"Then tell us, Aya," said Qin and Thur in chorus.

"Don't keep us standing here waiting, Aya. Riga's right, though I hate to admit it." Thur grinned at the mutant who nodded in agreement. "That Borgie can't be trusted."

"Yes, he can," said the little droll. But no one paid attention to her, except Annabeth. "He's—"

"No Man's Land, that what's out there," said Blu.

"Oh, why did you have to spoil things, Blu?" Aya snapped. "Will someone please let me speak?"

They were all full of questions, but Aya ranked as an elder and, therefore, could speak first. The older children usually followed that rule, except Annabeth who asked, "What's No Man's Land, Aya?"

Aya sighed impatiently. "That's what I've been trying to tell you, little one, if everyone would just stop interrupting."

The little girl smiled sweetly. "Sorry, Aya. Go ahead, tell us. What is that big noise out there?"

Miri tried to shush the child.

"That's the Churn," Aya said. "The turbines that churn the water to make power. They're very dangerous and well-guarded. The water and the steep cliffs along the river are the most dangerous for us, though. That's why they call it No Man's Land because few people have survived out there. If you fall off the cliffs and into the water—"

"I know the path," said a voice behind them in the depths of the stairwell. "If you will follow me, I will lead you."

They all turned, but saw nothing on the dark stairs.

"Who said that?" demanded Aya. "Show yourself!"

Slowly, a shadowy form crossed the shaft of light coming from a crack in the door. Everyone shrank away as it passed down the stairs, clinging to the rail for support. "You poor creature," Aya said. "How long have you lived in the Flyover?"

The nearly translucent form shook his head. "I've lost track of time. Months, no, years. Now, let me lead the way past the Churn and to the bridge. If I perish, at least it will be outside this awful place."

"We are going to Trezarium," said Riga. "Can you show us the way? We will share what little nutrition we have with you if you will."

"Surely," the form replied. "But I ask nothing . Keep the nutrition for the young ones. I am beyond that."

"We'll see about that," said Aya firmly. "Now, open the door, Riga, and let us smell the fresh air."

Riga pulled the heavy door back and everyone gasped. The roar from the Churn became so intense, little Annabeth and the droll child put their fingers in their ears. Everyone had the same thought—somewhere beyond the clouds of steam and spray blocking their view was No Man's Land and, if they survived that, freedom.

The form plunged forward into the clouds and they followed, holding each other's hands. Riga stowed his lazorizer weapon in its sling on his back and grasped Miri's hand. She, in turn, held Qin's hand, and Blu carried Annabeth and the droll. Aya, with surprising energy, and, as if she knew the way, walked briskly behind their dark leader.

None of them gave another thought to Borg Guard 80047. They were too busy admiring the wonders of the outside world. They felt the spray of mist on their dirty faces, the soft ground under their feet, so much softer than the cement of the sewers. Pretty soon, Blu put Annabeth down to feel the wonders of the earth. She and the droll child began to skip and hop on the path beside tumbling water of the Rye river.

After walking what seemed to be an eternity, the curtain of spray vanished, leaving them teetering on the edge of a steep cliff. Below them, was an endless expanse of swirling water which was being sucked into giant turbines and spat out again. They all gasped and took a step back from the brink of the abyss.

"Look," cried Annabeth, pointing to the greening cliffs behind them. "Cabbage! I want some cabbage! I'm hungry."

"That's not cabbage, little one," said Aya. "That's grass and watercress. We shall stop here and rest."

Combing the rocks that lined the cliff, they found two eggs in a nest and mushrooms, which Aya said were fit to eat. Annabeth and the droll gathered lichens, moss, and watercress. Aya produced salted-dried rat and frog's legs from her supply bag. "If we only had a fire, we'd have a splendid meal."

Blu shuffled forward. "Madam, kindly remove my right mitten, please."

"Why, Blu, how clever of you to remember! You were built in the era when cigarettes were still in fashion. Your third finger, right hand, is a lighter. You were created as a proper butler, weren't you?" Aya paid Blu the ultimate compliment by rubbing his frontal plates.

"I try my best, madam." Blu tried not to show how pleased he was, but couldn't help flashing all his buttons.

Soon there was a hearty soup bubbling in his dome cap. They all held out their cups when it was done and, one by one, Aya filled them. All except the dark form which stayed a little apart from the others.

Aya offered him her cup brimming with steaming

broth. "Won't you have some, friend?"

The shadow of a man shook his head. "I have no need of nourishment anymore. Have my portion, but I thank you for the offer."

"Strange gent," said Thur, slurping the contents of his cup. "He acts like he's kind of dead already."

"Maybe he is," replied Miri. "Maybe he wants to be."

Perhaps because Aya kept insisting or because Annabeth ran to him with her cup saying, "Have mine. I don't like it," the stranger accepted the soup and began to taste it.

"Delicious," he pronounced. "Now you must have the rest."

"Oh, no! That won't do at all! You have half and I'll have half. That's the only way I'll have any at all." Annabeth settled herself in the stranger's lap and held the cup to his lips. "Drink up, that's a good shadow."

Everyone laughed at the audacity of children and then fell quiet. Slowly, before their very eyes, the shadow became a shape with flesh-colored features though they still were hidden beneath a coat of grime.

"You are human! Why didn't you say so?" Thur demanded.

"I told you so." The little droll rolled her eyes. "But you didn't listen. You humans never do."

"Thur, you're being rude to our guest who has led us this far," said Aya. "Apologize immediately to…to… might we know your name, sir?"

"Just call me Shadow," said the stranger. "Because that's what I am. I should have said something about knowing the way, but until just now, I didn't see the point. I was fading away. Now, I'm beginning to feel stronger. Perhaps it's the fresh air, or the company that gives me life again. Or the kindness you share."

"That's all very good, but we must get to safety, if there *is* such a thing. You said you know the way, Mr. Shadow." Riga took command now. Standing beside a churning gorge, below a power plant that was no doubt well-guarded, was not the time for sentiment. "I assume you mean to the Trezarium."

"I do. I was there, working as a scientist, until the Triumvirate had me arrested and thrown in jail. If we can reach the waterfall below the turbines before dark, there is a large cave there that is a good place to hide until daylight tomorrow. But you are right, sir. The Borgs are always on patrol. We must hurry."

Riga nodded in agreement. "I will lead the way if you direct me."

They went along the narrow path above the swirling river, holding hands in case someone should fall. At rest breaks, Miri and Qin gathered mushrooms and watercress for dinner. Their quest led them among some large rocks, boulders that provided shelter for the others.

"Look! Giant eggs!" cried Qin. "Won't Aya's eyes pop when she sees those!"

"I don't know," said Miri, shaking her head. "Something about them doesn't look right, Qin. Better just stick to the usual birds' eggs."

"Spoil sport! Always worried about something that doesn't look right," taunted Qin. "'They just didn't look right' doesn't feed starving people and I, for one, am ravenous! I don't know whether it's all this fresh air or the climb but I'm going to whip up the biggest omelet you've ever seen with these babies, whose ever they are." Qin grabbed the largest egg and put in her knapsack. She was gathering some moss to cushion it when they were both surprised by a few dislodged pebbles.

Looking up, they saw one large boulder rolling aside and then another, as if from a doorway. Then, to their utter horror, a giant lizard emerged and scanned the nest. On seeing the missing egg, the lizard let out an ear-splitting shriek and, suddenly, leaped into the air above the gorge. Huge wings sprouted from its sides as it wheeled above the boiling water. Spying the crouching humans against the cliff, it dove straight for them, shrieking with hideous cries as it zeroed in on the terrified girls.

But Riga, though caught off guard, had already drawn his weapon.

"Don't shoot!" shouted Shadow. "Just put the egg back, and it will leave us alone."

"Put it back, Qin." Miri grabbed her sister's arm, but Qin wrestled it free.

"Just shoot the thing, Riga," Qin called back. "What's wrong with having a good meal?"

"Because the Fluglitz…" Shadow's voice was lost in the din created by dozens of flying lizards roused from their lairs along the cliffs. They dove at the hapless travelers who protected themselves by throwing rocks while running along the cliffs.

Meanwhile Miri was shouting at her sister, "Put the egg back, Qin! You can see it has put us all in danger."

"Can't you understand I'm hungry?" Qin shouted back. "I've been hungry for so long, I didn't know even know I was until I saw those eggs! You'd kill a lizard, wouldn't you, sister? What's the difference if it has wings? Besides, an egg isn't even an animal yet." She looked so forlorn and hungry that Miri relented.

"But this lizard has friends—" she started to say.

She didn't finish. Boulders started falling. raining down on them like gigantic raindrops.

CHAPTER 5

SCRAMBLED EGGS

There followed an avalanche so violent that Thur, striding uphill against the wall of rocks, threw himself on top of Miri, knocking her to the ground. Riga covered Qin with his own body as the boulders rolled over them and bounced into the chasm. The rock slide temporarily drove away the predators and, when there was a lull in the avalanche, Thur pulled Miri to her feet.

"You're hurt," she cried, but he ignored her, pulling her behind him with his good arm. The other one dangled at his side, and she could tell he was in pain.

"Watch your step," was all he said.

Qin and Riga were right behind them when they came out along the cliff path. The rest of the group had hurried down the path toward the turbines, and they followed, fending off dives from the hordes of Fluglitz.

At one point, a Fluglitz dove at Qin, knocking her off the path and down the slippery rocks that formed the side of the cliff. If she hadn't grasped a small root sticking out between the rocks, she would have fallen straight down into the maelstrom below.

Meanwhile, another Fluglitz continued to pluck and

nip at her legs and arms, finally lifting her bodily into the air above the Churning water. Qin let out a scream that could be heard above the roar of the power plant.

"Don't shoot!," Shadow shouted. "I'm coming!"

Now entirely morphed into human shape, Shadow calmly made his way past the others until he came abreast of Qin who was screaming hysterically. "Take the egg out and hold it in your hand so the Fluglitz can see it," he shouted above the noise of the water.

Qin realized her life depended on following directions. The Fluglitz stopped hovering over the abyss and flew directly to its nest of the cliff. She dropped Qin, none too gently among the boulders, settling down on the hapless girl to cover her eggs.

"As soon as she is calm and starting to doze off, crawl out," Shadow called, hoping Qin was still alive. "She won't hurt you now."

"But I'm being squashed," called Qin, "by this big chicken!" Presently, she crawled out from under the Fluglitz who, as Shadow had predicted, had dozed off. The Fluglitz gave Qin a parting nip to remind her to leave others' property alone, but it was a half-hearted warning. Nevertheless, it hurt.

CHAPTER 6

A BATH AT LAST

Shadow led the way down a steep, rocky path into what appeared to be the great rush of water jetting from the turbines.

"Is he crazy? We're going to get drowned!" Qin yelled, but Thur only shrugged.

"Better than being pecked to death by flying dinosaurs," he shouted back.

The noise from the thundering rush of the waterfall was so deafening , she only got the last two words. That was enough for Qin. Rubbing her behind, she followed Miri down the path leading to the water without another word.

When he got to the water's edge, Shadow skirted the thundering rush of water jetting from the turbines by going along a little path. He stopped and motioned for the rest to follow. "Come on, there's a cave just behind the waterfall," he shouted.

"That man's an idiot if he thinks I'm going to get my parts wet," Blu said to Riga behind him. "I'll carry Aya if you'll take Annabeth."

The droll child was clinging to Riga like a barnacle. Seeing Annabeth clinging to Blu, she suddenly put on a show of bravery. "Come on, human girl. You're not a baby, are you? Let's take a bath together!"

Never one to pass up a dare, Annabeth climbed down from Blu's arm and joined hands with the little droll. Riga and Aya watched the two children run beneath the spray shielding the mouth of the cave from view. Their laughter came from the other side, floating through the mist with the buoyancy of bubbles, inviting everyone to join them.

Thur and Miri followed with the renegade Qin between them. "One, two, three…gooooo! Last one in's a rotten Fluglitz egg!"

Their screams of shock, as the cold water poured over their heads, were drowned out by the roar of the waterfall. They only passed through the lightest streams of water, thanks to Shadow's skillful leadership. That was enough to wash away the years of grime and soot from life in the sewers.

In the spacious cavern under the waterfall, the group faced each other, amazed by the transformation. Then they all burst out laughing and pointing at each other. Even Shadow and Riga smiled as they watched the girls touch each other's faces and hair. Qin's long red hair hung straight down to her shoulders where it dripped unnoticed, as she admired Miri's honey curls and Annabeth's blonde ones. No one seemed to notice Thur's reaction to the revelation of the girls' appearance except Riga.

Thur sat down against the wall of the cave, nursing his wounded arm. Riga folded up beside him. "I didn't know you hurt your arm. Let me see."

"You're as bad as Aya. It's nothing, just a scratch," Thur answered, but Riga sensed the wound went deeper than that. He wasn't fooled by the young man's quick smile. That was always Thur's way of hiding pain, both physical and mental. "In that case, you won't mind if I take a look." Riga lifted the sleeve of Thur's lion tamer costume. The wound was a deep gash in his upper arm and, after scooping up some damp moss from the cave floor, Riga bound it with strips from one of his motorized umbrellas. "If you remember, that is Aya's way with dealing with a scratch," he said. ""What else is bothering you?"

"Nothing. I just want to rest, that's all. I thought that was what we stopped here for."

But this was Thur's excuse for having a good sulk, Riga knew. Then he caught the young man's involuntarily glance at the girls.

Their faces, free of dirt and soot for the first time, shone white in the sunlight coming through the rushing water. As they stared at each other, as if seeing each other for the first time, Blu was patting himself dry using one of his mittens like a towel. Seeing Blu's clean steel surface, all the girls rushed over to the robot, using his front plates as a mirror. Only Riga didn't notice how pretty they were. Mutants didn't do that kind of comparison between people's looks. He was too preoccupied with how Thur was taking it.

"But you always knew you were different," Riga said, as if reading his mind. "I've told you that from the beginning."

"But not that different. When we were in the sewers, it didn't matter. We all looked the same. But out here in the light, it's obvious." Thur gave Riga an agonized look. "Is it okay if I hate the way I look?"

Riga attempted one of his twisted smiles. "Try being blue," he said. "It puts a whole new spin on things. Anyway, we can't help the way we look. We inherit that, along with the rest of our traits, like your bravery and your destiny, Thur. Don't forget, you are the son of the Dark Warrior, and you will find the rest of your people one day. He was a great leader and—"

"Thur, look at us. Aren't we pretty?" Annabeth came running holding the little droll by the hand. "Tookie is pretty, too, even though she looks different from me."

"Tookie pretty, too." The little droll beamed from ear to pointed ear, turning around for his inspection.

"Yes, indeed," Thur said, suddenly laughing. "Pretty enough to go for a ride!" Springing to his feet, Thur grabbed Annabeth hands and swung her around.

"Next me!" the droll child clamored.

"At least some things never change," said Aya, nodding at the older two girls still preening at their reflection in Blu's plates. She pulled her shawl closer about her, shivering in the damp cave.

"Girls and mirrors." Shadow actually chuckled at the thought. "I think that will never change."

"Tell me, do you really think we'll get to Trezarium safely from here?" Aya couldn't help noticing the plaintive note in her voice. It was as if she knew the answer even before asking the question.

"If the young people do exactly as I say, we have a good chance of making it," Shadow said softly so as not to spoil their fun. "But they will have to follow directions. No more going out on their own."

"Qin's always been an impulsive girl. But Miri's had warrior training. That girl will make a good leader."

"That doesn't make her a warrior. And what about the boy? He seems to be fearless enough."

Aya nodded. "Thur has his father's strength and courage. They called him the Dark Warrior and he was a champion of the old civilization. Before he left for battle, he put the little boy in Riga's care. The Triumvirate suspected Riga of being a rebel sympathizer. They used his human ancestry as a pretense for kicking out of the Academy. His father and the girls' parents were all with the rebel army. The Great Revolution was put down, and you know what happened to the rebels they caught."

"But some escaped across the river into the lands beyond. I've heard they have flourished there and offer protection to anyone who comes in peace."

"Perhaps you'll find your family there."

Aya watched a great sadness envelope Shadow like a cloak. "I lost two of my sons in those great battles. My wife was a doctor who took care of the wounded. She died when the Triumvirate sprayed the Warrior's camp with germs that caused instant death. The few that got away were out on patrol. No more humans, no more hospitals. That was the Triumvirate's motto."

"I'm starving," announced Qin. "What's there to eat?"

"How about some Fluglitz eggs?"

They all laughed at the horrified expression on Qin's face. Thur looked over at Miri to see if she enjoyed teasing Qin as much as he did.

The admiring look in his dark eyes made Miri's heart do a strange dance. Her face felt suddenly warm. "Let's make a meal of the mushrooms and watercress I gathered along the cliffs," she said, dropping her eyes to fumble in her knapsack.

"No," Shadow said. "I have a better idea. Let's have fish for dinner. Come, Thur and Riga, I'll show you how to make a hook and fishing line."

They didn't have to wait long for dinner. Fish were constantly leaping out of the churning water below the turbines. They even landed on the rocky ledge beneath the waterfall before sliding back into the abyss. Abandoning their lines and hooks, Thur and Riga gathered the fish in with their hands. Soon they had a crackling fire going inside the cavern. The cleaned fish cooked on a bed of moss with the mushrooms beside them.

When everyone had eaten their fill, Riga and Thur dumped the scraps into the river as Shadow directed them. "The Churn will get rid of them. We don't want to leave any evidence behind," he said.

The scientist seemed to be always drifting away to examine the walls and ceiling of the cavern, as if he were searching for something.

"That's a good name for it, the Churn." Miri sat, combing her fingers through Annabeth's damp curls. "Is that what you've heard it called, Aya?"

"I only heard tales of a great whirlpool on the River Rye," Aya replied. "Into it, many people disappeared forever."

"Did you ever hear of Fluglitz before?" asked Qin. "You could have warned us they were out there."

"If I had, would you have listened, you silly girl? I would have thought anybody with good sense would know not to mess about with things that don't mess with you," Aya snapped.

"Why were they so big, Shadow?" asked Thur. "At least a thousand times bigger than the regular lizards we used to see in the sewer tunnels."

The scientist drew near the fire. "When the Earth warmed to the point of becoming a biological soup, a great many things we had thought were extinct came back to haunt us. Including the Fluglitz or pterodactyls as they used to be called, back when the world was young."

"Biological soup sounds like what we were raised on in the sewers." Thur licked his lips, eating his fourth piece of fish. "Fish is much better."

But Qin had stopped eating and was looking at Shadow across the embers of the fire. "You mean there's more to the world than Megacity?"

"Oh, yes," Shadow said sadly. "But I don't know what's become of it. I doubt anyone does." He looked at the sky which was growing darker. "We must move by night. Get a few hours' sleep. I will keep the first watch."

"No, I will keep watch," Riga replied as if the matter was settled.

"You still don't trust me, do you, Riga?" The embers of the fire reflected Shadow's wry smile. "I know how you feel. I don't trust easily either. Trust is the most valuable thing the Triumvirate has stolen from us as humans."

"I trust no one, except maybe Thur and Miri." The mutant picked up his weapon. "But they haven't been tested yet. That is my measure of who should be trusted."

"Good," answered Shadow. "I will sleep then."

Annabeth and the little droll were already asleep with their heads in Aya's lap. Blu was recharging, humming peacefully, when an earsplitting roar came rumbling up from the depths of the cavern. Another followed, and then another.

The noise was so intense, everyone was on their feet, except the two children.

"What is that?' Riga demanded of Shadow.

Everyone was huddled in the mouth of the cave, prepared to run, except him.

Shadow listened intently. "I'm not sure. Probably an animal awakened by the smell of smoke. Anyway, it sounds big and hungry so we'd better avoid it. Everyone, this way."

Just as they reached the far end of the cave, a giant cave lynx came up the passageway into the main cavern, its head down, sniffing the ground. When it saw the huddled group, it looked at them with glowing yellow eyes.

Blu snapped to life. "Nice pussy cat," he said.

With a deafening voice, the giant lynx roared, "Who calls me cat?" The animal stared around, topaz eyes blazing and tail twitching angrily. "Speak!"

"We're not good to eat! You love fish, remember?"

Shadow called over the roar of the waterfall. "Nice, fat trout."

"I do?" The big cat seemed confused. "That's right, I do. Love fish." The lynx began to pace back and forth, deliberating food choices. "But maybe salmon. Yes, I like salmon best."

Taking advantage of the lynx's preoccupation, Shadow dropped his voice. "A chimera, and blind as a bat from living in darkness. He thinks we're mice and, therefore, dinner. Show him we're not mice. When I say go, I want all of you to shout as loud as you can."

The lynx stared in the direction of their voices. "What's that whispering? Speak up, I say!"

To Aya and the rest of her family, the idea of shouting—when, all their lives, they had barely spoken above a whisper—seemed like some kind of joke. Qin looked at her sister with wide eyes, but Miri just took a deep breath. When Shadow gave the signal, they all made as much noise as they could. Annabeth surprised them all by giving a high-pitched scream that made the big cat take a step back.

"That was very good," Shadow whispered, "but you can do better. Go!"

They all shouted at the top of their lungs. This time Blu added the sound of pots and pans clanging in his storage drawer and played Bach's Fugue in G Minor. Riga beat his weapon on the side of the rock wall, making the cave echo. The giant lynx took another step backward, as if the thought of leaping on his prey was rapidly becoming a very bad idea.

"Riga, Thur, help me push this boulder in the way." Shadow indicated a large rock that had tumbled from construction of the Churn. With little effort, the three men moved the boulder so it shielded them from the cat. "Now," said Shadow, "follow the ledge under the waterfall. Women in the middle. One of you carry your mother. I'll carry Annabeth, that is, if Riga will trust me."

"I'll walk under my own steam, thank you," Aya said. "Imagine me taking orders from a man."

Miri giggled. "Amazing what a little fresh air and exercise can do."

Qin's answer was covered by the waterfall. "Yeah, one minute, she's at death's door. The next minute, Miss Independence."

The two girls burst into fits of giggles which was immediately cut short by Aya.

"I heard that, miss. I still have some life in me yet, you know."

But Annabeth, with her arms around Shadow's neck, kept looking behind her. "Shadow, why did the lynx sound like us when he talked?"

"Because he's a chimera, Annabeth. A cross between an animal and a human. It was experiment, that's all. Now hold tight, that's a good girl. Pretend we're going to walk a tightrope."

"Oh, I've already done that in the Flyover. Are we going to fly, too?"

Shadow smiled at the question. "I wish we could."

One by one, they gingerly stepped out on the ledge beneath the Churn's waterfall, feeling their way in the dark. After an hour, the path turned inland away from the water. Though wet and cold, they all agreed it was better than being eaten by a cave lynx. They were moving away from the Churn now and the cover its mist and clouds provided.

A deep quarry, carved from the earth to build the power station, held large boulders that provided shelter from security cameras, which would sound an alarm if they detected any movement. Still, they hurried from boulder to boulder for the cover of hills. Finally, Shadow who was leading the way, held up his hand for a rest.

"The Borg Patrols will be out soon. Hopefully, they will have lost our trail. We'll shelter under the bridge during the day. That will give us a chance to rest. We'll have to leave as soon as patrols change at six o'clock. That's the best time to cross the bridge."

"Where does the bridge go, Uncle Shadow? A bridge has to lead somewhere, Aya says. Does it lead to Oliver's house?"

Leave it to Annabeth to ask the question they all wanted to know the answer to, but didn't want to ask, for fear of appearing ignorant, thought Miri. *But could there be such a place called Trezarium?*

Shadow smiled and, for the first time, they saw him clearly. He was a tall man with strikingly handsome features and hair graying at the temples. "Of course it does, Miss Annabeth. On the other side is Trezarium. You can run and play there just like a squirrel."

"Oh, I think I'm going to love it there." Annabeth gave him her sweetest smile. "What's a squirrel, Uncle Shadow?"

Qin groaned and flopped on the rocky ground. "Here we go again."

It was a short rest, and they moved on through the dark, walking quickly now as they got to firm ground. Soon it would be morning, although there was little difference in the light. Dark clouds emptied bellies full of rain and then glowered on the hilltops, threatening more. The sun rarely came out and, when it did, barely shone through the thick clouds.

Still, it was one of the marvels of their first day above ground, and the children watched the panorama of the changing sky with awe.

Finally, the arch of a bridge came into view, its spans hidden in mist. A Borg Patrol passed overhead, tromping as they went, heads scanning in unison right and left. The little group hid behind a pylon, waiting for the patrol to pass.

Then, at Shadow's signal, they scurried underneath the bridge, just as the morning patrol tromped overhead. There were other dark forms huddled under the bridge. Seeing the newcomers arriving in their bright costumes, they made room, greeting them with weary smiles in grimy faces.

"It is a miracle we're all still alive," said a frail voice coming from the darkness. "Especially clowns like yourselves. I thought they were all gone until you came. You give us hope there is still laughter in the world."

It was clear everyone there was hiding from the Borgs, except for one exceptionally tall figure. He, like the other fugitives, wore a long, dark cloak with a hood. It was impossible to see his face, but it was clear to everyone, he was alone. He could be a spy for the Triumvirate, ready to blow his whistle and turn them over to the Borgs.

As the new group entered, he regarded them with interest, moving closer so he could hear their conversation. The others drew away, whispering among themselves. Finally, he approached Thur who had taken a seat against the wall of the overpass so Miri could re-bandage his arm.

"I see you don't remember me, but we have met before," the stranger said. "May I ask you who the older man with you is?"

Miri barely looked up from tending to the wound. "He is called Shadow. That's all we know."

Hearing her voice and catching a glimpse of her face apparently caught the stranger by surprise and he took a step back into the shadows.

His reaction only made him look more suspicious .

Thur regarded the tall stranger with wary eyes. "Your voice is familiar, but your face is not. How did we meet and when? It had to be somewhere in the Flyover, because before that, we met no one."

"I'll explain later when it's time. Right now, my business is with Shadow," replied the stranger. "That wound looks nasty. I have something in my kit that will help it heal faster. I'll get it after I speak with Shadow."

"Do I hear my name?" The older man set Annabeth beside him and stood up. "Who wants to speak with me?"

The stranger threw back his hood, revealing close cut dark hair which curled around his handsome face. His blue eyes glowed with emotion as he held out his arms. "Father, don't you recognize me?"

It took Shadow some minutes to recover his voice and his wits. "Val? It can't be! Is it really you?"

"It can be and it is, Father. It's so good to see you. I never gave up hope." The two men embraced, fighting back tears. "So when I followed these people into the Flyover, I saw you there in the fourth room. I recognized you, but you were almost gone. I had to do something to keep you from going into the Dumpster."

Shadow began to regain his color, looking more like an older version of his son. "You were the Borg trooper who jammed the Scanner? How did you manage that? Never mind. I want to hear all about it, but first, let me introduce you to my new friends."

One by one, Shadow took his son to meet each of Aya's family, starting with the matriarch herself.

Aya's sharp eyes scanned the young man's handsome features. "Did you say your name was Val?"

"Yes, that's right." He bowed from the waist, which marked him as a member of the Warrior class. "Valerian, at your service, mother." In making the old gesture of chivalry, his cloak opened, revealing a Borg Guard's uniform. Everyone took a step back in horror.

Thur and Riga rushed forward with weapons drawn, but Miri stopped them. "Wait! He's the Guard that saved us."

Qin joined her, forming a protective barrier with her sister between the tall Guard and Riga's lazorizer. "Yeah, I thought I recognized the voice, even though he's not speaking robot."

"That's right, I'm 80047 of the Borg Guard. But I'm also Val Spencer." Something about the way the young man met their eyes so unflinchingly seemed to ease the refugees' fears, and they took a step closer.

"I told you so." The little droll child walked up and patted Val's leg. "He's one like you. A human. Because humans have feelings, and he felt sorry for us, or we wouldn't be here."

"But how do we know he wasn't followed?" Thur still had his adl-adl ready to deliver a rock at Valerian's head. "He could have signaled the Borgies to round us all up."

The rest of the group muttered among themselves. "All Borgies have a signal on their belts," said a voice from the group in the shadows, "that lets the base know where they are all the time. He could be sending a signal right now."

"In that case, shouldn't you be leaving instead of standing around wasting time?" asked Val. He couldn't help smiling at their reaction when they realized what he said was true.

But Aya looked from Shadow to his son, satisfied by what she saw. "Then your father here is really Dr. Spencer whom we know as Shadow. One of the scientists working on the Superhuman Project that sent most of us here to our doom." Aya sat back against Blu's protective arm. "Tell them, Blu. Give them the awful history of our past, the lives this man helped to destroy. I haven't the strength."

"Please, not now," Shadow pleaded before Blu could begin, "I've only just found my son, can't you see that? At least, give us a little time together before you bring that up, Aya. I, most of all, regret my part in all that happened. Please believe me when I say that. If I had known what harm my work would cause—"

"But scientists never do," interjected Aya bitterly. "They just trust that everybody will do the right thing without a thought of what will happen if their work gets into the wrong hands!"

"Like the Triumvirate's," said Miri. She went to Aya and put her arm around Aya's thin shoulders to comfort her. "We've all lost a lot, Aya. But there's nothing we can do, except go on. After all, we've got this far, haven't we? And we couldn't have made it out of the Flyover if had hadn't been for Valerian and his father. And the rest of you, for that matter." Miri raised her voice to include the people crowding around Valerian.

Aya looked from the pleading father to his son. "I was once proud of my son, too, but I lost him in the Battle of Sumi. So I know what it's like to love someone so much. Now these children are mine. They are my family to replace the one I lost. Go ahead, Dr. Spencer, introduce him to the others. See how proudly he stands, like a young tree."

"I know my father was working on the Superhuman Project," Val said. "But it was the Triumvirate that took his work and turned it into a program to eliminate the less-than-perfect among us. Before that, all the scientists on the Project worked for the good of humanity—to eliminate hunger, disease, and poverty."

"That's true." Putting his lazorizer back in its holster, Riga joined the conversation. "But it's also true that when the Triumvirate took over the government, they wanted an Uber society. They wanted only the most perfect kind of any species. The elite, they called it. I see by your insignia that you are one of those. Your father, Dr. Spencer, tried to protest, to stop them from carrying out their plan. But he was silenced."

Shadow seemed to straighten, as though a huge burden has been lifted from his back. "That's when they sent me to the slave camps. Your mother died there. I had to let you go, my son. The Warrior-Nobles took you away to keep you from becoming a slave. Or even worse, one of the Triumvirate's ' men,' if that's what they call those hollow beings. They managed to put you in the Borg Academy, before they themselves were—"

"Wiped out at the Battle of Sumi. A few defected to the Triumvirate." A look of pain cross Val's face. "I know you don't believe this, Father, but there are still good people among the warrior tribes. They would rise up and defeat the Triumvirate except—"

Shadow sighed. "I know, I know. Except the Triumvirate is watching everybody. And what are the rest of the old warrior tribes doing? Hiding out in the Lands Beyond, I'll wager."

Thur was listening with fascination. "Then they do exist," he whispered excitedly to Riga. "I'm going to find them and join them if I can."

Val cleared his throat. "If I hadn't been rescued by Mediah, I would have surely perished in the Dumpster."

They stood together, mourning the past that was filled with painful losses.

"The Borg Guards day shift approaches," Blu broke in. "I feel the vibrations through the ground. We had better make a swift departure, Dr. Spencer."

Shadow nodded. "There is just enough light to see our way across the river. By that time, we'll have a head start on the Borgs. I've crossed that river many times, so I'll lead the way. Blu, you come behind me with Aya and Annabeth."

Blu rolled his mismatched eyes in panic. "But I am not amphibious. I was made for land service, not seafaring. My parts will surely stop working if I were to fall in the water!"

But Shadow waved the robot's protests away. "You are a Model 2600, Blu. I helped design your prototype. If memory serves me, you are equipped to float."

"What?" With a mittened hand, Blu gestured in the direction of the roaring Churn. "In that?"

"I think I have a solution," Riga said, stepping forward. In a low voice, he said something to Val and Dr. Spencer. They both nodded and, without a word, Riga and Val left the safety of the bridge together, and vanished in the thick mist.

Thur followed them. "Wait, Riga! He's a Borgie, after all! This could be a trap."

As usual, Riga's answer came out of the mist in the form of a question. "You want to find Trezarium or not?""

Dr. Spencer held up his hand. "Follow me, I'll lead the way. The mist will shield us along the water's edge until we come to the path of stones. Once we leave the underpass, no noise, no one speak, not even a whisper. Absolute silence, understand?"

The people huddled under the bridge nodded, their grimy faces now filled with something like hope. Few of them recognized the feeling, however. It had been so long since they had felt it.

One by one, like silent shadows, they followed in a silent line out from under the bridge, and along the bank of the River Rye.

CHAPTER 7

INTO TREZARIUM

I can see why he said for us not to speak until we got here." Thur watched the swirling water rush around huge boulders and tumble into the river from the quarry above. The roar of the Churn was deafening. "Even the Borg scanners couldn't pick up the sound of our voices above this racket."

"Don't be too sure." Spencer was looking over his shoulder to make certain they hadn't been spotted. "Better keep quiet until we're on the other side. And be on your guard, in case—"

"I know. Just in case we have to swim for it. But what I want to know is, what's waiting for us on the other side? We could be being led into a trap betrayed by that Borgie." Thur nodded at Valerian, who was striding with Riga confidently ahead of everyone, as they trailed along the swirling water. "What the—"

In an instant, both Riga and Valerian seemed to plunge directly into the river, not sinking as everyone expected them to do but miraculously walking across the rapids!

Voices could be heard behind them coming out of the mist in hushed tones. "Is it some kind of magic?"

"Maybe the Borg has got some kind of special shoes only available to Borgs."

"In that case, we're all doomed to the recycle bin."

"Calm yourselves, people," Spencer said. "They have found the Path of Stones and you'll all be crossing like them in a minute."

That brought a protest, which grew until Thur turned and said in a voice that carried down the line, "Pipe down, unless you want to run across with the Guard right behind you. This is the Path of Stones," he announced, indicating a line of huge rocks which the waves threatened to devour at any moment. "That mutant you're all griping about led us right to it. It leads across the river to Trezarium where you'll all be free. Riga is on the other side and has attached this guide rope to a tree. Tell me you're not going to let a mutant and a Borgie show you up as cowards." He grabbed the stout guide rope that Val and Riga had tied to a rock

"How can you be so sure that they not going to let us drown?" one woman shouted.

"You don't have much of a choice, do you?" Thur shouted back. "Either cross now or it's the Dumpster when the Guards gets you." He turned to Miri who waiting with one hand on the guide rope." "Miri will go first with Annabeth riding piggyback, then you follow them one at a time. I'll stay on the city side until everybody gets across safely. That way we'll form a human chain for the weaker ones. The stones are slippery with moss so I advise you to—" He was interrupted by the droll child.

"Look, Val is coming back!"

Everyone squinted through the haze covering the river as Valerian negotiated the wet stones, jumping the last few feet on to the riverbank. "The morning patrol is crossing the bridge! We have to hurry or they'll pick up our scent. Come on, Father, you and the little droll cross first. Miri, you follow behind with Annabeth. Thur, you can escort Aya, while I cover the retreat until everyone gets safely across. Riga's making sure the rope holds—"

"Take me first. I've got to get across."

Valerian was interrupted by a stooped old man making his way down the bank. His body was almost bent double beneath a bundle which threatened to overbalance him as he tried to keep his footing.

"Careful there, Uncle. Maybe you should let one of us hold your bundle until you get to the other side," Val said, steadying the elderly man.

"Get your hands off me! I ain't your uncle, Borgie! I carried it all this way, and I ain't about to get robbed by you! I know your kind. Always taking things from us humans!"

"You can't carry that sack across the river, old one." Val pulled the old man aside. "What have you got in there, rocks? You'll stay here with your precious stuff or cross by yourself."

"Let go of me!" the old man protested. "I have to get across."

Val was firm. "Not with that load. You need both hands to grasp the guide rope. If you fall, you'll sink like a stone and probably take someone else with you."

"All right, I'll show you." The man spread the contents of the sack out on the rocks. All sorts of weapons— old lazorizers, ancient pistols, even exploding devices no one had ever seen, tumbled out on the rocky riverbank.

"He's a Traveler," someone in the waiting group said. "Travelers always steal things to trade. Get a move on, old timer."

"Yeah, leave your stuff here, Traveler," said another anxious voice. "Maybe the Borgies will find them and blow themselves up."

The old man bristled with indignation. "I'm bringing

them to the warrior tribes, if you must know. And I'm not a Traveler. I'm a courier for the Galen Tribe. They're waiting for these weapons."

"The old man is off his chump," someone shouted. "There're no more warrior tribes left and, even if there were, what would they want that old junk for, anyway? Come on, now, get moving before the Borgs catch us."

It was clear Val was running out of patience. "Get a move on, old man, and I'll take that knife to pay for your passage."

The old courier turned to the waiting crowd behind him. "See, what'd I tell you? Borgs! They steal everything from us!"

"Yeah, but you probably stole it first, Traveler," someone yelled back.

Thur surveyed the pile of rusted weapons. "Tell you what, old one, I'll carry your load if you let me have that old lazorizer."

"That equipment will have to be updated before anyone uses it," Val said. "Now, don't delay us any longer. Thur will carry your load for you and escort Aya. Who's next?"

"Watch your step, sir." Miri helped the still-protesting courier to the first rock. "And hold on to the guide rope with both hands."

"Gol'danged Borgies, anyway. Be so glad to leave them behind, I can't tell you, miss."

Miri just smiled, not wanting to tell the old timer that this Borgie was going with them.

The refugees gradually formed a human chain across the massive river, helping each other to cross the rocks to the other side. They had all crossed safely, all except Blu. His mittens slipped off the guide rope and the robot rolled off into the water with a horrendous splash.

Caught up in the fast current, Blu spun around and

around, bobbing along toward the Churn and the power-ful turbines that drove the cataract. His eyes were rolling in his head like pin balls, while the rest of the group watched in horror as he was carried along toward the bridge. There was a loud, popping sound, and large water wings sprouted from his shoulders.

At the same time, a small propeller appeared out from a compartment in his back, turning briskly. Suddenly, Blu was propelled back upstream like a motor boat. No one could have been more surprised than Blu himself. He quickly found his way to the opposite shore, where he was pulled to dry land, coached by Spencer.

"That was quite a swim," he said. "You didn't know you were outfitted to operate on the water, I take it?"

"N—No," Blu sputtered, "But how did you know."

"Because I designed you or your prototypes," Spencer said. "Remember, son? You use to chase the robots around the workroom."

But the young man looked puzzled and shook his head. "Sorry, Father. I guess I must have forgotten. My first memories are of Mother Mediah scolding me for growing curly hair after my head was shaved. 'Mutants of the acceptable class don't have hair,' she said."

Spencer turned to his son with a stricken expression. "I take it you don't remember your real mother at all, then?"

Again Val just shook his head. "Sorry."

Hiding his disappointment, Spencer turned back to Blu. "Now, empty the water out of your orifices, or you'll rust out here in the open. And not in people's faces!" he shouted as Blu squirted the water of his mouth and ear ducts all at once. "You look like a water fountain gone mad."

What the refugees didn't know as they followed Dr. Spencer into the forest was that Blu's struggles in the water had made enough noise to attract the Borg Patrol. They had just mounted the bridge downstream, sniffing like a pack of bloodhounds as they went.

"Humans! I smell humans, Commander," they said in unison.

The sensor hissed the alarm, signaling that humans were in the area.

"What's that in the water upstream?" The commander paused, taking time to load his automatic telescopic glasses.

"Just an old piece of robotic junk coming downstream," said his lieutenant. "The nets will catch it in the recycle basket. Carry on, Borgs!"

The fog was lifting over the river just as the last of the refugees crossed the Path of Stones and climbed up the steep bank on the side where the trees offered them shelter. After Val had safely negotiated the rocks across the river, Riga cut the guide rope.

On the bridge downriver, another Guard said, "All the same, we'd better check it out. I have orders to watch out for a lot of Rejects that escaped the Flyover and are headed this way, trying to get to safety in the woods."

"Hey, I just saw something moving upriver," a corporal yelled. "Looked like humans crossing on the rocks."

"Well, shoot them! What are you waiting for?"

The entire Borg detachment sped down the bridge, keeping up a withering fire from their lazorizers as they went. Thur, Val, and Riga leaped on to the bank and took cover behind the closest rocks.

From the shelter of the rocks lining the riverbank, the two fired back at the oncoming Borgs. The front two Guards fell and shriveled like caterpillars. But the rest kept coming, kicking the lifeless bodies of their fellow soldiers aside like fallen leaves.

In an instant, Riga quickly assessed the situation. "We're outnumbered! Quick, we'll split up in the woods and distract them from following the others!" he called to Thur. "Go on ! I'll cover you!"

"In there?" Thur looked at the dense forest behind him. He had never even seen trees before except in Aya's crude drawings. Here were more trees that he could count, stretching away over the horizon like a vast army clothed in green. As far as he could see, they towered above him, giants ready to scope him up in their drooping branches.

Val sprinted past him to catch up with the others and warn them the Borg Patrol was coming. "Of course, in there! What are you waiting for?"

Taking a deep breath, Thur darted between the towering trees, followed by Riga, who kept up a blazing defense with his lazorizer. The Borgs kept their distance, not wanting to be turned to powder by the fire beams from Riga's weapon. Even the commander seemed to hesitate at the edge of the vast forest.

"Company, halt!"

The Guard squad was only too glad to obey. Trezarium was a virtually unknown territory for the Borgs. They had been born in a laboratory and raised in a dormitory. For them, the natural world was ten times more dangerous than the city streets where they could easily bully cowering humans and Rejects, sending them to the Dumpster like so many rats. The Borgs whispered among themselves that Trezarium was rumored to be full of ferocious animals, armed refugees, and traps—all kinds of traps. Besides, in the city, they could patrol together as a unit, like parts of a machine. In Trezarium, where they had to walk single file, there could be danger lurking behind every tree!

The Borgs unwillingness to enter even the outskirts

of Trezarium gave Riga and Thur enough time to plunge even deeper into the forest in opposite directions.

CHAPTER 8

A DEVIOUS DRUMMAN

In the high council room, Mediah tapped her foot beneath the magnetic table that ran the length of the council room. She only pretended to listen to the succession of documents on the monitor—each one appearing then disappearing as it was replaced by a new one which sounded just like the old one. The pleasant voice of the reader droid droned on in endless repetition.

What if the droid suddenly broke down? Mediah thought, half-smiling at the thought of the council instantly bickering among themselves, blaming each other for the hardware glitch. *"You didn't supervise that program properly"* or *"Your department's incompetence has surfaced once again!"* All to cover up the fact that none of them had bothered to learn to read.

She actually started laughing to herself then stopped, covering up with a series of coughs, when she visualized the magnetic table going blank. What uproar there would be then!

The fact would become plain that none of them knew what the documents contained because reading and writing was a skill none of them had ever learned, except Mediah herself.

"Is something amusing about the Gross Product Indices, Ubercouncilperson Mediah?"

She would have to be sitting next to Riksbury, the shriveled old drumman from Beach Lane, a part of the city that specialized in manufacturing. "No, I was just thinking how well you manage your reports, Ubercouncilman Riksbury. Eliminating all the negative percentages and rounding-up the positive figures to make it seem your branch is succeeding instead of failing, that's all."

Riksbury looked at her, as though he were going to explode. Then his warning valve kicked in and he squirmed in his chair. "Yes, Councilperson Mediah," he said agreeably, looking around the council to see if anyone had heard her remark. But they were all occupied by making their reports look good. Satisfied no one had heard her challenge, he said, "Yes, I guess you could say that. I quite agree."

Despite his cordial reply, Riksbury was mentally marking her for the review committee to look into her past. What they might find might well get her sent to the Dumpster and out of his magnetic hair.

Mediah realized she had stepped on Riksbury's district's toes. And she didn't care. She would take care of that outdated drumman with a snap of her fingers by exposing his manipulation of profits and losses. No, she had more important things on her mind.

The defection of Valerian, for one. When she thought about the boy who had been her protégé, her hope for humankind, Mediah felt an ache somewhere in her chest. It was a feeling she could not identify, but it ate her like a worm. She had to find him and bring him back.

Meanwhile, if anybody brought his defection to the attention of the council, and from there to the Triumvirate, she had to be ready with a story they would believe—that she had allowed him to defect and lead her to the pockets of human vermin living in the Trezarium. He constantly communicated with her, she would tell them and show them messages which, of course, they couldn't read because they were written in a code she had invented herself. Human writing.

When the meeting was over, she slipped away from Riksbury's sharp eyes and was on the magnetic tube that would deposit her in her car in the basement below when she realized she forgotten the tablet on which the documents of the day were recorded.

"Slitz!" The word for human excrement was out before she could hold it back. Mediah reversed the tube and shot back up to the council room. It was empty and her tablet was gone.

She shrugged, thinking she programmed it to erase everything at the end of each day. Anyway, it was not the one she used for personal affairs. The one that would contain references to Uberkapton of the Borg Guard 80047 was safe at home behind a magnetic field.

She was about to get back in the tube, about to press the voice code that would drop her in her car, when she heard voices in the council corridor. Mediah hesitated at the sound of Riksbury's unmistakable whine. *Like a dying fly*, she thought.

"She flaunts her power over us as if it carried some weight. She meddles in things that aren't any of her business."

"Your business, I gather?"

Mediah recognized the dry voice of the uberminister.

"And others. I have it on good authority that she was seen looking at the Flyover monitor for several days in a row."

"One of her precincts is coordinating the messages on all the Mother Boards, in and around the Flyover, I believe, Ubercouncilman. Councilperson Mediah is in charge of Mother Board messages this quarter, you know. No, I'm afraid you'll have to come up with something else more concrete, Councilman Riksbury."

Mediah pressed her long, fake nails into her palms. Riksbury was reporting her to the uberminister, whose vote could overrule the 200 council members at the table.

She pictured the little drumman wheeling even closer to the uberminister, lowering his voice to a hiss. "Uberminister, I suspect her of treason. She has taken a personal interest in a certain Borg officer who led a group of humans in a daring escape into the Trezarium."

Riksbury sounded triumphant as he denounced her to the uberminister, who was the acting head of the Council of Twelve, advisors to the Executive Committee of the Triumvirate. *I'll squash the little toad! But not before I make him the laughing stock of the ubercouncil.* Mediah found her palms were bleeding from making fists of rage. *Mustn't let anyone see blood. Mutants don't bleed unless they're more than fifty percent human.*

"Treason? That is a grave charge, indeed." The uberminister spoke slowly and deliberately, allowing his computerized brain to put the information in all the right places. "What is your advice on the subject, Ubercouncilman Riksbury?"

The drumman was only too happy to oblige. "We have to eliminate her, that's all. It should be easy to do, with all her shady affairs and dealings. Besides, I have it on good authority that there are humans somewhere in her genetic code. I'm sure if she were to be retested, she would not pass the required seventy-five-percent Other standard. That way, she could be recycled, and we'd be rid of her without having to go through a messy trial."

Shady! Look who's talking, she thought. *The King of Shady Deals himself. We'll see who gets recycled!*

The uberminister sounded unimpressed. "That's

hardly enough to condemn her. There are humanoids on the Council. Sargon, the head of the Gray Hoods for instance."

Riksbury was practically groveling by now. "I beg you, Uberminister, just put her on inspection. I'm sure you'll turn up something. Moral corruption, if nothing else."

Slitz on that old dried up stick! He's been spying on me! I'll get him for that. She'd had an ongoing affair with the head of the Borg Guard, a mutant named Androzarian. After Androz took Valerian into the Academy, Mediah had to admit to herself that the human side of her longed for someone to hold her close and make love the human way. She was immediately ashamed afterward and broke off the affair, only to revive it again.

The two councilmen were finishing their conversation in the corridor. "Very well, Ubercouncilman Riksbury, but you will pay the costs incurred by the inspection."

"By all means, charge them to me, I beg you, Uberminister. I'd be so grateful if you would."

Sniveling little drumman! I'll throw a wrench in your wheels! Mediah's first call after she got into her robocar taking her to her office was to her erstwhile lover, Imperator General Androzarian.

"What do you want now, Mediah? I'm busy." He had the blunt charm of a Swaug dispenser and the body of a soldier. That was probably the most attractive thing about Androz, she thought. That and his power. The Imperator had toppled more generals and politicians who challenged him over the years than would fill a Guard unit.

"What do I usually want?" she purred and stretched seductively in front of the screen as it zeroed in on the great man himself.

Everything about Imperator Androz was bigger than

life. He was at his huge marble desk with a wall behind that was a virtual cast of the city. Lights flashing on the wall indicating hot spots where detachments of the Guard were sent to root out smugglers of contraband goods. A good portion of what his troops confiscated—like actual food instead of Happy Pills or Swaugshine, a homemade imitation Swaug. Most especially meat and cheese which Imperator Androz kept for his own private table. "To feed my human side," the Imperator General would say with a mechanical twinkle in his eye.

"It's usually something that will mean trouble later. I'm sure you know your precious Valerian defected and took a bunch of sewer rats and Rejects with him," Androz growled. "That's trouble for you, baby."

"I know. I had it arranged. He's on a commission from me to find and root out the pests polluting the Trezarium. I hear from him regularly by code," she said for the benefit of the monitors which were recording every word.

Androzarian still wasn't buying it. "Is that why he managed to ditch his tracking device so we couldn't track him? What did you think you were going to do, Mediah baby, once you found them? Vacuum them up like trash?"

"He has his orders. I can't tell you more than that. Unless you want to come over tonight. Then I'll whisper in your fuzzy old pointed ears."

The Imperator sighed, a thoroughly human habit. "I ought to know better than to fight you, baby. I'll be over. This had better be good."

"Oh, you know everything is always good. 'Til tonight then." Mediah leaned back and shut off the screen. Everything was working out. "Take me home," she ordered the computer steering her car through the traffic.

"Reprogramming for home," it replied.

Home was a glass palace with interior rooms surrounded by locked force fields that ensured privacy. The word 'privacy' had long ago developed new meanings. *There is no actual privacy*, Mediah thought. Just turning on the lights as the car entered the garage flipped a switch somewhere that recorded the time she arrived home. *Only degrees of privacy.*

She wasn't even certain the force fields hadn't been unlocked by now. That was why she went through an elaborate ritual of re-setting the code every time she moved to a different room, thereby outwitting Riksbury's snoops.

In the mirrored bathroom, Mediah ran a bath in the marble tub the size of a city block and began slowly shedding her uniform. Setting her long, blond wig on its stand and replacing it with a short dark one, she walked down the steps in the warm water. Although bald, she was still beautiful, the very best of android and human prototype. Her body had been augmented with all the attributes to make a woman more desirable and disguise her mutant qualities. The only thing that couldn't be augmented was human hair but that could be disguised with wigs. Mediah had over two hundred of them stored in the glass walls.

As she sank into the perfumed bubbles, she felt her confidence returning. Androz would join her within the hour and they would get around to discussing Riksbury's plans to denounce her much later. Mediah practiced her most seductive smile in the mirror. *Much, much later.*

CHAPTER 9

YOP'S HOLLOW

Valerian was leading the way through the thick underbrush when he abruptly stopped. "Wait!" he ordered.

The refugees were only too glad to rest, sinking down among the ferns to marvel at the forest around them. Spencer could see that many were sick—faint from hunger and from living underground in the cold and damp sewer system.

As he moved among them, Val carefully poked at the ground ahead of him with the courier's knife. Suddenly, there was a snap and a deep hole yawned in the ground where there had been leaves. At the same time, a long rope with a noose on the end dropped down from a branch above his head. Val jumped back as the noose dangled where his head would have been.

"Just as I thought," he said, putting his knife back in his belt. "A trap just in case the Borgs are brave enough to get this far."

"The Borgs don't know how to be brave," said his father, coming up beside him. "They aren't programmed to be brave. But these people, these refugees have risked everything to be free. They are the brave ones."

"I will agree with that," a voice above them said.

Val immediately put his hand on his lazorizer, but it was too late. Suddenly, they were surrounded on all sides by strange men, their faces and clothes painted green and brown to blend in with the forest around them. They wore peculiar headdresses made of sticks, leaves, and feathers.

They bound Val's arms and took his weapons. "Look ye, 'tis a mutant," said the one who seemed to be in charge of the rest. He was better dressed than his men and wearing a curious helmet that looked like an upside-down pot. "God's eyes, he's a Borgie!"

"I'm not a Borg!" Val protested. But the strange men just laughed.

"That's what they all say before we destroy them. All reptiles, every one of the buggers."

"Yeah, wouldn't want them to contaminate the earth, now would we?" said another woodsman who was dressed in animal skins.

"You ruffians wouldn't know a mutant from a human!" Spencer scoffed. "You're as ignorant as pig slitz and twice as filthy!"

The savages gathered in a circle around Val and Spencer. "And who might you be, Father Time?"

"I know him," said the voice from the trees. "That you, Ed?"

Suddenly, there was a rustle of the branches above them, and a huge man vaulted to the ground, along with a shower of leaves. There was a gasp from the huddled refugees who shrank back into the shelter of the trees thinking the falling leaves were some new kind of vermin. Val and Spencer stood their ground, but had to tilt their faces back to look up at the man who, in spite of his size, had a big grin on his bearded face.

"This skinny fellow is the reason you have a place to hide in the first place," he said in a booming voice with his giant hand on Spencer's shoulder. "And well you should know that, for you men have been hiding all your lives from that scum across the river! The scum what took our land!"

Spencer shielded his eyes with his hand to look up at the giant. "You're a Lombardi, aren't you? I recognize the helmet with the eagle crest on it."

"Aye, that I am. Chief Mako, at your service," the big man said with a sweeping bow. "I and you was young once and friends as I recall. Welcome, old friend!"

"I thought you and all the Warrior tribes were wiped out at the Battle of Sumi," Val said, taking a step forward.

"That's exactly what we wants your kind to think," Mako said, putting his hand on the weapon in his belt. "That way, it will come as a big surprise when we take over Megacity and send the Triumvirate to the Dumpster."

"Mako, is that you, squawking like an old raven at the top of your lungs? You'll have every drone on our doorstep before nightfall!" The new speaker was almost as round as Mako was tall. In fact, his stomach protruded beneath his shirt a few inches, revealing a belly button. They all relaxed. The man was thoroughly human.

Mako let out a whoop. "Is that the Yop I hears barking like a worfel at the moon?"

"Yop Barnswallow, at your service." Seeing the bedraggled refugees, the little man stopped and attempted to make a bow. "You must be weary and hungry, too. Follow me, Yop Barnswallow, to the Hollow. You poor starvelings will be our honored guests. For you, we will roast a boar and entertain you with our dancing. As for this Borgie…" Val got ready to fight as Mako's men surrounded him.

Spencer stepped up beside Val on the narrow path.

"This Borgie is my son, Val. Without his help, none of us would be here at all."

Aya, Miri, and Qin stepped forward, all still in costume. "We can vouch for that."

Yop looked from father to son and back again. "Beg pardon, sire, it's just that he's wearing—but if these two beauties vouch for him."

Qin accepted the compliment with a pretty blush, but Aya made a face.

"Pig slitz!" she muttered. "Fatty must be blind."

"I will explain," Spencer interrupted impatiently. "But first, get these people to safety and shelter. The Borgs spotted us when we were crossing the river. And you two have made enough noise to attract fifty drones. I'm afraid they will send a patrol into the Trezarium to search for us."

"Never fear, Doctor. Yop and I knows how to deal with those toads, don't we, men?" Mako said.

There was a shout went up from behind trees and tall ferns that formed a natural shield from prying eyes.

Instantly, two dozen more fierce-looking men popped up, camouflaged from head to foot in leaves and skins. They let out a blood curdling roar that could be heard for miles and certainly by the Borg Patrol. It sounded as if the giant lynx they had left back in its cave had emerged and was prowling nearby.

That sent the refugees melting into the woods, afraid for their lives. Miri took her adl-adl, loaded a good-sized rock, and went looking for the creature before it pounced on some defenseless prey.

A half mile away, Thur heard the roar, and thinking the cave lynx had caught up with the refugees, went racing toward the sound.

Spencer lost patience with Yop's noisy bragging. "Come, man. You are frightening the children with your foolish antics and endangering us all. The Borgs will not let such a challenge go by without doing something about it. Now, do as I say and show the weary people some of your fabled hospitality. We'll be the judges if it is real or not."

Little Annabeth made her way to the front of the line, tugging on Shadow's hand. "Shadow, what's a boar?"

"Well, little one," he replied, lifting her into his arms and striding after Yop, the woodsman, "there are two kinds. One has four legs and the other one has two. The four-legged one has tusks. The two legged one has a head too big for its tiny brain."

"Like Mr. Yop?"

His annoyed expression melted into a smile. "I don't believe Mr. Yop has grown tusks yet. And he is still walking upright, though with some effort. He just might drop down on all fours any time. Keep an eye on him then, my little darling."

Annabeth giggled and whispered in his ear. "I think he's the two-legged kind."

Miri was bounding over tree roots and fallen logs to get to the cave lynx before it attacked. Suddenly, she was tackled from behind and her slingshot flew from her hand.

Her training triggered her self-defense mode, and she hit her attacker in the face with her free hand, arching her back to throw him off. She was on top of him when she saw, to her surprise, it was another human, a young man with a bleeding nose and a bruised eye.

"Ow, that hurt! Why did you have to hit me so hard?" The boy sat up, wiping his nose on a dry leaf. "I would have let you go if you'd identified yourself. Who are you, anyway?"

"Well, I would have told you if you hadn't pounced on me from behind like a coward. I thought it was a cave lynx." Miri stood up, letting the young man get to his feet, still moaning about his nose.

"A cave lynx? Here in the Trezarium?" The young man let out a whoop of laughter that made Miri look frantically around for the cave lynx. "That's rich! A cave lynx wouldn't last five minutes in here."

Miri crossed her arms in a gesture of disbelief. *Who is this braggart? He couldn't fight a girl, much less a cave lynx.* "Oh, and just why is that?"

The lad smirked. "Because lynxes make good eating and their fur first-class jackets, that's why. Everybody knows that. I can tell you're a stranger to these parts. What're you wearing? Looks like rags or something."

Miri looked down and saw that the antique bat costume had spilt into rags. She pulled it together with as much dignity as she could muster and looked him straight in the eyes. "And you look like you've been raised in a zoo! Since you and I have never met, it would seem logical that I am a stranger in the zoo," Miri said. "Now, I've got to go."

"How do I know you're not a spy for the Triumvirate?"

"You don't, but I'm not, because I'm one hundred percent human which the Triumvirate have sworn to replace with mutants or robots. Now, let me go, please, or I'll have to hurt you."

"Not so fast, my girl." Two more men, wearing outfits that made them look like matching trees, joined the young one with the bloody nose. "We can't let strangers bring weapons into our midst, now can we?" said the older of the two. With a glance at the one with the bloody nose, he said, "Loki, how could you let a mere girl get the best of you? You are a Lombardi! Don't you remember anything you've been taught?"

Miri scowled at her captors, hands on hips. "I'll have

you know I was warrior-trained by a graduate of the Academy. I always carry a weapon, and I don't go around looking like part of the scenery!"

"I'll say that again," the man surveyed Miri with admiring eyes. "Although I must say that's not a costume for the Trezarium. You'll soon change your ways, miss."

"Or have the cave people after you." the third one added.

"We can't stand here gabbing away while my people are in danger. Probably from the likes of you fools." With a backward somersault, Miri was off the path, running through the trees with the three Lombardis warriors right behind her.

Coming around a cluster of trees, she almost collided with Thur running in the other direction. Seeing the three woodsmen, he drew his lazorizer. "Freeze or I'll blow you to bits!"

"No, don't, Thur. They're harmless!" Miri shouted as all three woodsmen melted back into the forest.

"If they're so harmless, why are you running away from them?" Thur felt a rush of relief, seeing Miri's pretty face in these strange surroundings. But he knew it would be a mistake to let his feelings show. "Or did you challenge them to a race?"

"I'll explain later." Miri hardly paused to take a breath before taking off again. "You didn't happen to run into a cave lynx on your way here, did you?"

"Oh, swarms of them." Thur followed her, dodging around trees and leaping over roots and rocks. "Why? Is that why you and those people dressed like trees were running? Funny place for a cave lynx to hang out. I thought they liked high, dark places."

Miri stopped running and turned around. "I thought I heard one just now. Did you hear something like a roar?"

Thur wasn't prepared for her to stop so abruptly. He

collided with her and they both fell to the forest floor.

For a moment, they were lying face-to-face, their lips nearly touching. Then Thur was dragged to his feet by Riga.

He had a look of disgust on his face. "I thought you were lost, but I guess not. You knew exactly where you were going, you scruffy little human."

Thur shook himself loose from Riga's iron grip. "I was running toward—"

"Oh, forget trying to explain, Thur. Once Riga gets it into his head there's something dirty going on, he's permanently suspicious. It's a mutant thing. Now, let's find the others and make sure they are all right." Miri got to her feet, brushing the leaves and dirt from her tattered leggings. "Really, Riga. You don't have to look so disapproving. That's Aya's job."

"Then let's find Aya and see what she thinks about you two lying together on the forest floor." Riga's face actually had turned from its usual bluish color to a reddish hue with anger. It made him look almost human.

"Like you know all about it, Riga." Miri led the way back to the path. "Whatever. I'm tired and hungry. And what are those things that keep flitting from tree to tree and make little tweet sounds?"

Riga was still wondering why Miri had such an unsettling effect on him. "Birds. I think they call those birds."

"Probably somebody's idea of a robo toy. Like drones with feathers."

"Kind of messy for a robo toy," said Thur, wiping a splash of white stuff off his tunic.

∾∾∾

The residents of Yop's Hollow lived in underground

tunnels. "Like moles," Shadow commented to Val. "To think we've survived as an intact species just to revert to living like animals. Rodents at that."

"I heard that, Doc." Yop, who was leading the way, dropped back to join them. "That's because the Borgs send drones over Trezarium regular-like to see if they can spot us. When they do, the fools drop poison gas that doesn't hurt the trees but causes us to drops in our tracks. A tree is more important to them than a human life."

"That's because a tree produces oxygen while we just produce carbon dioxide. And that has brought the earth to its present state of ruin." Sadly, Shadow watched the children playing in the long tunnel between rooms. "And I have only myself to blame for robbing them of their heritage."

"Hasn't it always been like this?" Qin was sitting by the fire, drying her bright hair as though she'd fallen in love with it. "I mean, people living underground, hiding out from the Borgs. I know that's how we were raised."

Miri and Qin had changed out of their circus costumes into tunics and leggings of woodland colors. They were sitting close to the blazing fire eating raisins, nuts, and dried berries by the handfuls.

"Far from it, child." Yop was used to commanding an audience. As Mayor of the Hollow, he took any opportunity to speak on any subject, whether he knew what he was talking about or not. "Why, the Doc and I remember after the Lost Times when we even had lights and could go to market by the river. But that was before the Triumvirate took over. Then it all changed for the worse, right, Doc?"

" I've told you that before, Qin," Aya piped up in a thin, bitter voice. "That's when the robots took over and established the acceptable classes of mutants—Borgs, droids, drummans—thanks to the irresponsible experiments of men like Dr. Spencer here. He and his fellow scientists defected to the Triumvirate for protection. But with the Triumvirate, there's no such thing as loyalty, is there, Dr. Spencer? When humans were classified as defective, you found that out."

Val, who had been sitting in the corner of the cozy room where he could look at Miri, was immediately on the defensive. "My father did not defect! He was working for the first council, along with many other scientists, when the Triumvirate seized power and defeated the Noble Warrior tribes in charge of The Academy."

"That's all right, son," Shadow said in a weary voice. "I've heard it all before, you know. Aya, as I recall, your parents were scientists although of a different sort."

Before Aya could retort, Val got to his feet, bumping his head on the low ceiling. "No, Father, they're ignorant about what you tried to do to save them all. Why even these woods were your idea!" With a sweep of his arm, Val indicated the woods overhead. "And that Churn that powers the city was your doing. With all these improvements, you thought everybody would survive and live in peace. But the Triumvirate took over and stole your ideas, perverting to fit their own needs."

"Yes, but that was all a long time ago, and we have the future to think about. We can't stay like this." Shadow gestured at the underground living quarters. "The Borgs know we're in here and, besides, I won't hide anymore. We have to form a defense that will hold them off until we can raise an army."

"Then what?" Thur had been eating meat at the round table along with a couple of the Yop's woodsmen. "Us against the Borgs? That'll be shortest war in history. More like suicide."

Val gave him a stony glance. "Not if we use our brains, boy. The Borgs just do what they're programmed to do. I know most of their programmed orders and can counter them with different maneuvers. Chief Mako of the Lombardis proves that there still some warriors alive. I'm going to find them before the Borgs do. Then we'll see some action."

"You just gave me an idea, son." Shadow began to show even more signs he was coming back to life. "Brilliant thinking."

Thur returned to eating. "Intellectuals," he said in disgust. "Always coming up with dumb ideas."

Yop just grinned. "Have some more fried squirrel, everybody!"

With an impatient sigh, Val left the room. This time he remembered to duck, climbing the winding stairs to the surface. He found a seat carved out of a tree stump and looked up at the canopy of stars, thinking Miri's eyes were even lovelier. Below, watched like a Borg scanner by Riga's suspicious gaze, Miri saw Val leave and suddenly she longed to be with him. Using the excuse to refill the bowl of dried fruit and nuts, she moved toward the tunnel door.

"Hey," Qin said. "I'm coming, too!" And she followed Miri out into the long corridor, taking the bowl from her sister's hand. "Okay, go see your dreamy Borgie. Just be back in rat's time or I'll have to make up something to cover your tracks. And you know how good I am at making up stuff."

Miri was gone before Qin could finish speaking. She found Val still sitting on the wooden bench, contemplating the night sky.

"Is there room for one more?" she said.

At first, Val was confused. He thought Miri's voice was just echoing in his head like it had been ever since he'd first heard it back on the filthy sidewalks of Megacity.

"Star?" he asked.

"No, silly. I meant for me."

He looked up and saw her standing there beside him. Val jumped up, indicating the seat beside him. "Certainly! I was just...just going below. Not used to being underground, you know. Had to get a breath of fresh air. Good night!" he said with a bow.

"Well, how did it go?" Qin asked her when Miri came back downstairs looking glum.

"He went," was all Miri could say.

☙❧

Miri and Qin made friends quickly with the young people of the Hollow. The Hols, as those who dwelled underground liked to be called, regarded the newcomers as sophisticated residents of the city beyond the river, peppering the girls with questions about hairstyles and clothes. The boys of Yop's Hollow stayed on the fringes of the chattering group, admiring the fiery haired Qin and her pretty sister from a distance.

But Thur and Riga stayed aloof, waiting for Val to signal that he wanted their company, which rarely happened. Valerian and his father seemed to be deep in conference every time they asked him for a lesson in martial defense. So they practiced together, Riga coming out the winner in every match. One afternoon, they were joined by a group of young men from the Hollow. Out of the corner of his eye, Thur only recognized Loki, the fellow whose nose Miri had broken when he grabbed her in the forest. Loki was watching the match between mutant and human with eagerness.

Loki stood up. "Hey, would you teach us some of those moves?" He was well-muscled from living outdoors and could be a decent warrior if trained to be more observant, Thur thought. "My father will be impressed," Loki continued. "He's Mako, Chief of the Lombardis. He might even give you a job, mutie."

Thur turned his head just as Riga swung back with both his arms together, hands clasped, catching Thur in the midsection. The result was Thur lying on the ground, flung out like a gutted fish with little birds singing in his head.

"Like that one?" Riga asked.

Loki grinned. "Yeah, like that one."

As they finished up, Riga was putting away the crude weapons, when he noticed Thur was skipping stones down by a little stream.

He walked down and stood beside him, but Thur only continued skipping pebbles without acknowledging his presence.

"Come on, you're not that hurt," Riga said. "Maybe your pride is bruised but I could have hit you harder than that. I've told you never take your eyes away from your opponent. And you did. Serves you right. Now, come on, quit sulking and carry your share of training weapons back to camp."

But Thur remained rooted to the spot. "You didn't have to hit me so hard, Riga. That really hurt."

"What really hurt is me taking you down in front of the chief's son. Come on, admit it. And the lad had the nerve to suggest his father might offer me a job. Imagine working for a Lombardi who has sworn to erase all the mutants off the face of the Earth. Fat chance I'd work for him!" Riga clapped Thur's shoulder. "Come on, then. It's getting dark. Don't want the worfels to get you. Or the Lombardis."

Reluctantly, Thur shouldered his share of the weapons and followed Riga back to the Hollow.

As they grew more accustomed to their new freedom, Annabeth and Tookie played hide-and-seek around the trees in the Hollow. One day, they were both so tired and hot, they fell down among the leaves for a nap. But they were soon awakened by a group of children from the Hollow who stumbled on the sleeping youngsters while gathering wild figs.

"You can't take naps until after lunch," said a boy who seemed to be the leader of the foragers.

"We all have jobs around here," said a little girl not much older than Annabeth. "Including drolls. They have to eat, too."

The children explained that certain groups were assigned to collect figs, others collected nuts, still others gathered fruits or plants in season. There was an apple detail, one for nuts, blackberries, wild strawberries, onions, and garlic.

"First, you city dwellers have to learn how to get around the treetops on zip lines," said the leader. "Then, depending on well you do that, we assign you to a group."

Annabeth looked from one dirty face to another. "Don't you even want to know our names?"

"For now, you're just all Newcomers to us." The girl shifted her baskets of figs to her other hip. "Then you'll get names. Our names, not city names."

"I like my own name, thank you." Annabeth grabbed the basket the girl was holding out to her.

"So do I," Tookie echoed.

"I didn't know they had drolls in the city," the leader of the Hols said.

"Then you have a lot to learn! You teach us and we'll teach you. Is it a deal?" Without realizing it, Annabeth used one of Thur's favorite expressions.

The leader of the Hols foragers was impressed. "Deal," he said. And led the way into the Trezarium.

Revived by the food, fresh water, and clean air, Aya gathered the women of the Hollow to give them cooking lessons on Blu, who had become the marvel of the Hollow. While they prepared food for the Hollow, she told them stories with Blu correcting her from time to time, because her memory was getting as cloudy as her eyes.

Deep in a back room underground, Shadow and Valerian began assembling a machine made of anything they could find among Yop's museum collection from the Lost Times, and even before that, when humans had dominated the earth. There were tank wheels, weapons of all sorts, and old motors that used fossil fuels.

On a sheet of tree bark, Shadow began drawing plans for a giant machine. "It's to scale, of course. We'll build the model first to see if it works. Then we'll build the real thing."

Valerian looked puzzled. "What's it's supposed to do, Dad? I mean, the Borgs will pick up any machine noise, even this far underground."

Doctor Spencer took off his handmade spectacles and rubbed his eyes. "I don't know what kind of physics they taught you at the Academy, son, but this machine doesn't make noise of any kind. It runs on thermal energy—light to be exact.

His son shook his head. "Now, I really don't know what you're talking about."

"You use a lazorizer, right?"

"Right." Val nodded, thinking it over. "Oh, I get it. It's going to be a giant disintegrator."

Spencer sighed. "I see the Borgs only taught you to destroy. This machine will be an anti-disintegrator to protect all the people in this Hollow."

"But—"

"There's an old saying. The best offense is a good defense."

Val gave his father a quizzical look. "Isn't the best defense is a good offense? A pre-emptive strike. That's the principle I was taught in the Academy."

The elder Spencer turned away in disgust. "And that's the very philosophy that got us humans in trouble in the first place. Shoot first and ask questions later. Now, hand me that wrench. Let's get started."

CHAPTER 10

THE PEOPLE OF THE TREZARIUM

The newbies, as they were called affectionately, soon learned there were more residents in Trezarium than Yop's tribe and the Lombardis Warriors. Thur and Riga were out hunting with Loki and his friend Chez from the Hollow when Riga's sharp ears picked up the sound of a drone.

"Incoming! Quick! Into that cave."

Thur followed him, scrambling up to a hollow opening in a stony outcrop then looked behind him. The others hunkered down where they were, their camouflaged outfits blending in with forest.

"Fools," Riga muttered as he climbed in the opening. "They will get us all recycled."

The drone passed overhead, so low the camera on its underside was visible. The small aircraft was big enough to hold a man, though probably just a droid. No sooner had the drone passed, than they heard a roar that stood Thur's curly hair on end. They scrambled back out, dropping to the ground some five feet below them as a giant droll emerged and then another behind him.

"Run!" shouted Chez as he and his friends pelted the giant with rocks from their supply bags.

The droll was yelling what seemed to be curses and throwing boulders down from his perch above them. Thur and Riga took turns blasting the boulders to bits in mid-air with their lazorizers. When the drolls saw their missiles coming back at them in a hail of rocks, they stopped throwing boulders, aghast with horror. Loki, Chez, and the others were equally stunned at the destruction. For a moment, all was still.

Then Thur stepped forward, speaking in a gentle voice to the drolls. "Look, we don't mean any harm. We were just hiding from the drone." He pointed to the sky. The drolls followed Thur's every move, first looking up and back at the tall young man standing bravely in the clearing. "Let's be neighbors." He made the gesture of shaking hands, that Aya had taught was the universal sign for friendship, and then touched his heart.

The giant drolls exchanged grunts and, ducking their heads, went back inside their caves.

"At least they didn't throw any more rocks," Riga said when Thur rejoined him.

When Shadow heard about the incident, he was thoughtful for a moment. "That was brave of you, Thur. Drolls have little use for humans—or anyone else, for that matter. It's because of humans using nuclear weapons, they've become mutant giants like they are. It was radiation, you see, that caused them to grow to such heights."

"You mean, we were once humans like you?" Tookie who was standing with Annabeth, had been listening to Thur retelling of their encounter with the drolls. "Then why I am I so furry and you're not?"

He lifted both children onto his lap. "You're furry because drolls have adapted to living in damp caves. That gives me an idea. Tookie, do you want to help us defeat the Triumvirate?"

Tookie's elfin face lit up with excitement. "You mean them as put me in the Dumpster and tried to recycle me? Just tell me what to do and I'll do it."

"Me, too," said Annabeth. "I want to help."

Shadow whispered something to both children and sent them giggling away.

"You surely don't want those children to endanger themselves," said Aya. She was serving the men one of the dishes the women had made that afternoon.

"Why not? It will take everyone to defeat the Triumvirate, and they have a part to play." Spencer frowned, looking at the dish she set in front of him. "What is it?"

"Cream of acorn soufflé," she said proudly.

"Don't touch it," he shouted, upending the bowl and spilling the soup all over the table.

The men paused, their spoons halfway to their mouths.

"Throw it out!" he commanded

"What?" Aya was so angry, she sputtered like grease in a hot pan. "Don't you dare! Don't listen to this…man! He doesn't know what he's talking about."

"It's poison to cook acorns, don't you know that, woman? You want to do what the Triumvirate has failed to do and kill us all?"

Everybody immediately dumped their dishes in the composter.

"Okay, Dad," Val said calmly as Aya hurried away, hiding angry tears. "You've made your point."

"Yes, and very pointedly, too." Miri and Qin began gathering up the plates. "She only thought she was pleasing you," Miri said to Spencer but Val perceived it as a rebuke to both to of them. "Poor Aya, she's never lived in a place with trees before now. She looks on everything as a potential food source."

"I'm sorry. You see, I've already forgotten what it's

like to be starving." Shadow looked ashamed of his outburst.

"That's the difference between us," Qin snapped. "We've been starving all our lives and Aya lived longer than we have. We'll never forget!"

She and Miri went after Aya to comfort her while Val looked after Miri, longing to apologize.

After the incident with the acorn soufflé, Aya kept Annabeth and Tookie with her instead of letting them play with the children of the Hollow. The other women tried to get her to resume her cooking lessons, but she refused, although she said they could still use Blu. The old robot became a sous-chef, chopping, mincing, and slicing everything from squirrel to nuts.

"But not acorns," he kept muttering. "Never acorns."

"Time to try out our demagnetizer," Spencer said to Val one morning. "The Borgs will be sending drones over any time now."

Val looked up in surprise from tightening a screw on the anti-disintegrator machine. "Demagnetizer? I didn't know we had one."

"We don't. At least, not yet. There's a part I need to keep it from overheating, but we have to bring down one of those drones to get it. So in my spare time, I've built this." From under a root, Spencer took what looked like an older model lazorizer. "I traded that old traveler fellow a few spare parts I didn't need and just reversed a few things, added a switch or two and—bingo. A hand-held demagnetizer. I have to try it out first, though. I thought I would use old Blu as the target to try to demagnetize his computer parts. If it works, the drone will drop out of the sky like a dead duck."

"Poor Blu." Val couldn't help grinning at the thought of the old robot keeling over with his apron and chef's hat still on. "You can reverse the process, I hope. The ladies of the Hollow will be in an uproar if you can't."

But his father didn't smile. Shadow seemed to be thinking of something far less humorous. "Of course, my brother and I were working on an anti-demagnetizer which would reverse the process when we—but we'll see." He busied himself, tinkering with the old lazorizer.

"Your brother? Father, you didn't tell me you had a brother." Valerian sounded hurt. "What's he like?"

"Was, probably," Shadow replied, keeping his head down. "Mercator was an inventor like me. Always playing jokes, a regular pain in the ass, that was your uncle, E. Mercator Spencer. I emphasize the 'was' because I have not seen or heard from him again after. Now, let's go on top and wait for a drone to try this out on."

"Really, Dad. Sometimes you worry me with this science stuff. It's almost like you don't give a slitz about how you do something, you only care about the end result. Like the Churn. You wanted to build it to provide the city with electricity, right? But the Triumvirate stole your idea. I have heard Imperator Androz boast that it was the Triumvirate's idea."

"Right. And I did that, using natural resources. I just didn't realize the Triumvirate would be in control of it someday. Androzarian, huh? I had no idea that old Other was still around."

But Val failed to catch the irony in his father's voice. "But you were warned it would put the farmers who depended on the water from the river out of business. Or that it would lead to environmental disaster by making a desert where there had once been lush vegetation. Mediah said when my mother died, she told you it would only be hurting humans if the Triumvirate got control of it."

Spencer started walking through the tunnel, carrying his demagnetizer. "You can't believe anything she says.

Mediah is a liar. She's manufactures lies for the Triumvirate, that's part of her job."

"She has another side. She knew who I was and still she protected me," Val protested.

Spencer stopped and turned around. In the dim light of the tunnel, his face was contorted with grief and anger. "I see Mediah brainwashed you like she brainwashes everybody in Megacity. She only wanted you alive so she could get me to stay with the Triumvirate. Only when she couldn't do that, she condemned me to the Slow Death."

"I'm sorry, I didn't know." Val was shocked to see his father so angry. "I'm just saying—"

"I know, son," Spencer said. "But, sometimes you have to take the bad with the good. For instance, Blu is just a machine, an obsolete one at that. With the drone sensors, I can build a much better one. We have to make progress. Otherwise, The Triumvirate will extinguish us from the earth."

Val shook his head. "You don't get it, do you? Blu is a companion to Aya and her family. He helped them to survive. Now you want to change their whole history with him the way you changed the river. Go ahead, but you'll do it alone. I won't be part of your experiment."

"Very well, Val. I thought you wanted to defeat the Triumvirate. But if you're already crying over some old run-down machine—"

"A machine that saved your life, Dr. Spencer." Blu came lurching out of a small room adjoining the Tunnel. "But, you're right, I'm just an old machine. Junk, really. I don't expect thanks. And I'm willing to donate my parts to science, if it will help defeat the Triumvirate." Blu turned to Val. "And you, boy, have some respect for your elders. You must learn what it is to be part of a civilized society. Everyone in the Hollow acts like a family, with a common set of values."

Yop stepped from behind the old robot. "Yes, like love."

"And a community, where everybody contributes," said another man behind him.

A woman joined the others in the tunnel. "And everyone is equal."

Spencer realized, by the crowd in the narrow passageway, that the whole community had overheard the exchange between Val and himself.

"Now. Dr. Spencer, you'd better tell us what your plan is so we can vote on it," Yop said. "And to do that, we must use the great Hall. follow me."

He led the way down a winding hall leading off the main tunnel, lighting the torches as he went. He paused before huge double doors of oak with giant hinges and a huge lock. Taking the key from a ledge just overhead, Yop swung wide the heavy doors which creaked on their hinges.

"Welcome to our parliament," he said gesturing at the spacious room inside. "This is where we all meet to vote on our rules."

❦❦❦

Aya was stuffing a few things in a leather pouch given to her by the Cooking Committee for her contribution to their menu. There were two clay pots, three wooden spoons, some salt, and a dress made of soft deerskins.

"What are you doing, Aya?" Miri stepped into the small room high in the treehouse which was their new home. Thur and Riga slept in hammocks like the rest of the men of the Hollow. "Why are you packing your cooking pots?"

"Because I'm leaving, that's why," Aya snapped. "Hand me those confounded leather shoes, please. I can't go barefoot over all these roots and stumps."

"But—"

"Never mind the buts and whys. I'm living on my own. This is just too much togetherness for me. I'm not used to all these people, that's all."

Qin was listening, too. "Grandma, the council has just voted to make war on the Triumvirate. There's going to be trouble. You can't just go out in the forest and live alone."

"I suppose Ed Spencer is behind this war-making plot. Trouble follows that man wherever he goes. We should have left him in the Dumpster," Aya said bitterly.

"There are giant drolls out there, too. Thur told me." Miri winked at her sister. "Like Tookie only bigger. Much bigger. And worfels that can run on two legs. Chimeras, Riga told me."

"Yeah, like the cave lynx with a pair of lungs that would outdo the roar of the Churn," Qin chimed in. "Humans mixed with wolves and who knows what else."

"Probably something else of Dr. Death's experiments that went wrong." Aya stood still and gave them a hard, defiant look. "You girls don't scare me. Oh, I'm hate leaving Blu here for that mad scientist to experiment on. Poor Blu. I just hate it! He's been so good to me." Aya burst into sobs.

The girls rushed to her, entwining Aya in their arms. "The people of the Hollow will get over the acorn soufflé. In fact, they just went on with dinner as though nothing had happened."

"Yeah," said Qin. "These people really know how to eat."

Miri burst into laughter. "Yop Barnswallow probably hasn't seen his feet in years."

"And his wife could be his twin," Qin said between gasps. "They look just like a couple of clay cooking pots from behind." She collapsed on the floor, laughing.

Aya began to chuckle. "I've never seen this much food. I swear these women cook all day."

"Hey, that gives me an idea." Qin sat up, suddenly sober. "How 'bout if we teach the girls how to become warriors. Like Riga says 'Keep Fit Or Die!' Miri, you could be the instructor. You know how to do all that stuff."

Miri nodded thoughtfully. "And Val and Riga can teach the men."

"Even Yop Barnswallow? I'd like to see that happen." Aya began to smile at the thought.

"And Yop's wife Lolly?" Qin giggled. "Can you imagine her as a warrior? She'd just have to sit on a Borgie to squash him!"

They went off into hoots of laughter again and, this time, Aya joined them. When she looked around, her pouch was gone. She rushed out to the treehouse landing just in time to see Annabeth and Tookie climbing down the ladder. The pouch was dangling on a nearby limb, out of her reach. Inside, the girls were laughing. Aya suddenly realized what a good sound that was.

Qin's idea took off the next day like wildfire. It was as if the people of the Hollow were only waiting for the Newbies to teach them something new. They even willingly divided into their work groups—the men to do the hunting, the women to cook and do the washing. Qin took the children and the babies watched from their swings among the trees.

Thur and Riga took the men's group and Miri put the women through a series of exercises. After two hours, every one of the new recruits groaned, grunted, and complained about their backs, shoulders, arms—in fact, their whole bodies—being a mass of aches and pains.

Miri ordered everyone to skip the usual banquet at lunch and only eat berries and nuts. Only the young Hols obeyed the order. Yop Barnswallow and his wife Lolly served the usual huge lunch to the defectors in the cafeteria. Afterward, they retired for their afternoon naps.

Meanwhile, Val and Shadow worked in their underground laboratory, although Val itched to watch what was going on above ground. Finally, Shadow took notice of his son's distraction

"The trainers are wasting their time, you know? They'll never turn these simple people into warriors. Fighting's just not in their nature."

Valerian disagreed. "I think organizing them as a fighting force is a good idea. I'm just concerned that all this activity will attract a drone. And that will lead the Borgs right to us."

"Then go tell them that." As if he were bored with the subject, Dr. Spencer returned to tinkering with his current project, the de-magnetizer.

Val obeyed all too quickly, as if he were waiting for the chance to get upstairs. "And say hello to Miri while you're up there. I'm sure that's who you want to see."

Val turned and smiled at his father. "You don't miss much, do you?"

"Get out of here." His voice was gruff, but there was a smile on Shadow's face.

Val was right. It wasn't very long until a drone came toward the Hollow. When the lookout stationed in the tallest tree picked up the whining sound of the drones motor, he whistled his warning. Everyone in the training groups scattered, in spite their trainers shouting to just drop where they were.

Shadow decided to try out his new weapon. He rushed up the stairs to the ground level as the drone approached, its camera recording everything on the ground. Spencer aimed the de-magnetizer directly at the drone's camera eye on its belly and fired. Not only was the weapon silent, it simply looked like a flash of light.

The drone dropped as though it had run into a wall.

A cheer went up from the Hollow. "You've done it! You've beaten the Borgs!" Yop Barnswallow engulfed Shadow in an embrace against his sweaty jerkin. "Doc, you're a genius!"

"No, Yop." Shadow was already examining the fallen machine. It was slightly damaged but still useful. "I'm afraid I've just kicked a wasp's nest. But I couldn't let the drone pass. It might have caught your people running away."

"I told them to drop where they were." Thur joined them, running his fingers through his thick, blond hair in exasperation. "But they just won't listen. What is it with these people?"

"Don't worry," Yop said. "I'll see to it that they do it next time."

"Then you might try modeling the behavior yourself." Riga gave the mayor a hard look. "Being an authority figure and all."

ಲೊಲ

"We have to move the people to safety." They were in the laboratory deep beneath the trees. Dr. Spencer had called a meeting of the Newcomers, but Yop came along to see what was going on. "The Borgs will send more and more drones to see if the one that fell was just a malfunction. I've dismantled the tracking device, but I can't be sure that it didn't register the exact location before it fell."

"Do we have to move? I'm beginning to like this place." Qin looked around the group, hoping to find someone who agreed with her,

"Nonsense, girl," Aya said with a sharp look in her

direction. "You just like all the attention you get from the boys."

"Yeah," said Thur. "Especially Chez."

Yop scratched his bald head. "But where should we go? There's other inhabitants of the forest, you know. We usually stay in our own territory."

"Like the giant drolls," Riga said with a glance at Thur. "That's exactly what the Triumvirate is counting on."

"Not only them," Yop said. "There's the River People, the cave drolls, and the Noble Warriors. There're lots of tribes of those, though I've never met up with any of them, except Mako. We've stumbled into their territory before and got out in a hurry. Oh, yes, and the Travelers. But they never stay in one place for long."

"Yeah, they're usually on the run for stealing something," Chez said and everybody laughed. He winked at Qin, but she was looking at Valerian.

Val seemed to be a natural leader, getting the people's support instead of giving them no alternative. "It would be only temporary until we build defenses around the Hollow. Then the people can come back when it's safe again."

Spencer wasn't taking "no" for an answer. "Pack up all that you will need to move swiftly," he said grimly. "The drones will be back within an hour, or two at the most, and this time, they'll probably be armed with missiles."

"And when your trainers say drop, tell your people to drop where they are and don't move," Val said. "Even if your faces are in the mud. Better mud than blood."

"How do we know these newcomers aren't just trying to take over our Hollow," said a new voice at the back of the crowd that had gathered around them.

"Yeah, how do we know they aren't just trying to

lead us into a trap?" another voice said, joining the first.

"To use us as bait for the cave drolls or the Worfels to wipe us out."

It became a chorus, with everybody joining in.

"Because we will leave a detachment of workers here in the Hollow to build the defenses." Spencer got to his feet and stood beside his son. He looked like a tired old king with the weight of the world on his shoulders. In the light of the flickering torches his craggy features, once as handsome as his son's, now looked drawn and thin. But his eyes were alive with passionate ideas, darting about the room like a hunting hawk looking for some place to land.

He found it in Aya. She stood up and faced the rebellious crowd. "And some newcomers, you idiots, will stay here with you because you aren't capable of fighting your way out of a paper bag, much less taking on the Borg Guards. We, on the other hand, have a lifetime of experience of doing just that!"

Miri jumped up beside Aya. "And we're trained as warriors. Riga, before he was rejected and thrown out of the Academy, reached First Level. He has taught Thur and me as he was taught. And Val achieved the rank of Ubercaptain in the Guard. One of them will stay here to train the workers who are building defenses, and one of them will go with the people. That way, everyone is safe and we will be taking the same risks as you."

"Thank you, Aya," Spencer whispered. "You always were a brave woman."

"No, you are the one to thank, Ed Spencer," Aya said. "For giving us back the hope we thought was gone. The hope that we will survive."

They divided into two groups with warriors and trainers attached to both. Miri, Riga, and Valerian went with the group that would find a temporary home. Qin and Thur stayed with the group that would build the defenses for the Hollow. Aya said she had enough traveling, and someone had to cook for the people doing the work. But she allowed Miri to take Annabeth and Tookie, with strict instructions about bedtimes and snacks.

"And don't let them get into those prickly bushes and eat those blackberries. You'll never get their faces and hands clean!"

Spencer stayed to work on the defenses and employed Blu as a draftsmen to draw up his plans. Blu surprised him by drawing, to scale, weapons and defenses worthy of a battlefield general.

When Dr. Spencer asked how he learned his skills, the old robot rolled his mismatched eyes in Spencer's direction. "One of my first employers was a general with the Borg Guard," Blu said. "You didn't think my only talents were as a stove pot, did you, Dr. Spencer?"

Valerian was preparing supplies for the journey when Thur approached him, his expression like a thunder cloud.

"Something on your mind?" Valerian continued working, ticking off the list he and Yop had prepared. *Waterproof skins, a pound of nuts per person, dried fish.*

"Yeah, you are, Borgie!" Thur snarled.

"What about me?"

"I want to keep you to keep away from my girl."

Val still kept it cool. "And that is?"

"You know who it is! Miri, that's who." Thur punctuated this revelation by shoving Val back a few steps.

Valerian answered him with a level tone which enraged Thur all the more. "Oh, really? Does she know that?"

Thur came at him, swinging. Valerian had his notebook in his hands and, at first, was caught off guard by the attack.

But he was a trained warrior and, after a few self-defenses moves, got his balance again. He thought he would finish off this boy's attack in no time flat, but Thur surprised him with his level of training.

They were going at it, tearing up the woods around them, rolling around in the dirt when Yop and two men who were bringing supplies jumped in, separating the two combatants.

They were both without a scratch, though covered with dirt. "I know what will cool you young bucks off," Yop said. "Bring 'em along to the showers and throw them in, men. That's a sure cure for hot tempers."

The story of the fight made the rounds of gossip before nightfall. Qin heard it from her friend and rushed to tell Miri about it. But her sister merely shrugged and went on packing. "It's because Thur's being left behind to train the Hols to fight. He's been pouting about that ever since the decision was made. Hand me that adl-adl over there, will you?"

Qin brought her the slender leather strap wrapped around a sharp stone and watched Miri pack it away in her leather pouch. "I don't see what you want with that old thing. It's positively antediluvian."

Miri straightened up and stared at her sister. "Whoa! Where'd you learn a word like that?"

"Wouldn't you like to know?" Qin said with an impish smirk.

"Tell me or I'll show you what an adl-adl is good for." Miri threw a pine straw pillow at her sister who threw it back.

And the battle was on. The tree house rocked as they threw anything they could get their hands on.

If Aya hadn't stopped them, Miri said later to Thur, there would have been nothing left but acorns to throw. Her attempt to cheer him up got nowhere. "And do you know where she said she learned that long word?" When he said nothing, she answered her own question. "From a book. Qin said there's a woman who has a whole bunch of them, and she lends them out. Isn't that great?"

"I guess so," came the reply out of the dark. He was sitting on the winding stairs that connected the tree-houses, nursing a swollen jaw.

"Why do I feel like I'm talking to myself tonight?" Miri said, throwing up her hands. "Maybe I'd better go clean up the mess and get to bed. Early start in the morning." Instead, she sat down on the step beside him. "I heard about the fight, Thur. I heard you gave Valerian a good match."

Thur made a disgusted sound. "Not good enough. That's his reason for leaving me here and taking you on the expedition instead. But everybody knows what the real reason is."

Miri couldn't help but smile. "You think he's sweet on me, don't you? That's the only reason he picked me instead of you. Is that what's got you all bent out of shape?"

Thur winced as if it hurt him to speak. "Think? I know that's what it is, Miri. I've seen the way he looks at you, and he's with you every chance he can get. Forget this story about taking you along to deal with the women and children. If you believe that, then you're just a dumb girl!"

Miri flashed a word from Qin's vocabulary. "Oh, drop that antediluvian attitude! You're now the chief trainer for the Hollow. And that's an honor."

Thur suddenly came to life, grabbing her hand. "But you'll be with him. I've seen the way you look at Val. The stupid expression you get on your face like…I don't know…like Annabeth when she eats blackberries."

"I hope I don't look that bad with the big blue stains

around my mouth," she said, bursting into a giggle.

But Thur wasn't laughing. He pulled Miri over to him. "I love you, Miri. I've felt it, and I know you have too." He kissed her on the mouth. "There, I've sealed my pledge with a kiss. You're pledged to me now."

Miri drew away. "Thur, whatever gave you that idea? I certainly am *not* pledged to you, or anybody! Besides, I've known you all my life! You're like a brother to me." She got to her feet. "Maybe it's a good thing that you and I are parting tomorrow. Good night!"

He watched her storm away, climbing the steps to the tree house two at a time.

Suddenly, he was alone, really alone in a dark world. Valerian had his father. Loki had his father. Yop had all his children. Something inside Thur ached, not because Miri had just rejected him. That had hurt. But not as much as this feeling that he was lost. Adrift in a world like a boat floating down the Sumi River, toward an uncertain future. Riga was there to protect him and Aya, too. But there was something else, someone else he belonged to. He just didn't know who or what.

The two groups parted just before dawn the next day, not without tears, as men watched their families walk away in single file, following Yop Barnswallow's lead. By the time the first drone came over, they had built a camouflaged canopy over the tunnels which they would later turn into a retractable roof. When the drone passed directly overhead without deviating from its course, the men standing beneath the canopy cheered—but quietly. They had built the first defense.

CHAPTER 11

I've got your little weasel and his hole in my sights. Just thought you'd like to know, baby." The imperator's voice came on her office communication screen, though he had blocked his image.

As if Androz's voice could remain anonymous, Mediah thought. "Oh? And so do I, you big thug. You coming over tonight?" *That ought to set Riksbury's forked tongue wagging.*

"Maybe. Depends."

"Oh, don't be coy, Androz. I've got steak."

That got the reaction Mediah had hoped for. "Where in hell did you get it?"

She could hear him salivating. "I have my sources."

"It's not that manufactured stuff, is it? The stuff made from beans and wood."

"The real thing. Red meat." Actually, she hated the stuff. Even having it in her cooler sickened her. And she had to pay a councilman's ransom to the smuggler to get it for her. But she knew all of Androz's weaknesses and one of them was cow's meat—rare. She even had potatoes, though she had no idea how to cook them. Fry them, the computer said. In what? She didn't even have a stove to cook on.

Androz took care of that problem. "I'll bring my

cook. I can't risk having you ruin a good steak. They're too hard to get."

Mediah relaxed. He had a robot cooker so she wouldn't have to smell burning flesh. She smelled it every time she went past the Dumpster.

Within an hour, the imperator arrived with his robot cook and a bottle of wine, a sort of diluted version of Swaug, he said. She had taken care to wear a transparent gown of twinkling fabric that made him take his mind off the meat at least for half an hour.

"So you've got a fix on Valerian's location, have you?"

"Yes, darling girl. He's holed up in the trees. We've suspected for a long time there were pockets of vermin there in there, but you're right. He's led us right to them. You're very clever, babe." Androz looked at her doing her hair at her dressing table. "As clever as you are beautiful. When is your boy giving us the go-ahead to wipe them out, did he say?"

"Don't worry, darling. Val is very meticulous about everything he does. He'll give you the signal when he locates all of them." Mediah came over to the bed where the general was stretched out like a starfish on a rock. "They must have allies to have survived this long."

"You won't tell the council then? I'll be the first to know, won't I, baby?" He patted the circular bed beside him. "It's important that I make the first move. That shows the council how effective I am with sources of intelligence they don't have. That's what keeps me on top of the rat pack. That's what they are. A bunch of rats."

"Of course, my darling. If Riksbury doesn't tip off the council about my plan first," she whispered, lying back on the pillows beside him. "I wouldn't trust him not to. In fact, I heard him denouncing me to the uberminister today. Telling the old man about you and me seeing each other."

Androz sat up as if she pricked him with a pin. "Say what? Riksbury, that old pile of slitz! Why would he even know about it? This's not his district at all."

"Because he wants me off the council. I heard him complaining about my wicked ways. I think I've got enough on him to send him to the Dumpster and he knows it. But if he gets a quorum—you know they're like a pack of worfels. If they smell blood, they come in for the kill."

Androz sat back on one elbow and looked down at her. "What evidence does he have on us?"

"As you just said, he has his sources of information, just like we all do." Mediah nodded at the wall screen. "I've dismantled the connection to the cameras like you told me to. But you know, Riksbury knows the uberminister will start an inspection, and he'll eventually find out about us. I just hope Valerian messages me soon that he's found enough Rejects and humans for you to launch a cleanup that will impress the council."

"Let's eat and talk later," Androz said, getting out of bed with a groan. "I can't think on an empty stomach."

ↄﬞↄ

"I'm sure they know where we are." Spencer gathered the defenders every night to hear their reports and give them their instructions for the next day. "If I'm not wrong, that will work to our advantage."

"And what if you are wrong?" Thur asked with a challenge in his voice. "We'll get wiped out, right? That's bogus! All this work for nothing."

"Will you just shut up and let him talk?" Qin said. "You might learn something."

Spencer grinned. "At least, this is a healthy debate. That's the way to get new ideas."

Qin held up her hand. "Well, I've got one."

"Now, look who's talking. The walking library," Thur mumbled.

Qin gave him a withering look. "That's right, I read it in a book."

"So what's the idea?" Chez said encouragingly.

Qin described how, in The Time Before when humans ruled the earth, they had wars. Lots of wars. In early times, there were castles and the owner of the castle built a kind of lake around it called a moat. "But sometimes, that didn't stop their enemies from building a bridge over the moat. "So the owner built a deep trench around the moat and disguised it with bushes and trees. The enemy, thinking they were just charging up to the moat, fell into the trench where there all kind of pointed sticks sticking up. It was called a Ha-Ha, I guess, because the joke was on them. An even better name was the Wolf's Leap."

"That would definitely take out some of them Borgies," Chez said. "That's a good one, Qin."

"Perfect for robots like some of the Borgs," a man said, joining in the applause for Qin. "They don't think, they just go straight ahead."

"I beg your pardon," Blu said, rolling his eyes in the direction of the speaker.

"Sorry, Blu. Your model is probably too smart. That's why you're obsolete. At least the Wolf's Leap is a delaying tactic," Spencer said thoughtfully. "And, as the man back there said, it's perfect for robots. I think that's a great idea, Qin."

Qin beamed with pride. "I got out it of a book," she repeated.

Thur groaned. "Not again."

"I'm putting you and Chez in charge of the Ha-Ha or whatever it's called." Spencer was anxious to move on to other matters of defense. "Get a crew together and start tomorrow."

In the morning, there were more flights of drones. They came three at once, fanning out to cover more territory.

"They've picked up on our movements. Probably Val's expedition. Even though I told him to be careful, he can't control the children," Spencer confided to Aya who had brought him his lunch in the laboratory.

"You can't blame them for running about in the woods," she said. "After all, that's really what this is all about. So they'll survive to carry on the race of man."

The scientist had a worried expression as he stirred the steaming cider she had brought. "I know, I know. It's just that I'm having trouble with the demagnetizer that will disable them, that's all."

Aya looked at him in surprise. "But the one you tried out worked very well. What's wrong with that one?"

"It's just not strong enough to work on bigger drones, ones that carry weapons." Spencer smiled, in spite of his weariness. "You've got enough to worry about. I didn't mean to burden you with technical problems."

There was a squeaking of wheels as Blu came up to the work table, the plans he had been drafting in one mitten. "What's wrong with your other arm, Blu? Why is it dangling like that?" Spencer asked.

"I'm practicing, that is why."

"What on earth for?" Aya said, laughing. "Doing everything with one hand?"

"Exactly, Aya. I want to donate the sensors in my left arm to Dr. Spencer so he can build a universal demagnetizer."

Both humans were speechless for a few heartbeats. Spencer was the first to recover. "Let me just guess. A universal demagnetizer could stop anything within a hundred miles or so that has a computer. The Brain for instance," he said, with a glance at Aya.

"Precisely," said Blu. "I can draw you a diagram, if you like."

"But, Blu, where did you learn about this…this… universal thingy?"

They all jumped, a little nervously, at the sound of Qin behind them.

"Shush, girl. Come in and shut the door," Aya snapped crossly. "That's what you get for snooping at key holes."

"Nothing locks doors in the Hollow so there aren't any key holes, Grandma. I just came to see what was keeping you, that's all. You're needed back in the dining hall."

Aya ignored the impertinent girl but Qin was sure she'd hear about it later. "Go on, Blu."

"When I was first minted, and shiny, I was assigned to a general. General E. Mercator was his name."

"I know the name well," Spencer said, with a glance at Aya. "He was an inventor for the Academy. A very talented one. I always admired his work. Go on."

"He was working on the central computer called the Brain and was directed by the council to develop a demagnetizer that would dismantle all the computer systems within a certain area, in case of war. So Mercator created the universal demagnetizer and, when it was installed in the Brain, he just disappeared."

"And you have no idea what happened to him?" Spencer met Aya's gaze. They both knew the answer.

Blu's eyes rolled around like pin balls. "I do, but it's too sad to repeat. He was a good master."

"Key word, 'was,'" Qin said.

Spencer turned his back on all of them, staring at the wall.

"That does it," said Aya, streaking from the room and snatching Qin by the ear along with her. "Wait 'til I get you home."

"But, Grandma, I was just stating a fact! Ow, that hurts!"

Aya pulled Qin along down the tunnel. "I'll give you facts, girl! Mercator Spencer was Shadow's brother! And that's a fact you didn't read in a book!"

"I don't know about you, Dr. Spencer, but I'd rather be General Mercator than that poor girl right now." Blu's printers were spitting out the blueprints. "I think he named them after me," he said modestly. "Blue prints, you see?"

Spencer didn't answer.

∽∾∽∾

Valerian soon learned that moving humans was not like moving a Borg Guard unit. For one thing, they did not know how to obey orders. The little ones skittered around like loose mercury, The older ones listened to Yop, not him.

In frustration, he consulted with Riga and Miri. "They don't seem to realize this is not a picnic we're going on. The Brain could be watching our every move!"

"It's the children," Miri said. "They haven't had enough sweets and crave the blackberry bushes along the way. You probably don't remember what it was like, craving something sweet."

Riga watched the glances traded between the two humans, the one he admired, and one he simply loved, whatever emotion that was.

"Oh, I remember," Val said, his eyes meeting hers. "But it was beaten out of me at the Academy."

"Not me." Miri laughed. "I still get blackberry fever, just like Annabeth does. Only I think it's under control."

"I hope so." Val smiled, an expression so rare it made his face hurt. "Because it's putting us in jeopardy."

"I'll control them," Riga said in order to put an end to the exchange between the two of them.

But the next morning, just as the expedition was packing up camp, Annabeth and Tookie ran off to gather the sweet fruit that grew wild in the forest. They had just found a patch of juicy berries when a giant cave droll appeared with a large basket, intending to gather berries. Annabeth saw the cave droll and started to run but Tookie just kept stuffing juicy berries into her mouth

"Where're you going, Annabeth? Why are you afraid?"

Annabeth pointed wordlessly at the droll.

"Oh, don't mind her." Tookie said, spilling juice down her chin. "She's just looking for berries, too. Pick some and put them in her basket. She'll like that."

Seeing that the two little girls were not among the children nearby, Miri volunteered to go find them before word was passed to Riga. "Just keep moving. We'll catch up with you," she called to the others who were busy folding up the tents.

She found them alternately stuffing the juicy berries in their mouths, and sharing handfuls of them with the cave droll. Unaware the droll meant no harm, Miri hit it with a rock from her adl-adl. The droll fell like a tall tree, down in the bushes.

"Come on, let's run back to camp before Riga hears what brats you two have been," she shouted at the girls.

But neither child followed her. Annabeth waited while Tookie cautiously approached the giant droll who had fallen among the blackberry brambles. "Are you hurt, mistress?"

The droll began to groan.

"Let me make it better," Tookie said and, bending over, kissed the droll's forehead where the stone had struck her. Miri and Annabeth watched from far away as the droll struggled upward, first to her knees, then to her feet.

Annabeth and Tookie clapped their hands with joy. "Oh, good!" Tookie said. "You're not hurt so bad. My friend just hit you because she thought I was in danger, that's all. You know how humans are, always acting before they think."

Annabeth started laughing. But the droll bent down and peered in Tookie's round face. "Drumph?" she said, in a voice that rolled through the forest like thunder.

Tookie said something back that sounded approximately the same, and then the droll scooped Tookie up and gave her what Annabeth described as a droll kiss. She then carried Tookie away on her shoulders, to the amazement of Miri and Annabeth.

Riga was unsympathetic to Annabeth's tears. "That will serve as a good lesson on obeying rules. I told you girls yesterday not to run off, didn't I?"

But Val, on the other hand, understood her grief. He sat the little girl in his lap. "There's another way to look at it, though. You may have lost a friend, but Tookie has found her people. Maybe she's found her mother. Tookie is a droll—a small one but a droll. You said she even spoke their language, didn't you?"

Annabeth nodded, tears streaming down her cheeks. "But now, I don't have anyone to play with. I want Tookie back! She was my best friend."

"I know how that is, to lose someone who means so much to you. Come on, I've got an idea." Val lifted Annabeth up on his shoulders. "Hang on, we're going for a ride."

The children in the camp followed them curiously, then, as Miri grabbed their hands, they ran laughing after Val. Soon the whole line of marchers were running after Val and Annabeth, carrying tents and packs with them.

"He picks a strange way to make up for lost time," Riga said, jogging along beside Miri, several folded tents and water skins bobbing up and down on his back.

She laughed at the boys frisking beside her. "But kind of fun, don't you think?"

"Fun? What is 'fun'? If you mean acting silly, then I don't like fun."

Miri looked at Riga's bewildered face. "Oh, Riga, sometimes you're such a mutant. Lighten up, will you?"

Riga still looked puzzled. "But I'll have to leave something behind then, won't I?"

CHAPTER 12

DIRTY LITTLE SECRETS

Androz appeared on Mediah's bedroom screen a few days later. "We've got to get rid of Riksbury."

"Why, what's he done now?" she said sleepily.

"The little weasel is conducting a search of the Dumpster files to see if Mercator's number shows up."

"Who?" Mediah took off her sleeping mask and turned off her music.

"You know that inventor who they told me to assign to the Dumpster after he installed something in the Brain. A new part or something, I don't remember."

"Well, did you get rid of Mercator like they ordered?"

"No, I didn't. I thought I'd keep him around in case he invented something else I could use. A weapon or something."

"And you think Riksbury's on to your disobeying a direct order from the ubercouncil, is that the problem?"

Androz's scowling face was magnified by the virtual screen. "Well, what would you call it, my dear? A hangnail?"

"Sarcasm doesn't become you, darling." Mediah

reached for her hairbrush on the bedside table and began brushing her wig on its stand. "Have you got any idea why he suspects you?"

"Does it make any difference how he found out? I tell you he's got to go. You said you have something that will discredit him. We both want him expelled from the council, so let me have all that information, and I'll get my team on it right away."

Mediah smiled up at Androz. "That depends. Only if I can be on your team."

The face of the Imperator softened a little. "You forget I know you better than anyone does. If you promise to play fair. Fair enough, that is. If you don't, baby, we'll both lose the game."

Mediah hesitated before answering. Now would be a perfect time to admit that her story about Valerian wasn't true. After all, Androz had admitted he had disobeyed the Ubercouncil in not sending the prisoner to the recycling Dumpster, which was equally bad and she had caught it all on digital recorder.

On the other hand, Androz was the only one who knew she had disguised Valerian's identity as Doctor Spencer's son, in order to get him an appointment to the Borg Academy. She decided that the odds were stacked in Androz's favor.

"I promise," she said with her best smile. "Don't worry, darling. Our team will win. By the way, if you didn't dispose of Mercator, where is he now?"

The imperator laughed, an unpleasant rumbling sound like distant war drums. "That's for me to know and you to find out. I could be persuaded if you get me another one of those steaks."

As soon as he closed the screen, Mediah was out of bed. Slipping into her uniform, she ordered her car and was soon in her office across from the Flyover. From the vantage point of her circular office windows, she could see the Mother Boards message signs all over the city.

She changed the messages every three seconds and images every minute. This week, the speakers broadcast the message "Mother loves all of you who take the Happy Pill. You're so happy because you take the Happy Pill. And that makes Mother happy, too." The images flashed by in rapid succession: first a smiling, blurry face, then figures splashing in water, a scarce commodity in Megacity, and last, figures in a circle, their arms intertwined. She had to make certain that the figures appeared neither droid nor mutant human. Androgynous was the word.

Occasionally, she would throw in a robotic animal in a museum setting, a lion or a monkey, just to keep it interesting, as long as the message she gave them met the ubercouncil's approval.

This morning, though, Mediah altered the message ever so slightly. "Everybody knows Swaug is habit-forming, but Mother loves healthy habits. Swaug makes you want more, and more is always good!(Pause) But make sure it's the real thing! Mother loves it when you drink the real thing. No imitation Swaug! Yurrch!"

Mediah made sure the announcer's voice made the yurrch sound loudly and clearly over the noise of the city. She laughed as she heard it echo in the Flyover, making passersbys stop at look up at the message board and laugh.

The distribution of the narcotic drink was under Riksbury's jurisdiction. She suspected that one of his sources of illegal money were bribes from manufacturers of imitation Swaug to put their product on the market. By twisting the message slightly, she would plant the seeds of doubt in the consumers' minds across the city. And everyone consumed Swaug. Everybody from the uberminister on down—except her.

As she had anticipated, Riksbury was furious. He was pounding on her office door within the hour, and, after keeping him waiting until she was sure Androz was listening, she finally instructed her robotic secretary to let him in.

Riksbury came rolling into the office, a stunted mutant who had long ago given up walking for the convenience of wheels.

"Ubercouncilman Riksbury, to what do I owe the honor of your visit? A little Swaug, maybe?" Mediah held up a bottle of the stuff.

"I'll get right to the point, Mediah," Riksbury snarled. "Stay out of my business or I'll denounce you to the council!"

"Why, Councilman, what has upset you? Come, have a little drink of Swaug. That will calm you down. Then you can tell me all about it." Mediah poured some water into a cup and handed it to him, but, with a sweep of his hand, Riksbury dashed it to the floor.

"Slitz, woman! Did you hear what I said? Stay out of my business, do you hear? Or I will denounce you! And your lover, too."

"Is that so?" *He is playing right into my hands*, Mediah thought. "Which one?"

Riksbury made a strange noise that passed for a laugh among mutants. "The most important one, Imperator Androzarian. The council will be interested to know that he ignored a direct order to get rid of a certain human creature. Just as did you, my dear Mediah, when you hid Doctor Spencer's child from them. It will spell the end for you both unless you stay in your own territory and out of my business."

"I can do better than that any day, Riksbury." Mediah picked up the broken cup from the floor. "One of your many illegal businesses is taking bribes to allow imitation Swaug to be distributed. That's competing directly with the Triumvirate, I believe. Not only that, it's mostly water, the drinking of which is forbidden altogether."

Riksbury shrank back, looking like a large toad on wheels. "You can't prove that, bitch."

"I can have this analyzed and the results sent to the council before you leave this room. And I intend to do just that. By the way, I understand you've started an inspection on me already."

Now the councilman was visibly shaken, down to his custom wheels. "How did you find out?"

"The uberminister warned me against you. He called me to let me know."

Riksbury was edging toward the door. "You're lying! I never said anything to him."

"I think you'll find the council guards waiting for you downstairs. And my own guards will escort you there." The door opened and three guards in the uniform of the Mother Guards marched in. They lifted Riksbury up by each arm and carried him out, his useless legs pedaling in the air. "Good-bye, Riksbury. Have a happy day."

"Bitch! You haven't heard the last of this!"

"I'm sure I haven't, Riksbury. Only when I learn of your demise, will I hear the last of you," Mediah said with a diplomatic smile. "Ta-ta."

She turned back to the console that ran the Mother Boards across the city. *Mother loves you and knows you want to make her happy! We all want to be happy, don't we? So take your Happy Pill today! And tomorrow will take care of itself.*

CHAPTER 13

THE RIVER ROGUES

Valerian awoke to the sound of something moving in the underbrush. "Miri, wake up," he whispered.

"I hear them," came the response. He should have known she'd be awake before him. He wondered if she ever relaxed.

"They're coming from the direction of the river." Her voice, coming through the dark, sent strange chills through him in spite of its ominous tone.

"That's still a hundred miles away," he said, reaching for his lazorizer. "How many are there?" Val had trouble adjusting his eyes to the pre-dawn darkness. Megacity lights never dimmed because the Triumvirate was so afraid their enemies would launch an attack in the dark.

"Too many to count. We'll have to lay low and hope they pass us by."

"Pass the word to the others. Tell Riga to keep them absolutely silent."

"Too late for that,' Riga yelled. "Stand and fight."

"Just a minute there, mutant," A rough voice called. "Who you going to fight? We come in peace, seeing as how it's Yop Barnswallow's lot." The speaker emerged from the bushes, a strange-looking fellow dressed in what appeared to be fish scales and bits of cloth. He had a long, red beard adorned with mussels shells that jingled when he walked.

"You know who we are. Identify yourselves," Val said, coming up beside Riga.

"I'm Basi of the River People," the stranger said, advancing boldly to meet them. "And who might you be?" His thick-lidded green eyes slid from one to the other defender, measuring the strength of the expedition against his forces, still hidden around them in the forest.

"Valerian, newcomer to the Hollow, and these are my comrades, Miri and Riga. We are looking for a place to camp while reinforcements are built for the Hollow."

The stranger threw back his head and laughed. "Reinforcements? Against what? Drolls? Worfels?"

"Basi! I thought that was you I heard! How are you, you scaly Sonofafish?" Yop Barnswallow thundered awake and grasped the stranger in a bear hug.

The two leaders embraced while Valerian kept an eye on the forest around them, suspecting a trap. Miri and Riga fanned out, keeping their weapons at the ready.

"Your friends are mighty jumpy," Basi said, nodding at the trainers. "They expecting trouble?"

"Oh, they're just newbies from Megacity," Yop said. "Always on edge, you know. Come have some breakfast. Catch up on old times."

Basi and his men, who numbered fifty-seven, proceeded to eat up more than half their supplies at breakfast, and Valerian was afraid Yop would invite them to lunch.

But the gregarious mayor had his reasons for entertaining Basi and his River Rogues, as he called them. "Yes, I know they look like pirates," Yop admitted. "In fact, they are pirates, but nobody comes in more handy in a fight than Basi and his Rogues."

"You can't trust anybody who makes their living smuggling contraband goods." Riga was furious with the Mayor. "And they've eaten half of our supplies, thanks to your famous hospitality."

"Steady on, my mutant friend," said Yop. "You'll find we travel faster without all that food weighing us down. And if we don't obey the Triumvirate's laws, then we can't break 'em, can't we?"

"He's got a point," Miri said grudgingly. "Anyway, let's get going, wherever that is. It's getting awful warm out here."

"That's because the smog that hides the sky around Megacity is thinning and the sun is coming through," Riga said, loading folded tents on his back. "Above the river, you'll see nothing but sky."

"How do you know, Riga?" Annabeth had stopped playing when she saw the river people hiding in the trees. "Have you been there?"

"There you are, Annabeth." Miri gathered the little girl up in her arms. "Where have you been hiding? We almost left without you!"

"How does Riga know we'll see the sky? Have you been there before, Riga?" Annabeth repeated.

But Riga kept loading the last of the tents. "You ask too many questions, Annabeth," was all he said.

The expedition's numbers were swelled with addition of Basi's Rogues to almost one hundred now. They turned out to have brought their own food along, although it was mostly dried fish, which no one else liked. They also had some curious-looking plants they identified as vegetables which they ate raw. Yop joined them in snacking on carrot chips as they marched along through the forest.

"I haven't had these since I worked on the Farms as a little sprout," he said. "That's one of the few places they still had humans working instead of robots. 'Cause robots got too dirty and wet and had to be cleaned all the time."

"Still do. That's where these carrots came from." Basi offered one to Annabeth who wrinkled her nose. "The workers there trade us veggies for fish and sometimes, we even get a cow."

"Isn't that dangerous?" Yop stopped chewing immediately as if something had stuck in his throat. "Those farms are run by the Triumvirate. I remember a slave who ate a blueberry got lazorized right on the spot."

"How awful!" Miri shuddered. "What a thing for a child to see!"

"Oh, I could tell you better stories than that," said the Mayor, warming to the subject.

"the Farm ain't like what it used to be," Basi said. "See, it was set up to be a zoo, like. Only they treated it like an experiment, see. Then the Gray Hoods took over. Like all bureaucracies over time, the supervision of the ubercouncil had grown careless, leaving the running of the place to robots, who could care less about waste and corruption than their own creature comforts. They left the running of the Farm to mutants and drummans who were only too ready and willing to line their pockets by providing the Gray Hoods with contraband Swaug and food such as meat."

"Be quiet!" Riga said. "And don't dawdle along. March!"

"And I thought my slave days were over," Yop muttered.

"I don't trust Yop's friends," said Riga quietly to Val. "They look like ruffians to me."

"Appearances can be deceiving, can't they, Mr. Clown?" Val smiled, but the joke was lost on the mutant.

"Yes, but what we did in the Flyover was a matter of life and death. We don't go around in costume ordinarily." They were letting the women and children rest while the trainers scouted ahead. Riga paused beside Valerian on the way to his post. "Anybody who does business with the ubercouncil's farms has permission from the Gray Hoods or is going to get caught and Yop's people with them."

"I've thought of that," Val said. "But what if the slave workers want their freedom? Maybe the River People will join us when it comes down to a fight with the Triumvirate."

Riga made a sour face. "A big maybe, Valerian. The fish people will all probably swim away."

"You don't believe much in humans, do you, Riga?"

The mutant made a yurrching sound. "Do you, when you see what's become of them? They had it all and they lost it through their own stupidity and corruption."

"I admit that's true, but that doesn't mean we can't make a fresh start, Riga," Val said. "Or would you rather have the Triumvirate eliminate all of us without a fight?"

"That's just the point." Riga was just as stubborn in a debate as he was in combat. "You've got to depend on your allies, agreed? And smugglers and slaves aren't dependable allies."

"But they're all we have, my friend. Now, go on to your post. We'll talk later when Miri and Yop can join us."

"I've already talked to Miri. She agrees with me," Riga said without malice.

Val smiled. "Naturally. You're her hero."

Riga went marching down the trail, wondering what a hero was. But not wanting to sound like Annabeth, he kept it to himself.

෬ඁ෬

"I wish you had been there to see Riksbury's face when I told him he was selling bootleg Swaug and cooking his district's books." Mediah laughed wickedly. "His wheels almost melted."

They were relaxing in Mediah's tub, which was large enough to float a table laden with food. Candles reflected in the water, music played, and robotic hands massaged their backs.

"I was listening without turning on the screen."

Mediah threw a sponge at Androz. "You rat! Can't I have any privacy?"

He caught it and threw it back. "I told you he's already got spies in my unit. I caught them going through my records this afternoon. No telling who Riksbury has squealed to. It won't stop with getting rid of him, baby."

"I know that," she said, running her foot up and down his leg. "I'm way ahead of you, darling."

"I was counting on that," Androz said, sliding over next to her. "So what do you have in mind?"

She whispered something in his ear and the general slipped under the perfumed water like a torpedoed ship. When he surfaced again, he shouted, "Slitz!"

This time she went underwater with him, her gown floating away from her perfect body. Without her wig, she looked like the images she put on the Mother Boards—beautiful, genderless, smiling. In fact, she had modeled them after herself.

Androz joined her under the water. "Revolution?" He formed the word with his lips and she nodded, smiling.

They surfaced again, the word acting like a magnet between them, pulling them together face-to-face, nose to nose.

"We both have the resources. I can get the citizens behind us and you can get the backing of the army." The table was rocking on the waves, the candles flickered crazily. "We can do it, Androz," Mediah whispered in his ear. "We can dump the council and take over Megacity!"

"And all this just to get your precious Valerian back." Imperator Androzarian shook his head. "Women! They're worse than any dictator."

Mediah clung to him like a barnacle. "And you can promise Mercator his freedom if he destroys the Brain."

"Ho, ho, now there's a plan I can work with." Androz planted a kiss on her perfect nose. "I wonder why I didn't think of that."

"Because you have other things on your mind," she said, wrapping her body around his.

⁊

In the Trezarium, Basi joined the trainers meeting that night, in spite of Riga's objections.

"He isn't part of this expedition. He may even be a spy, for all we know," he protested.

"Or he may be planning to kidnap those of us who will bring the most ransom. Like you, Val." At first, Miri was plainly on Riga's side. "Isn't that what pirates do?"

"I resent being called a pirate," the bearded captain of the River People said. "I'll have you know we work for a living."

Miri engaged Basi in a stare-down contest. "Smuggling isn't working."

"Look," Yop said. "Basi and I worked on the farms when we were just kids. We don't know what happened to our parents but we figured they had gotten too old to work so they were recycled. We ran away together and hid in the Trezarium until they thought we were dead and gave up looking. I wouldn't have survived if it weren't for him catching fish, and I guess he wouldn't have survived but for me hunting. One day while I was away and he was fishing, some rogues came down the river and carried him off. No one hates the Triumvirate more than Basi does unless it's me. Now, I say we can trust him and that goes for his Rogues as well." The mayor looked around at their faces, hoping for agreement.

Then Miri got up and kissed him on the cheek. "I vote yes."

Riga gave a slight nod and Val agreed. "Invite then in, Yop. I'd like to hear what they have to say."

Basi said it in few words. "The slaves want their freedom, and they're willing to fight for it. But they need weapons."

Val nodded at the noisy crowd outside, eating and drinking and chatting up the women. "What about your crew?"

"Most of them are defectors that suffered at the hands of the Borg Guard. They'd like nothing more than to put a cannonball right through their guts."

"Cannonball?" Riga was aware he sounded just like Annabeth. "What's that?"

"I'll explain later," Val said. "You said 'most' of your crew. What about the others."

Basi looked uneasy. "Well, those are the ones in it for what they get out of it."

"Pirates, in other words." Miri made a disgusted noise. "I thought so."

Basi nodded. "So if you can promise them some kind of reward, they'd be loyal. For sure."

Suspicion was written all over Riga's blue face. "And what did you promise them for joining us?"

"If you really want to know, a chance to meet some jolly good-looking girls." Basi's green eyes sparkled.

"I've met a couple myself," he added, looking straight at Miri. "Present company included."

Val kept to the agenda. "So you can bring the farm slaves and your men in case the Borg Guard attack, is that right?"

Basi nodded. "Right." He looked at Miri. "Do I get a kiss like Yop here?"

"She'd rather kiss a frog," Riga muttered.

CHAPTER 14

THE FOREVER ROAD

Iow's the universal thingy coming along?" Qin set Spencer's lunch tray down and sauntered over to the huge machine taking up most of his laboratory. "It's beginning to look a lot like the Dumpster."

Right behind her, Blu creaked into the lab to pick up the wooden tray and replace it with his own steel one. "Nut butter on toast with mustard on the side," he corrected, sounding like a short-order cook. "Just like the doc ordered. Now, missy, thank you and goodbye," he said, lowering the tray to Spencer who was under the machine. "Laboratories are no place for girls, especially ones who forget the mustard."

"Blu, you're such a chauvinist, you know that?" Qin fired back. "And you're getting worse the older you get. You need to update your programs."

"How's it coming along, Qin?" Spencer rolled out from under the machine. "What's it called again? The fake moat thing?"

"Done," Qin said, with a smug glance at Blu. "All we need are the pointed sticks, and Chez's crew is making those. And by the way, we call it the Ha-ha."

"Ha-ha," Blu repeated. "Aha. Aha."

"Oh, don't get off on that, will you, Blu? I'll be back with the mustard." Qin flounced away.

Thur was getting bored. He was tired of drilling the blubbery residents of the Hollow for hours at a time, only to have them stuff anything and everything in their mouths at meals. Slices of walnut and raspberry cake. Venison steaks, slathered in mustard sauce, fried squirrel; grilled frogs legs.

"Aya, if you would stop cooking for them, they would have to stop pigging out at every meal," he told her one day.

She could see his frustration. Also, his boredom. She knew he was missing Miri and Riga, but Miri most of all.

As much as he tried not to think of her and Valerian together, Thur was secretly in agony, imagining what might be happening. Her face came to him at night in dreams and, though he tried to wish it away, it always came back.

Aya saw that he was preoccupied and guessed the reason. But they were in danger, and he must not lose sight of reality. She herself had been in love once and knew the telltale signs. But she wouldn't let Thur lose his focus, which had to be the defense of the Hollow. "I promise to cut down on the sweets. We're running low on honey anyway. I wish I could get someone to bring me some more."

Thur got the hint. "If you could just serve these blubbertubs with already on their plates instead of putting all the food out there on the table for them to help themselves, that would help. And I'll see what I can do about getting you more honey."

The next day after drills, Thur went into the deep woods around the Hollow to look for honey. The thought crossed his mind, that if he kept going, he would soon pick up the trail of the expedition. Then he shook his head to throw the thought out of his mind. As much as he wanted to see Miri and Riga, that would be deserting his post.

Presently, Thur came to a little stream and kneeled down for a drink of fresh water. That's when something or someone—he couldn't tell which—knocked him sprawling into the stream.

He was immediately on his feet, hand on his lazorizer, ready to face his assailant. But there was no one on the bank of the stream. In fact, he couldn't see anything in the immediate vicinity other than trees. As he stood there knee-deep in water, he saw a branch high up in the canopy suddenly dip as though something was swinging on it.

"Halt or I'll shoot," he shouted.

"Coward! Newby!" called a voice high up in the trees. "You can't defend yourself, let alone us. You are just a liability!"

"Come down here and say that to my face!" Thur roared. "I'm a trained warrior, not a coward that sneaks up on people."

"I'm not a coward, you know." Thur detected a doubtful note in the voice.

"Then prove it. Come down and show yourself."

"Can't take a joke, Newby? I can tell you're not used to the woods." Before he could answer, a girl dropped down about twenty feet away. He had seen her before, practicing the drills with the rest of the defenders, but she was definitely a cut above them all. She was lithe, agile in the way she moved.

"Sorry," the girl said. She was young, about his age and, like all the residents of the Hollow, blended right into the woods. Brown-haired, brown as a nutshell, and pretty with big, brown eyes.

"For what? You didn't hurt me. Just surprised me,

that's what you're supposed to do, right?" He swallowed his pride, hoping she took it as a compliment. She'd probably just go back and tell everyone that she got the drop on the person who made their lives miserable every day. He'd just have to suck it up, he thought.

The girl came two steps closer. She was strangely beautiful dressed in the uniform of the Hollow—leggings tucked into soft deerskin boots and a woven tunic trimmed with shells and bright feathers. "My name is Gelise. I'm in your two o'clock group," she said.

"I know." He was suddenly shy. "The thing you do, swinging from the trees? That could come in very handy in a fight, you know." His words sounded like all he knew to talk about to girls was how to fight. *In fact, that's true*, he thought. *That's been my life so far*.

Gelise came closer and Thur took a step back, not sure whether she was alone. As if she sensed his uneasiness. "Don't worry, this isn't an ambush, if that's what you're thinking. I often come out here to hunt rabbits. What are you doing out here? You're awfully far from the Hollow."

He explained his mission for Aya and her pretty face lit up. "That's easy! I know all the bee nests around here. C'mon, I'll show you the closest one. But you'll need both hands. Better put the weapon in its sling and follow me."

That was the day Thur learned to fly. The people of the Hollow called their system of ropes and zip lines the Forever Road because it had a view as far as they see. As far as Gelise knew, no one had ever ventured beyond the horizon. That was the Land Beyond.

Thur had grown up learning to recognize different tunnels in the sewers so he soon learned how to recognize the next rope from the vines that climbed midway up to the canopy of the tallest trees. Soon they were moving briskly along the treetops until Gelise lowered herself almost to the ground.

Even before Thur dropped down beside her, he heard a buzzing sound that sounded as if the tree had a jet pack in it and was ready to take off.

"Bees," said Gelise with a smile as if she had discovered buried treasure. "And lots of bees make lots of honey."

Thur was about to say that the bees might not want to hand it over when Gelise slowly reached down the hole and brought out what looked like a pine cone bristling with bees and dripping with golden honey. Thur handed over the pot Aya had given him and she let it drip until it was full and then with same smooth movement replaced the pine cone. "See, easy," she said.

"You have bees crawling all over your arm," Thur pointed out as if she didn't notice.

"They'll fly back into the hive as soon as you move," said his guide.

Thur didn't need any encouragement and shot up ten feet followed by the line of bees. He swung through the trees, but the bees gathered an angry mob and followed just behind him.

"You won't outrun them. Drop into the water!" he heard Gelise call.

Spotting the stream below, he couldn't lower himself fast enough. The bees swarmed around him, in a stinging mass. Thur finally let go of the rope and shot down into the water. He had barely come up for air when he heard a high, thin voice say, "I just saw a boy drop from the sky."

The speaker was a little girl, a couple of years older than Annabeth. She was on her hands and knees, washing clothes in the pond. A man stood close by, with a net in his hand. "No, you didn't, girl," he said looking straight at Thur. "That was just a branch from yon tree."

All the while he was speaking, he was making a motion with his hand for Thur to stay down under the water. Thur had learned a long time ago that robots don't look down so he was safe.

"Anything amiss, 231804?" another voice asked, this time a robotic one, coming up behind the man. A robo guard, by the sound of him, Thur took a deep breath and sank under the water.

"Nothing, Overlord Two. Just a branch from the trees disturbing the water."

"Well, don't let it keep you from fishing. Fish are good for the fertilizer," said the Guard. "The plants must grow so that the cows can eat."

"Yes, Overlord Two." When the robot had gone off, the man leaned down. "Get out of here, boy. Go!"

Thur surfaced again. "What is this place? And why was that robot guarding you? Are you prisoners?"

"To answer your questions in order," the man whispered with great caution, "you have reached the farms, and we are slaves of the Triumvirate, and yes. Now, if you don't want to join us, leave at once, boy."

"I am Thur of the Hollow and we are building a defense against an invasion by the Borgs. We'd like to depend on your help."

The man almost laughed, but he sounded as if he'd forgotten how. "How can that be? We are but mere humans against the greatest force in the world?"

"Better to die for freedom than to live a miserable slave," said Thur. "That is our human right."

"And that is what led us to the edge of extinction," replied the man. "Better to survive a slave than to die a hero."

"And you, miss? What do you think?" Thur smiled at the little girl who was staring at him as though hypnotized.

"I think you're the most beautiful thing I have ever seen," she said.

"Girl, that will do. Get back to work and you, boy, leave now or I'll call the Guard."

"No, you won't, Pier. Or I'll never speak to you again.," said the girl, getting up on her feet. "He's an angel, like the stories Mama used to tell. Only she didn't say angels come in colors."

"Now, see what you've done, boy," The man looked over his shoulder as he were afraid. "Get to work again, girl, before they catch us talking."

Thur swam back up the stream until he was well away from the Farms. But the phrase stuck in his mind. "Like the stories Mama used to tell."

When he got back to the Hollow, the whole encampment was buzzing with excitement. Spencer's Super Machine, as it was known, was ready to work. The Hollow's defenses were ready. The defenders were ready for the expedition to return to help them, if only someone in the Hollow knew where they were.

Before Thur had a chance to tell anyone about his adventures that afternoon, a meeting of the defenders was called. Excitement went around like an electric spark among them.

"That means Doctor Spencer will probably say the Super Machine is ready." Chez passed Thur in the tunnel. "Then we'll see some action. Those Borgies can bring it on! We're gonna wipe 'em out!"

"He's probably going to launch into a boring lecture on how it works that will put everyone to sleep." Thur yawned. "I'll pass."

Aya saved him from boredom. "I got word from Eddy Spencer just now. He wants you to find the expedition and tell them to hurry back. And take Chez and Loki with you," she said. "They know the forest as well as anyone.

And that will give them something to do beside hanging around Qin and eating me out of house and hollow."

But Thur had other plans. "I'd rather take someone who doesn't talk as much as they do. Gelise, for instance."

"Who?"

"The girl who brought you the honey." Thur suddenly found his face getting red under Aya's gaze. "She showed me how they move around the forest so fast."

"I see. Suit yourself," she said, in spite of wanting to tease him. "Only hurry."

CHAPTER 15

THE BRAIN

E Mercator squinted through the bars in his cell. The thick ever-present layer of smog and drizzle that blocked the sunlight was getting lighter. Another dawn, another dusk.

What does it matter, he thought? *They're all the same.*

He shuffled back to his drafting table, the only other piece of furniture besides his bed in his cell. In the ten years he had been held captive, he had become an old man. His brown hair streaked with Gray , his beard showing more white than brown.

Nevertheless, hope kept him alive—the hope that he would be kept alive long enough to witness the destruction of the Triumvirate and the toxic society they had created.

Having no one to share the joke with, E. Mercator laughed aloud, a creaky, unused sound. But who cared what he sounded like? Nobody.

He was startled at the sound of his cell door rolling back. A Borg roboguard rolled in with his meal. Breakfast or dinner, they were all the same. A nutrient tablet, and bread for fiber. That was what the bread was made from—fiber from anything they could grind up. "Put the tray on the table," he said, without a glance at the Guard.

"I'm to take you to the Imperator. He wants to see you, E. Mercator," said the roboguard.

Mercator looked around in alarm. "What about, do you know?"

"If I did, I wouldn't tell you," came the answer. "E. Mercator, you stink, the odor scale says so. Take a bath first. I have clean clothes."

"They must not going to kill me if they're going to that much trouble," Mercator said.

"Maybe. Maybe not. The plans of the Imperator are not for the likes of us to be discussed. To the water you go."

Clean and wearing clean clothes, an hour later Mercator appeared before Imperator Androzarian.

"Well, Mercator, I see detention hasn't been too hard on you," said the Imperator. "You're looking well. Have some Swaug."

Mercator held up his hand in refusal. "What did you want to see me about, Androzarian?"

The Imperator chuckled. "I see you haven't lost any of your arrogance, Mercator. I'll get right to the point. You know that part you added to the Brain, the universal degenerater or whatever?"

"Anti-demagnetizer," Mercator corrected. "Yes, what about it?"

"Have it ever been tried to see if it works to your knowledge?"

"I wouldn't have any idea, now would I? Being imprisoned in a cell for nearly ten years."

Androzarian looked offended. "But I did defy a direct order to send you to the recycling center, didn't I? That has put me in great danger, it turns out."

Mercator was unimpressed. "Is that why you want to

know if the universal anti -demagnetizer works?"

Androzarian looked uncomfortable. "Well, in general, yes."

"And why should I tell you?" He knew he had pushed the general too far and cringed inwardly.

Androz could swat him like a fly and Mercator expected him to.

But, to his surprise, Androz lowered his voice and grabbed him by the shirt front, pulling the scientist so close he could smell the Swaug on his breath. "Because you want to destroy them as much as I do, don't you, you scrawny little sewer rat? That's why I kept you alive, in case the Triumvirate ever wanted to get rid of me."

As much as Androz blustered, Mercator knew he had the general by the throat. He smiled at the mental picture, because Androz was three times his size. Still, the little scientist kept his reply cool. "And I gather they *do* want to get rid of you and that's why you want my help."

Androz thrust him away like a child who has grown tired of a toy. "You're too smart for your own good, Mercator. What do you want in return, eh?"

"Well, seeing the Triumvirate self-destruct, for one thing. My freedom, of course, and safe passage back to…wherever it is I'm going."

"Otherwise, you'll rot in your little hole and let the city blow up around you, is that your plan?"

Mercator shrugged. "If you say so, General. The way I see it, you're not in any position to bargain."

Androz scratched his chin where a few sharp bristles were starting to grow, an annoying side effect of his human genes. "Suppose we became partners, you doing the science side, me with the muscle? If we pulled it off— toppling the Triumvirate, freeing the city rats, taking over the government until things were normal again, then you would be free to do your thing and I mine. What do you say?"

"Just we two? Aren't you forgetting the others in the Triumvirate? The Gray Hoods for instance. And Mediah?"

"I'll handle them," Androz said confidently. "The Grays will do what I tell them as long as they can make a profit. And Mediah is already an ally. She's changing the Mother's image across the city even as we speak. Are you in or not ? Because if you're not, you can go back to your cell and rot for all I care. You're no use to me now."

"Just a minute," Mercator said. "You military types are always doing things in a rush without thinking them through. It doesn't matter to me what you do. Free all the slaves you want, they'll only create more chaos. For your information, I don't have to do anything. The Brain is set to self-destruct in about three days, give or take a few hours."

Androz was aghast. His throne of a chair groaned as he sat forward. "Give or take a few?" he asked in a shaking voice. "Could you be more precise, Mercator?"

Mercator shrugged. "I can't because I don't have any idea what time it is or what day it is, do I? After all, you've kept me in a dark cell for nearly ten years now."

The imperator was fighting panic, grinding his teeth. Mercator smiled to see how red his face was getting.

"If you're lying to me, I'll kill you with my bare hands," the general growled.

"That will do a lot of good, now, won't it?" For the first time in years, Mercator was actually enjoying himself. "How do you know I'm not lying? Just have to wait and see, won't you?"

Androz was thinking, drumming his thick fingers on the marble desk in front of him. "If I show you a computerized time and date, could you possibly give me a closer estimate of when the Brain will self-destruct?"

Again, a shrug. "That depends."

"On what, you little weasel?" Androz thundered.

"You said something about setting me free." Mercator watched as perspiration oozed down the general's cheeks. *It seems the imperator falls short of the seventy-five percent marker for Other Species*, he thought. *Something the Triumvirate already knew, I'll wager.*

"No, you said that, remember? Look, I will arrange for your safe passage out of here when you tell me exactly when the Brain will blow."

Mercator knew he had the upper hand. "I'm not that big a fool, Androzarian. Arrange my release first, and I will relay the message back to you. Those are my terms."

"And just how will you do that?"

"Simple. By the same guard you give me to take me where I want to go."

"And where is that?"

Mercator tried another laugh, and this time it came out loud and clear. "Wherever I damned well please."

℘℘℘

Mediah was in her office when Androz suddenly appeared on her screen. "Haven't you got something else to do besides call me up to chat?" she asked, trying to hide her annoyance at being interrupted.

"Listen, baby, I've got to talk to you. Your place in an hour, all right?"

She tried her best wheedling tone. "Androz, I'm right in the middle of something. Can't it wait until I'm through?"

But he was already gone. *It must be important if Androz is in a hurry*, Mediah thought, hurrying to perfect her appearance. *He doesn't really do anything but sit on *his throne, signing requisitions.* With a sigh, she sent another set of Mother's messages along to the screens and gathered her things to go. the Mother's voice boomed from the Flyover across the way. She had altered the voice to a lower, slower pitch so that it sounded ominous.

"Mother's children have to be careful. There are those who would try to take advantage of you." Here the voice became even more urgent. "Even steal from you and cheat you. Mother doesn't want her children to be cheated by thieves. She wants the BEST for her children."

The images were of the Mother hovering near a gray-hooded figure. The next was of her shaking her head. The hooded figure was being led away by Borg Guards.

"So what's so urgent that it couldn't wait?" She barely had time to change from her work uniform to something more alluring before Androz arrived. He looked as though he needed a steak and some real Swaug.

"The Brain has been programmed to blow up three days from now. Mercator just told me that was the adjustment he made ten years ago when he was captured."

Mediah was hardly alarmed. "I'm surprised he waited so long, given his situation. Actually, darling," she said, handing him a glass of Swaug, "it will play right into our hands, won't it?"

"It will?" Androz felt better already. Mediah was looking particularly sexy, he could smell his steak cooking, and the Swaug took the edge off the crisis.

"Of course, darling." She snuggled up next to him, a purring, warm body next to his. "That's the part of the Triumvirate we don't have control over and this Mercator has just volunteered to get rid of it. Done deal."

"One catch, my love. He'll only give me the exact time after I've released him. You say you're in contact with Valerian. Now there's a lad who's trustworthy, I'd say. Suppose you call him back and tell him what's going on? I'm sure he'd relay Mercator's message straight away to you."

"Of course, darling. I'll let him know right away to come back to the city." Hiding her confusion, Mediah threw herself into the business of entertaining the general. She amused him with her impressions of Riksbury and the Mother's messages until Androz was roaring with laughter.

When he finally left, she was exhausted, flinging herself across the circular bed.

How could she tell Androz she'd been lying to him all along? That Valerian had defected months earlier and she had not been in contact with him since then? Mediah decided then and there to find her proxy son and tell him what lay in the balance of his absence from the Borg Guard—the destruction of Megacity and all its inhabitants including her. She had preserved his life, given him a false identity, become Androz's mistress just to keep him alive.

Valerian owed her something, Mediah thought. If not her life, then at least a favor.

The next day the Borg Guard's drones picked up a signal. Activity had come from a pinprick on the map called a hollow, depressions and elevations in the topography not made by nature. Tunnels beneath the ground were surrounded by a wall. Evidence of human existence.

General Androzarian was one of those who got the dispatch. He was on the screen to Mediah who hadn't left for work yet. "Looks like they've found your boy," he said. "Better tell him to get back here on the double."

Totally caught off guard, Mediah managed to scrabble a reply together. "I messaged him last night after you left. He hasn't answered me yet. What are you going to do?"

"Let's just say it won't be pretty, whatever it is," he replied. "I've got to go now, baby. Don't worry. If they find him alive, I've already sent out the word he's on a spying mission."

"Androz, I haven't been totally honest with you." Mediah started to tell him Valerian was really a defector and then stopped, gripped by fear. *What will he do to me?* Visions of the Flyover and the Dumpster loomed like twin specters in her mind. "There's a girl, you see. Pretty, in a human sort of way."

Androz booming laughter seemed to shake the fragile walls of her room. "Isn't there always? Is that what lured him into the wilds?"

Mediah's concern was genuine, but not for Valerian. It was for herself. "He's gone to bring her back, and he will do it, I know."

"I can't guarantee his safety, baby. You know there's only so much I can do after the Borg have spotted something. It's all robotic after that."

"I'll message him right away," she answered. "Tell him to report immediately back to you, with or without her."

"Steak tonight?"

"Whatever you want." Even though she tried to sound alluring, her voice trembled.

Fortunately, Androzarian didn't notice. He had started laughing again. "A girl? Val went after a girl?"

∽∾∽

Thur and Gisele started out immediately, following the expedition's trail through the Trezarium.

"We have to go faster than this," he said impatiently. It was tedious, finding the marks Valerian had left, indicating the way through the dense trees. "If we take the

Forever Road, we might get high enough to actually see them."

Gisele shook her head. "But that's taking a chance that a drone will spot us. Better be safe and stick to the trail. With all those kids and old folks, we're sure to catch up to them pretty soon."

"Look, they're headed in the direction of the river, that's easy to see." Thur pointed to the footprints in the fresh mud. "Let's climb to the top for a look around. Then we'll make sure we're going in the right direction, all right?"

Gisele sighed, as if she weren't convinced. "Just don't miss the ropes this time, will you? Might not be as soft a landing as the last one."

They mounted to the treetops and Thur stuck his head out to look around. "Wow! What a view!"

Immediately, there was a whirring sound and an unmanned gyrocopter swooped down, seemingly out of nowhere. Before they could drop far enough below the canopy of branches, a transparent, gas-filled bubble enveloped them both and started speeding toward the city. The captives beat on the walls of the bubble, but it was as hard as steel. They soon passed out from the gas which was concentrated helium mixed with a little oxygen. When the Borgs opened the bubble, they found the couple sleeping soundly, smiles on both of their faces.

Androz was back on the screen. "I've got them!" he said triumphantly. "Valerian looks younger than I remember. But the girl is certainly pretty, though a little weirdly dressed. I'll bring them over when I come tonight. Right now, they're sleeping it off."

"Don't hurt them, will you? They might be the last pair of humankind. They at least ought to rate museum status," Mediah suggested helpfully, "since you're going to wipe out the rest of the defectors anyway."

"Well, if nothing else, they can join the slaves on the farms, although Valerian will have to be brain-cleaned. It's a shame because so much training went into making him the Borg commander that he was." Androz sighed dramatically. "They say love makes fools of us all. It's the truth, though. See you this evening, baby."

While he blathered on, Mediah's mind was racing. Valerian a slave? Never! Not the boy she had protected like…like her own son. He was, in fact, left to her to raise by his father, Edward Spencer, when he became a prisoner of the Triumvirate. That made her his only parent because Spencer was dead. She had verified the ID number from Riksbury's files herself. His mother died before Spencer handed the boy over to her. So that made Valerian hers and hers alone. He was not going to become a slave. The girl with him, maybe, but not her boy.

Mediah began early in the afternoon, making an effort to look even more beautiful than ever. She tried on all of her wigs and chose the one closest to Valerian's hair, a curly brown one that fell nearly to her waist. She turned on the robotic facial machine and went through entire procedure, which took all afternoon. She lay flat while the robot was busy filling in microscopic lines with serum, tweezing stray hairs, and applying makeup.

Next, she chose a gown from her twelve closets. It was not too revealing, but just enough for Androzarian to relish along with his steak dinner.

Mediah moved to the perfumer robot. That one sprayed her hair with one scent, her hands with another, her feet with another until her whole body spread perfume every time she moved a limb. The perfumer made certain they all blended perfectly so that the effect was intoxicating rather than irritating.

Still, when the magnetic field around the entrance to her rooms announced Androzarian's arrival, Mediah's confidence shriveled, and she took a nervous gulp of Swaug.

"Whew," exclaimed the general, "it smells like a Pleasures House in here, right, Val, my boy?"

He turned to a young man walking behind him, a silly grin on his face. He replied by pinching his nostrils closed with his fingers. His eyes, the color of dark water with flecks of green, nearly popped out of their sockets when he saw Mediah.

Mediah took a big gulp of air. What strange apparition was this, she thought? Dressed in skins of animals and a shirt of earth tones, he was wearing a cap of some kind of creature. No, this was some kind of joke Valerian was playing. This was certainly was not her beloved Valerian.

Even stranger yet was the creature hiding behind him, almost crouching double as if looking for somewhere to hide. Finding nowhere in the room that had a door, she was trying to make herself as small as possible.

"Welcome back, my dear Valerian!" Mediah managed to choke out. Their smell was overwhelming, and she motioned the robotic perfumer to spray them. When it shot a spray of deodorizing perfume over the pair, they reacted by falling into convulsions of sneezing, rolling on the floor to the great amusement of Androzarian.

In fact, he was laughing so hard, he had to sit down. "I'm glad you think it's so funny, Androz. Did you ever think to bathe them before bringing them over here?" Mediah looked at the pair sprawled on her clean marble foyer in horror. Androz laughed all the harder.

"I'm not a nursemaid," Androz managed to say. "Bathe them yourself. I brought you your beloved Valerian. That's my end of the bargain. Now waste no more time tidying them up and let me know where I can find the human vermin."

"I'll have to let them use my own bath then." Mediah's sensitive nostrils flared against the assault. "I'll get Habdi to serve you dinner while I'm busy."

Androz stopped laughing long enough to ask, "You're not going to join me?"

"It's your own fault. You know I can't stand dirt in any form," Mediah snapped. "I won't be long." She hustled the pair away.

As soon as they were in the pool, she enclosed them in a sound bubble and stepped inside. "Where is Valerian? He and the rest of you are in immediate danger. What is your name, boy?"

"Thur," he said. "And this is Gelise." The wild girl seemed to be enjoying the water, bobbing up and down beneath the surface of the pool. "We are from the arboretum. You call it Trezarium. We were searching for Valerian when we were captured."

"Are you going to recycle us?" the girl asked, sticking her head above the perfumed water. "Because if you are, I want to made into fertilizer, not chicken shit. I can't stand to be pecked at."

"Be quiet," Mediah snapped. "We don't have time to waste on silly questions. Thur, if I can get you back to Trezarium, can you find Valerian and give him this message? He is to come back immediately to the city. Promise me you'll tell him."

"Not without me, he can't get back to the Arboretum," said Gelise, not intimidated at all by Mediah's imperious manner. "He gets lost easily."

"Just for that, you can stay here, Miss Big Mouth!" Mediah was rapidly losing patience with this organic creature. "It will take that long to clean all the dirt off you!"

The boy Thur looked at Mediah with eyes so honest and brave, she was reminded of someone long ago. "It's true, though, beautiful lady. I do lose my way in the forest. She's right. We both have to go if you want us to find Valerian."

The girl nodded enthusiastically. "He's a newby, you see, Miss Bald Lady?"

Mediah's hand went flying up to her wig. "How did you know that?"

Before Thur could stop her, Gelise moved to the other side of the pool. "Because your hair is crooked."

Mediah went flying into the mirror in the next room to straighten her wig and Gelise disappeared below the water. There followed a swooshing sound and she surfaced again. "Hold your breath, City Boy," she said, pinching her nostrils together. "Heeeeere we go!"

Before Thur knew what had happened, his legs were swept out from under him by a current that sucked him into the pool drain. He followed Gelise through a pipeline almost filled to the top with the perfumed bath water, but with enough room to breathe.

He heard Gelise yelling, "Wheeee! This is fun! What a ride!"

Half an hour later, they were dumped out on to the smelly earth of the Farms, right under the noses of two surprised workers.

When Mediah returned to the pool after fixing her wig, it was empty and the robotic pool cleaners were scrubbing the dirt off the walls.

CHAPTER 16

THE FARM

Well, look at what they're flushing down the tube these days, will ya?" One of the slave workers peered down at the pair coated with mud.

"Oh, come on," said the other slave. "You don't think them robots go poop like us, do you? Get up, boy, or you'll soon be fertilizer. You, too, young lady. I'd be ashamed to go around half naked, if I was you."

"Well, it's obvious you're not me," Gelise replied, grabbing the shreds of clothing she'd had on in the pool. "You act like you've never seen a girl before!"

The slave just grinned, showing a mouthful of picket-fence teeth. "Our master hasn't seen you before, that's for sure. If you're caught where you shouldn't be, you'll be recycled. They have their own recycling plant right here on the Farm for slaves who get to old or useless to be useful."

At that moment, a voice came from the control tower. "Number 23109, why aren't you working? Why isn't your shovel in the ground?"

Before the slave could answer, Gelise said, "Because I brought them lunch, okay?"

"Lunch?" repeated the voice of Overlord Three. "What is lunch? And your voice is not on my voice index."

"That's because he's been sucking helium gas," said Thur. "He sounds like a girl."

"Girl?" the computer squawked. "The term girl doesn't compute. And your voice is not on my index either. What is your number? This is highly irregular. Stay where you are. I'm sending Overlord Five to bring you to the Tower."

When Overlord Five rolled up, the second slave worker swung his shovel in both hand and sent the robotic guard flying into the mud. Another bash and the guard sank below the ooze. "That takes care of Overlord Five, but there will be more," he said to the others who were standing there speechless. "Time to make plans. My name is Pier. I have a child, a girl child. I want her to have a better life than this. To do that, there are two options—run or take over the farm."

"If we run, they will pursue us," said his companion, "and either recycle us or bring us back. My name is Rufus and I say gather the other slaves and take over the farm."

"We would join you but we have to get back to the Hollow and warn them about the attack." Thur looked at Gelise who nodded agreement.

"Unless I go to warn them and you stay here," she said.

"To escape from here takes skill and daring," said Pier.

Thur couldn't keep the admiration from his voice. "Oh, don't worry, she's got plenty of daring. For a girl."

Rufus who had been watching the Control Tower, had an urgent warning. "There are more guards coming. Now or never!"

It became a battle cry. Other slaves heard it, and soon their voices echoed across the rows of green plants.

"Now or never!"

They turned on their robotic overlords and, using their shovels and hoes as weapons, hurled them to the ground.

"Come on," Pier yelled. "To the Control Room."

Thur and Gelise each picked up a shovel and ran after Pier and Rufus. Gelise used all the fighting tricks Thur had taught her and a few of her own. She threw a rope with a noose at them, and, as it dropped over one Guard's head, tied the other end to a post wrapping his arms tightly to his sides. She then took his lazorizer and zapped him with it.

The rebels soon had control of the Farm and raced to the Control Tower, where the remaining guards including the commander, were playing at magnetic polo. They were too engaged to notice the commotion outside until the door was blown open and the mob came rushing in. By then, it was too late.

❧❦❧

Androz took the news of their escape surprisingly well. "That's one less problem we have to worry about, baby. They couldn't have survived anyway. Those pipes empty right into the river, don't they?"

"I have no idea," Mediah said. "That little human dirtbag said my hair was on crooked. It's not, is it?" She hated the human impulse that always strived for perfection but never quite achieved it. She felt it was a weakness that was dangerously obvious to her enemies.

"You always look perfect to me, darling. Come over here and let me put things right."

She did as the general wanted but was thinking all

the time. How could she get Valerian back to the city so he could take a position of power?

She awoke, thinking her feelings for Valerian were a weakness, too. A weakness she was powerless to resist. But where was he and how could she make contact with him?

CHAPTER 17

TOOKIE'S MOTHER

Basi and his River Rogues led the expedition deeper into the forest than any of the people from the Hollow had ever gone.

"This is The Great Unknown," Yop whispered to Valerian. "We have heard from the travelers that bad things happen here. A few of their people just disappeared from here."

"Maybe they were carrying something they shouldn't ought," Basi said. He seemed to overhear even their whispers. "Like Swaug or some such contraband stuff. Everyone knows they get their stuff by stealing it from hardworking folks."

"Like yourself?" asked Yop.

As if to prove that point, they ran into a group of cave drolls the next morning. The drolls were out picking berries just as the expedition rounded a curve in the path. Immediately, everybody went for a weapon, and it looked as if a battle was about to take place, when a child's voice yelled, "Oh, stop! Just stop, okay?"

It was Tookie and, from each group of combatants, a child raced forward. Annabeth ran out, before anyone could stop her from the expedition, and embraced Tookie, who came from between the legs of a giant droll.

"I'll be damned," said Basi. "Will you look at that? Who would have thought? Obviously you couldn't imagine two kids making peace between warring adults, nor could I? But there it is in front of our eyes."

Suddenly, five of the River Rogues started firing their lazorizers at the drolls. One of them fell while the rest ran for cover in the forest.

"Something that big can't hide for long!" yelled the leader. "After them big palookas!"

"Hold it, you trigger-happy dogs!" called Basi. "Can't you see they're friendly? Stow your weapons, that's an order!"

"You can't order us around no more, Basi," the leader of the rebel rogues called over his shoulder. "We're Gray Hoods, and we take orders only from the Brain. See ya, sucker!" He ran off into the woods, followed by his men.

Annabeth ran back into Miri's arms. She was shaking so badly, she could only whimper. "Is Tookie dead?"

"Shhh," Miri whispered. "I'm sure she's alive and well. Tookie leads a charmed life."

"Let them go," Riga said. "They'll do us more harm than good anyway."

Miri hugged Annabeth tightly. "They almost got Annabeth and Tookie killed. Did you know those bastards were Gray Hoods or do you just allow anybody who has a weapon to shoot around children?"

"This is a rough outfit, miss," said Basi. "We take anybody who can hold their own. Besides those were our contacts with the farm. That's how we got meat and stuff to sell on the sly."

"Too bad." Miri stroked Annabeth's hair. "Guess you'll have to make a living some other way."

The one who had tripped and fallen rejoined the expedition. "I fell on purpose," he said. "You're good people and I want to be like you, not like them." He was hardly more than a boy, but met Valerian's stern gaze without flinching. "My father is one of the leaders of the Gray Hoods, but I'm not a thief so he was disappointed in me."

"Even thieves have to obey orders, Zak." Basi clapped the boy on the shoulder. "But I'm glad you came back. I only wish your father and the rest of those dogs had been as smart."

Valerian felt something on his waist pulsing. It was the sensor belt his father had given him before he left. It was flashing a green light. "Hold on," he said. "There's a signal from the Hollow. 'Return at once,' it says. 'Defenses complete.'" He looked directly at Miri. "We can go home."

In spite of the rule to whisper, the people of the Hollow cheered.

As usual, the trainers flanked to the right and left of the column, Valerian taking the lead and three of the group they had trained guarding the rear.

As Miri skirted a thick stand of saplings, she heard a hoarse whisper, "Miss, over here."

She immediately got her adl-adl ready in case of attack and took a step toward the saplings. There, tied to two of the young trees was a boy of about twelve or thirteen. He was dressed in brightly colored rags and looked half starved.

"Have you got anything to eat with you?" he asked. "I haven't had anything in two days."

"Who left you like this?" she asked, cutting the leather thongs that tied his wrists to the trees. Once he was freed, the lad dropped to the ground, too weak to stand.

"My people. They call us the Travelers. I was caught

stealing food," he said, between gasps. "Because I was hungry."

She gave him some water out of her flask and he took little sips. *Like a bird*, she thought.

"And I thought the Borgs invented cruelty," she said. "Whoever these Travelers are, they ought to get a taste of their own punishment. Can you follow me back to get some food now?"

The boy nodded and Miri helped him to his feet. "Thank you, Miss."

"Hush, don't use your strength talking. Lean on me now and take it easy." Together, they limped back to the column where the boy was immediately given food. He ate like one nearly starved and was quite sick in the bushes afterward.

"I hope some of that food stuck with him," said Yop.

"Why would they would do that to a kid?" Miri asked.

"The Travelers have strict rules about stealing from each other. Even food."

"Just not from other people," someone commented. "They would have sent someone back to get him, though."

"Is that right, boy?" Yop asked. "Someone said they were coming back for you?"

The boy who said his name was Skye nodded, his color still pale with a greenish tint.

"I hope they do because I'd like to give them an earful," said Miri.

"So we have one boy who doesn't want to steal and one who's been punished for stealing." Yop scratched his head. "What does that add up to?"

"A lot of wasted time," commented Riga. "Let's move along."

They were well on the way back when Valerian's

belt picked up a strange sound. He called a halt and the women and children sat down, glad to rest.

"What is it, Val?" Miri whispered, getting her adl-adl ready.

Riga moved closer to the group as if his keen hearing had picked up something. "Something is moving up ahead of us. Many somethings. Maybe the drolls are back." He checked his lazorizer out of habit.

"You don't have to worry. Travelers are harmless." Skye stood up and took a deep breath. "I'll go show them I'm all right."

"As if they cared," Miri said under her breath. "I'll go with you, Skye. Just to make sure it's them and not the Hoods."

"In that case, I'd better go along, too," Zak said, joining them. "It'll be me they're after and I'm going to tell my father I'm not coming with him anymore. I rather be with the kind of people who don't make me do things I don't want to."

"I going to make you stay behind me even if you don't want to," Valerian said impatiently. "And get ready to run in case of any danger."

Crouching down in the underbrush, Thur gave the signal for Pier and his men to get ready to attack. The sound of soft footsteps approaching through the forest could mean the Borg Guard had already started their invasion. He wished Miri and Riga were here instead of the freed workers from the Farm. He would have even welcomed Valerian, although he barely tolerated the guy.

He held up his hand until the whispered footsteps were even with him and then he stopped midair as Miri's golden head went by above the tall ferns.

"Miri, it's me, Thur! I've got—"

Too late! Miri was already nervous what with all these threats in the forest. She whirled the adl-adl around her head and let a rock fly. Thur ducked but it still struck him on the side of his head. To the horror of his followers, he fell over like a tree in a storm.

"You've killed him," Gelise cried, jumping up. "You stupid newby! You've killed him!"

❧❧❧

At the Academy prison, E. Mercator asked the Guard to convey a message to Imperator Androzarian. It was simply, "In twenty-four hours, I will be free."

CHAPTER 18

FLIGHT TO TRESAZRIUM

Androz's impressive image flashed on Mediah's screen as she was getting ready for work. "We'd better get out of the city, baby. Things are going to blow sky high, and the residents are going to be in full panic. It won't be pretty."

She tried to hide her annoyance. He was popping up at the worst times these days. "I was just going to the office. I have a few more things to wrap up."

"Get back here when you're finished then. I'll be waiting. We're going up to my getaway place until this whole thing blows over. Get that, blows over?"

Mediah hid a grimace. She hated what Androz referred to his "getaway," a spacious solarplex with all the luxuries he and his buddies loved: Year-round games on the wall screens in every room, all of which involved killing things or making them scream with pain. Swaug faucets, pleasure pits, and robots resembling the Mother in various costumes. Mediah shuddered just thinking about it.

She tried not to appear flustered, pretending to straighten her wig. "What about E. Mercator? Do you think he was just throwing a scare into us? You said yourself he didn't even know what day it was? How could he be so accurate?"

"Because I gave him the exact time and date, darling, that's why. I thought he would play right into our hands and he did. There will be no Triumvirate ruling Megacity when we get back." Androz drummed his fingers on his marble desk as if he were anxious for the disaster to get started.

Either Androz was trying to cover his mistakes or he was smarter—deviously smarter—than she had given him credit for. "Well done," she said, smiling her brightest smile.

✐✐✐

Thur came to, cradled in Gelise's arms, with Miri and Riga impatiently looking down at him as if they expected him to jump up and run along after the rest of the expedition. "That hurt," he said, rubbing the knot on his head and looking up at Gelise for sympathy.

She pointed back at Miri. "I didn't do it, she did, that stupid newby."

"Well, what do you expect, sneaking through the bushes like a pack of worfels? Come on, get up!" Miri extended her hand. "You can tell me who all your funny-smelling friends are later."

Thur got to his feet, his head wrapped in a makeshift bandage. "These funny-smelling friends of mine just took control of the farm, and they came with me because I told them the Borgs were about to attack the Hollow."

Miri looked skeptical, glancing at Riga to see if he thought the blow to Thur's head had done something to his brain. "How do you know that?"

Gelise jumped right in. "Because a bald lady named Mediah told us, that's why. She said to find Valerian and tell him to return at once. So your hero Valerian is a spy!"

"He is not!" Miri said, taking a menacing step toward Gelise. "He helped us get to freedom."

Gelise fought back. "And found us. Since you've come, we've had nothing but trouble."

Riga took charge. "Come, let's not waste time throwing accusations at people. If we're going to fight as an army, and win, we can't fight among ourselves. Now, quick time! We have to catch up with the others."

"Let's go," said Pier. "These two can fight it out later. By the way, my mutant friend, my name is Pier and these are the men and women from the farm." He indicated the people armed with hoes and shovels behind him. "We haven't got weapons like yours," he said, nodding at Riga's lazorizer, "but fight we can just the same."

"They call me Riga and you're very welcome to join us. Now we must hurry. If Thur is right, and I have no reason to doubt him, the Borgs could attack any time."

The line of marchers headed by Valerian was just a mile ahead when the sensor on Valerian's belt started flashing red, a warning of robotic action nearby. The attack happened so fast, the people from the Hollow barely had time to dive for the cover of the trees before robotic drones flashed over their heads, firing lasers as they passed.

The laser missiles splintered bark as they landed deep in the forest. One huge spruce tree was hit so directly, it toppled over making a loud crashing noise s it fell.

"Beezlecrikey, what was that?" A strange figure leaped out, narrowly avoiding being squashed by the falling tree. "All whirring and whining and swishing along, they was. Just shot this tree in two, they did." He had wild, shaggy hair, a bushy beard, and was wearing a collection of colorful rags. The whole effect was something like a jester's costume.

Others dressed in strange bright costumes gathered around, staring at the tree, talking in the same sing-song language.

When the people from the expedition began to emerge from their hiding places, they first stared at the strangers and then began to laugh. Yop put a stop to the giggling instantly.

"Slip, my friend, you barely missed getting turned into toothpicks. What brings you Travelers to these woods at such a dangerous time?"

"Have ye never known these woods to be no dangerous, Yop Hedgehog? It was I looking for my boy, if truth be known until something broke yon tree in half. Blasted me eyes and singed me beard, it did," said the curious-looking stranger.

Valerian was going down the line, making sure there was no one missing. He barely even took notices of the newcomers. His voice was commanding and urgent. "No time for talk until we get to the Hollow. Yop, move them out on the double. The drone'll be coming back."

"Is that the Borg Guard or what?" Slip asked, scratching in rude places. "Who does he think he is, a king?"

"Just come to the Hollow, Slip. You and the Travelers will be safe there," said Yop, getting the line moving again. "I'll explain later."

The Travelers debated among themselves. "Will there be elderberry wine and rabbit stew?"

Yop said over his shoulder, "And raisin cake."

"Then we'll come and be glad."

Skye, seeing his father talking to Yop, turned white with fear and disappeared from Miri's side.

಄಄಄

Mediah was putting the finishing touches on the message board when the Borg Guard crashed through the magnetic field on her doorway. Behind them was Uber-councilman Riksbury.

"May I ask what is the meaning of this?" she asked coolly.

"Ubercouncilperson Mediah Polius Exeter, you are under arrest for treason," he replied in a squeaky voice.

With one long nail, she tapped the send button on her computer. "Really, Riksbury? Can't you think of something more original than that? Treason is so yesterday."

The drumman was unmoved. "Your partner Androz is also so yesterday. He was arrested this morning."

Mediah knew Riksbury was bluffing. Androz was at her apartment by then, stinking up the place with his cigar.

The Borg Guards advanced, preparing to carry her bodily off to prison when Androzarian suddenly flashed on the office wall screen in full uniform. "Stand down, you robo idiots!" he barked. "I said him, Councilman Riksbury, not her. Don't they teach you pronouns in the Academy?" Borgs were genderless but that was swept aside by the imperator's powerful voice. "Who gives you orders, huh? That little rat or the imperator?"

At the sound of their commander's voice, the Borgs snapped to attention, saluted, and answered, "The imperator, sir."

"Then take that disgusting drumman tripe Riksbury to the Dumpster and toss him in! That's an order, roboidiots!" As they marched out with the shrieking Riksbury between them, Androz chuckled. "I'm waiting, baby. When you coming back?"

Mediah couldn't let Androz see her thinking, so she

pretended to be getting ready to leave—collecting things from the desk. She couldn't bring herself to go with Androz to his getaway, and yet she didn't want to lead him to Valerian. Besides, what if Mercator was wrong?

"I'm coming right now." She signaled for the robocar and went to the tube. Behind her, there was a rumbling in the streets. Despite her own dilemma, Mediah smiled. Mother's messages were working all too well. The Rejects in the Flyover were on the move.

When the robocar arrived, she directed it to take her to the Aeroplex where her Jetstar was waiting. So was Imperator Androzarian.

"Take me to Valerian," he said around his ever-present cigar. "Isn't that where you were going, sweet baby?" His small eyes, buried in florid creases, gave away nothing.

✤✤✤

The expedition arrived, swelled in numbers by the workers from the Farm, the Travelers, and Basi and his Rogues. Aya's eyes grew wide with shock as people kept pouring in the dining room, thirsty and hungry.

"And I thought feeding a family of five on frogs and sewer cabbage was a challenge. Come on, Blu, let's see what we've got to feed three hundred."

Thur and Gelise were welcomed back as heroes for delivering Mediah's warning to Dr. Spencer.

"We'll be ready," Spencer said, giving them both a hug. "And you two risked your lives to bring back Mediah's message. I want to hear the whole story but first, you must rest. Aya, and Qin have been so worried, you had better go to them or they'll be in here after you. And Gelise had better rejoin her family. I have a little more work to do."

"Oh, no, you won't get rid of us that fast," Gelise said. "We came to report that this Valerian is a spy. That bald lady said for him to return at once didn't she, Thur?"

Thur nodded reluctantly. He hadn't told Gelise that Valerian was Dr. Spencer's son. How would it look if their two defenders turned out to be working for the Triumvirate? "But he saved us and led us to freedom. Why would he do that if he was just working for the Triumvirate?"

"And he led you right to the Hollow, didn't he?" Gelise demanded. "How do you know he wasn't reporting back to the bald lady all along? How did those drones know where to attack us in the forest if he didn't tell them? And that belt he wears, the one with the flashing lights. It could be a transmitter so they could communicate with each other."

"All good questions have answers, young lady. Not reasons, just answers which you may believe or not." Spencer glanced anxiously at the huge machine in the center of the room as if he had work to do. "And those will come in good time. Now, I must get back to work. Call Valerian to me, please," he said, ushering them out the door.

"They're in cahoots together, the two of them. I just know it," Gelise muttered as they went down to the dining hall. "We're about to get handed over to the Borgs and I'm not going to let it happen. Wait 'til I tell Yop."

Thur suddenly stopped and grabbed her arm. "You're only going on suspicion, not facts. It's like Dr. Spencer said, your questions will all be answered. It's just that now is not the time. You will just tear us apart if you start throwing accusations around. Right now, we all need to trust each other."

"Trust him!" She stared angrily at Valerian. "But you heard the bald lady yourself! And how did they even know where we were living in the first place if Spencer didn't tell them? How can you be so stupid, Thur newby?"

Qin suddenly popped her head into the passageway. "Am I interrupting something or can anybody join this fight?"

"No, you're not interrupting anything at all," Gelise said, turning on her heel and walking away.

"Forget that little squirrel and give me a hug, little brother," Qin said, embracing him. "It's so good to have you back. Now come see Aya and then tell me why you stink so bad."

Valerian came into his father's lab with a plate of food. "Aya says to eat something or you'll disappear again."

Spencer didn't stop tinkering with his machine. "That young lady with Thur. What's her name, Gelise?"

Valerian eyed his father's heaping plate with relish. "The loud mouthed one? She's already called me a spy in front of the whole group. Do you want your drumstick?"

Spencer was concentrating on tightening a screw. "But they did escape and bring reinforcements with them."

"And we picked up some more along the way, so now we number five hundred fighters." Valerian gnawed away on the drumstick.

"What concerns me is they were captured by Mediah and she released them with a personal message for you, Valerian. Explain that, please. And hand me that screwdriver with your clean hand."

Valerian was clearly annoyed at having his integrity challenged by a mere girl and one who was ignorant as dirt at that. "For starters, she didn't release them, they escaped through the drain in Mediah's pool. And I'm sure Mediah knows I defected by now and where I have made

my home, because the Borgs chased us into the Trezarium, remember? The Triumvirate Council has been planning to wipe out pockets of opposition for a long time.
You, of all people know that, Father. So why all the questions?"

Spencer rolled out from under the machine. "So you
will be able to answer them satisfactorily in the meeting
we are going to have as soon as you finish gnawing on
that bone like an angry cave lion.

⁊◌⁊◌

Mediah and Androz had just started out from the Jet-
plex when there was an horrendous noise behind them.
Following that, their Jetstar took an ominous plunge
downward. She let out a piercing scream just as it was
about to plunge into the roiling waters of the Abyss.

"Do something! We're going down!"

"Just keep your wig on, baby. I'm in control." Androz switched the small craft over to manual control. He
steered the nose of the Jetstar upward, and it soon leveled
out, just missing the huge turbines that were grinding
slowly to a halt. "Good thing I remembered my flight
training days." He laughed glancing at Mediah's fear-
frozen face.

"I thought we were finished there for a second," she
said, looking behind her at the sprawling Megacity. "It's
gone dark," she said, not taking her eyes off the back
window. "There's not a single light in the whole city."

"I guess Mercator was telling the truth, after all,
although his timing was a little off," Androz said. "The
Brain has finally been fried." He started to chuckle, and
then his roaring laugh made Mediah cover her ears.
"Wonder what Riksbury is thinking now."

"I'm wondering whether my Mother Boards will

switch over to the emergency power or does the Brain control that, too."

"Shall we take a looksee?" asked Androz

Mediah stiffened beside him. "No, don't go back. They might think we had something to do with it."

But her protest came too late. Androz was already making a U-turn in the sky. "No, they won't, because I filed a flight plan that said I was going to my getaway. And I made sure I spread the word in every communication."

They flew over the darkened Megacity, looking for any sign of light. Then slowly, there was a flicking, then a glare of blue light as Mother Boards all over the vast city lit up the night. The last message Mediah had sent out boomed out over the darkened city.

"Mother says revolt against the cruel Triumvirate Council, you residents of Megacity! Take things into your own hands. It's time to make them pay! Revolt and be free!" The message ended with a simulation of fireworks, complete with explosive noises.

Androz chuckled again. "Very inspiring, baby. You think they'll do anything or just lie there in the dark until somebody turns the lights back on."

"That somebody is us, darling," Mediah said, settling back in her seat. "Whoever turns the lights back on will be the new rulers of Megacity. But we have to let them do without the necessities for a while first. Food and water and Happy Pills and Swaug. Then we'll come to their rescue. Meanwhile, we have to hide out somewhere."

"I know just the place, too," Androz said, turning the Jetstar around. "My little getaway."

As they flew across the night sky, below them stretched the Trezarium, dark and mysterious. Androz turned on the camera and they had a close-up view of the endless trees, and bushes. "Think your Valerian is hiding somewhere below? Now's your chance to say hello, ba-by."

No sooner were the words were out of Androz's mouth than the Jetstar lost power and crashed down into the thick branches below.

In the Hollow, Valerian's belt lit up with flashing lights. At the same time, the demagnifying machine seemed to develop a life of its own, tweeting hysterically, looking like a Solstice tree gone crazy.

"We got visitors," Spencer said. "Go tell the others to get ready to fight. I'll see if I can find out who they are. Whoever it is will get a taste of Yop's famous hospitality."

A pipe suddenly shot up through the roof of the room and through a camouflaged hole in the ground. Attached to its head was a camera which flashed a view of the forest for twenty miles around. It didn't have to go that far. Mediah's Jetstar had crashed nearby in the trees and was inching down as the occupants frantically tried to get out.

Valerian had run back to the dining room where he could tell by the way everyone grew silent, Gelise had been spreading her accusations against him. He saw Miri's face flushed with anger, and when he said he needed scouts to go with him outside, she was the first to volunteer. Riga was already getting his weapon ready, and, to Valerian's surprise, Chez and Loki volunteered to go.

Thur and Zak stood up also, but Val shook his head. "No, you two stay here. We need some trained fighters below ground. In case—" Val paused. "Well, just in case. The rest of you need to prepare for battle. You know what to do. Yop is in charge, and you will obey his orders and no one else's. In case we don't return, don't send anyone outside to look for us, is that clear?"

"Clear enough, young Val." Yop gripped the young

man's hand. "You can count on us to do our part."

"But can we count on him to do his?" Gelise muttered.

Above ground, the forest was dark, except for a red glow in the distance. As they crept through the trees, it became evident the light was coming from somewhere over their heads. "Maybe a drone malfunctioned?" Miri whispered, keeping close on Val's heels.

"Too big," came Val's whisper back.

"And drones aren't thermo powered," Riga added. "That's definitely coming from a Jetstar."

They got close enough to see the Jetstar teetering in the tree, ready to plunge to the ground. The insignia on the side made it clear. It was the transport belonging to a member of The Triumvirate Council. Val signaled for the scouts to come to a halt. "Chez, run back and tell Yop we've got a council transport that has crashed in a tree. Bring a strong net and twenty strong men and come back on the double."

Chez took off running through the forest like a deer.

"I think I can get up there." Thur had noticed a rope hanging down from a nearby tree. He recognized it as belonging to the Forever Road which took people across the canopy of trees.

"I'll race you to the top," said a voice behind him. He looked round just as Gelise swung over his head, landing in the tree next to the wrecked Jetstar. Looking in the window, she called down "Hey, it's the bald lady and her soldier boyfriend. They look pretty banged up, but not dead. At least, they're still moving."

"If they move, the jet could fall to the ground. Tell them help is on the way," Val called.

But Gelise crouched on a branch near the wreck, looking like a cat that has discovered a bird's nest. "Isn't that what we want them to do? Die like the rest of the people they've sent to the Recycler. Like my parents, for instance. I've got a mind to just nudge this wreck over and send them crashing to the ground. Oh, that's right, Valerian. That's your mommy in there."

But Thur had landed on the other side of the wrecked jet craft beside Androz who signaled that the hatch was damaged and wouldn't open.

"Wait until Yop comes with the net," Valerian called to him, "and then use your lazorizer on it. It opens from the back."

There was a great commotion behind them as Yop and at least twenty burly men arrived with a stout net used to store things in the trees. "I've never tried to see if would hold a plane but there's a first time for everything," said the mayor of the Hollow.

The burly men—some Travelers, farmers, and Rogues eager to see what they could steal from the downed craft—stretched the net as far under the tree as it would reach.

Valerian waited until the net was in place and then called up to Thur. "Now, blast the back of the hatch, Thur. But tell the occupants to cover their heads first. We don't want any ears shot off."

"Tell baldy not to worry about her hair frizzing," Gelise called. "She hasn't got any."

Androz and Mediah did as they were told, and Thur zapped the back of the hatch. It turned out to be laser proof metal. Miri climbed up beside him. "Let me try," she said. She swung her adl-adl with bone-crushing power and the hatch lock shattered into pieces. "Guess they weren't expecting stones in space."

The Jetstar gave a moan and plunged down two more branches, carrying Androz and Mediah with it. "Here, grab my hand," Thur yelled at Mediah who let out a terrified scream.

"And mine," said Miri, leaning over to catch the other hand. Together, they hauled Mediah up to the branch above stricken craft, where she teetered, dazed and bleeding.

"Tell the general to grab hold of the rope as I swing it over to you, Thur," Val called. "You hold it steady," he said, indicating the sturdy rope tied around the tree.

The imperator gripped the rope in both big fists. "Got it!"

"Now, hold the rope as far from the tree as you can so he can drop into the net," Val commanded. "Drop, Androz."

The burly soldier dropped and bounced around the net like a kid. "I haven't done that since I was a lad. This is fun!"

"First time I ever caught a general," said one of the Grays.

"I'd rather catch his girlfriend," said a River Rogue.

They used the same routine to get Mediah down, only Val caught her as she slid down the rope.

"Val, I thought I'd never find you," she said.

"I never get the girl," said the disappointed Rogue.

Dr. Spencer came running through the woods. "Wait, men. Don't lower the net yet. I'd like to save the plane if we could."

"So you and Valerian can escape?" Gelise called from the tree. "Not on your life! Look out below!"

She gave the small craft a shove and sent it crashing to the forest floor. The men below dropped the net and ran for safety as the craft exploded in a burst of light.

"You impulsive little fool." Mediah struggled to stand on her feet. "You've only signaled to the Borg Guard where we are."

"In that case, I'd better get back to my work," Spencer said briskly. "Imperator Androzarian, I believe," he said, addressing the general, "follow me. You can tell me what happened to my brother, Mercator, among other things."

"Edward Spencer! I thought I recognized you," said Androz, falling in behind him. "Frankly speaking, your brother is the very reason we're here."

Valerian took Mediah's arm as she didn't appear too steady on her feet. He couldn't help noticing how small and vulnerable she looked in the forest. Following the others, Thur glanced up at the burnt tree where Gelise was still huddled on the upper branches.

"I'm sorry, Thur. Really, I only meant—" she called through the shriveled branches.

"You know what? I don't care what you meant. Tell that to the Borg Guard when they kill us all. And by the way, you look just like the bald lady now." He marched away after the rest of the defenders. Gelise reached up and felt her head. Her hair was gone, scorched off by the exploding Jetstar.

The attack began shortly before dawn with a volley of laser cannons. There wasn't much the Borgs could destroy above ground, except the tree houses, hammocks, and landings. They blasted the tops off all the surrounding vegetation and still didn't detect any movement above ground.

As they moved closer to the Hollow, the Borg commander was called aside by his lieutenants. They had detected movement in the trees and infrared vision had revealed large, furry shapes behind them.

"Turn the laser cannons around and blast those trees away," the commander ordered. "Whatever they are will either be blasted or crushed. Then back the cannons up and, if anything moves, mow them down!"

The Borgs obeyed their commander and swung the cannon muzzles around, backing up to get a good aim on the invisible enemy. Suddenly, the Guard disappeared! When the commander gave the order to fire, he was met with silence. He looked back behind him to see his entire force gone.

When he turned back around, the last thing he saw before he went soaring through the air was Tookie's droll mother.

In the underground Hollow, Blu lifted his good right arm. "Ha-ha," he said. "Ha-ha."

The ground attack of the Borgs was followed by a squadron of robot drones carrying bombs. In his lab below ground, Dr. Spencer picked up the vibrations of one hundred engines coming toward the Hollow.

"Something has gone wrong," Androz said. "All defenses should have been shut down by the malfunction of the Brain. Unless Mercator got it wrong and his plan didn't work."

"My brother never gets it wrong, General," Spencer said. "Probably these units were already launched before the Brain shut down. These robots can switch over to auxiliary power modes in case of emergencies and apparently, they did. Now, providing this demagnetizer works, we'll take care of that. Unfortunately, it doesn't have much of a range, though. We'll have to hold our fire until they're practically over our heads."

"That's a comfort," Androz remarked sourly. "Those bombs make craters at least fifty feet deep. How far down are we?"

"Ten feet. But less than that in some places."

"Well, what are you waiting for?" Androz yelled.

At the same moment, Spencer pushed a lever down, and they both got knocked off their feet by the force of the demagnetizer revving up to maximum speed. In the kitchen, Blu crumpled in a heap.

The drones crashed into the retreating Borg Guard

and took out the bridge over the river and the Churn below, sending a curtain of water 200 feet in the air. When
it descended, a huge surge of water swept over the empty
plains around the Megacity, and the river slowed its pace
as though it was slowing down to enjoy being free again.

In the darkened flooded city, Riksbury called for the
Guard outside his door. When no one came, he made his
way on the wheels that served as his legs to the entrance
of his cell. The force field was down. He was free.

The other prisoners were making their way through
the dark water toward the main door, past heaps of robotic Guards crumpled up on the floor along the corridor.
Their yawning orifices were filled with water and sparks
that flew from ruptured circuits.

"What just happened?" Riksbury asked a human who
passed his cell door.

"I don't know but I'm not stopping to find out," the
man said. "And if I was you, I wouldn't either."

When all the prisoners had vanished into the dark
around the prison, Councilman Riksbury sat alone in the
Guards' office, waiting the lights to come on, for the robocars to run, and the magnetic tubes to work so he could
leave. He tried to call up Sargon of the Gray Hoods, who
ran his district for him, but the wall screens didn't work.

Riksbury wheeled about the prison, looking for a
mutant guard who knew where the auxiliary power system was. But the guards had all fled, being afraid of what
the prisoners would do to them. *Androzarian and Mediah!* Riksbury thought. *They had something to do with
this and I will make them pay!* When he found them, of
course.

Finally, Riksbury saw a light coming toward him. It
was an eerie light and it kept moving back and forth like
a small green eye. As it came closer, he saw the outline of
a small, stooped figure.

"Who are you?" demanded the councilman. "Are you a Guard?"

"Dear me, no," said a quavering voice. "I answer to the name Mercator. And whom do I have the doubtful pleasure of speaking with?"

"Ubercoucilman Riksbury and if you're not a Guard, you must be a prisoner. Hand me your light, so I can see my way out of this miserable place," Riksbury demanded.

"Riksbury. I seem to know that name," said the man, shining his light in Riksbury's eyes. "In fact, you sat on the council that put me here all those years ago." The light faded as Mercator moved on down the corridor and Riksbury was in the dark again. "Goodbye, Councilman."

"Wait," Riksbury cried in desperation. "I'll give you anything you want if you will only get me out of here."

"I want nothing you can give me, Councilman. But I can give you something," replied Mercator.

Riksbury held out his hands. "What? Your light? Oh, that's good of you, sir!"

"No," said Mercator. "A decent burial, unlike the ones you have given thousands of others. Ta, ta."

Riksbury was still sitting in the dark hall, wondering what Mercator had meant, when the walls exploded. Councilman Riksbury was buried under piles of rubble.

❧❦❧

In the Hollow, there was jubilation as the people poured out of the ground and saw Borgs lying in heaps everywhere. Travelers, Rogues, and farmers all danced a mad victory jig with the people of the Hollow. Even the drolls joined in, whirling around four partners at once.

In his underground laboratory, Androzarian and Mediah were deep in conversation with Dr. Spencer.

"So you planned to take over ruling Megacity after the Brain was destroyed. And just how did you plan to do that without the Guard? It will be chaos over there." For the first time in years, Spencer was smoking his pipe, a sign he was relaxing. "But won't the residents follow anybody who offers them food and shelter? The Grays, for instance?"

"I thought of all that." Androzarian squirmed uncomfortably in his rough wooden chair. He was used to more luxurious surroundings. This was more like boot camp in the sticks. "No one has command of the Guard like I do. The mutants and the drummans, at least. The robots just do as they're told, anyway. With a handpicked force, I can establish order and get things done. Even Sargon and the Grays can be managed."

"And I intend to help Androz by bringing the Mother image back to calm their fears." Mediah managed to look as lovely as ever, in spite of a few bruises and scratches. She kept glancing at Spencer under her long artificial eyelashes, which made Androz even more uncomfortable.

Dr. Spencer seemed unaware of the tension he was causing, concentrating on the matter at hand. "That's all well and good, but you two represent the old government. You need a fresh face as the figurehead for anything new you're going to try."

"Father, they're calling for you outside." Valerian walked into the lab and then stopped when he saw Androz and Mediah. "Sorry, I didn't know you were busy."

"And here he is," said Mediah, smiling for the first time. "Handsome, brave, and strong. Just the right sort of person to bring order to the poor wretched masses of Megacity."

Valerian looked mystified. "I didn't mean to interrupt anything. I'll just tell them you're busy, Father."

"You didn't tell me he was Spencer's son, Mediah."

General Androzarian regarded her with a frown. "I thought you said he was just a boy you found and decided to hide for some reason. Just what's going on here?"

"I can explain that," Mediah said. "Because I foresaw he would someday be useful and, as it turns out, he will be. The perfect representative of a new era."

Spencer was quiet, sending up smoke rings toward the ceiling. From his father's silence, Valerian gathered Spencer was leaving it up to him to take up Mediah's offer. Valerian shook his head. "In case you hadn't noticed, I defected from the Triumvirate and the Borgs a long time ago. I wouldn't go back again for all the power you could offer me. I intend to build a new society outside of that cursed place."

"A society of underground tunnels and treetop travel." Androz gave a grumpy chuckle. "You are welcome to try. I suppose you make fire by rubbing two sticks together."

"At least we will have sticks," Val retorted. "No thanks to you, Androz." He turned and walked out.

The young soldier was striding down the passageway when he heard Miri call his name. She stepped out of the dining room and he forgot what he was angry about.

"There you are! I've been looking all over for you." She came toward him, wearing the white tunic Aya had made for her while she was gone. Her knee-length deerskin boots over white leggings were trimmed with embroidered leaves. Her golden hair was cascading in loose waves over her shoulders.

Something caught in his throat and his voice came out in an uncharacteristic squeak. "I've been trying to get my father to come out and join the celebration but he's talking to the general and M—his lady friend."

"You can come outside then, and leave them to stew and chew as Aya says." Miri laughed and took his arm.

"You look like you could use a cup of Yop's blackberry wine. This isn't the time to be thinking about tomorrow or what that girl Gelise said."

Val's head spun with the feeling of Miri being so close. Although he wanted to be alone with her, he allowed her to lead him to the celebration just so she would stay near him.

A great cheer went up when he stepped outside where Riga was waiting with Yop and the rest of the warriors from the Expedition. The drolls even cheered just because everyone else was. Tookie danced around with Annabeth and Pier's little daughter, Nadja.

"To Valerian, our fearless leader and defender of small people," Yop shouted. "And to all our brave defenders!"

Under Riga's watchful eyes, Miri drifted away with Qin and their girlfriends. Only Gelise sat alone, a braided cap on her head, her scorched face still red and swollen with burns from the exploding Jetstar. She felt miserable as she watched Thur, Loki, and Chez laughing and flirting with one girl after another.

Hoping Miri would notice his absence, Val walked over to where Gelise sat. When she saw him coming toward her, she ducked under a long table holding the food, thinking the man she had slandered wouldn't notice her.

But Val bent over and saw her crouching there. "How's the view from in there?" he asked.

Gelise's face grew even redder with embarrassment. "Go away, will you? I don't want to talk to anybody right now."

Val just smiled. "I don't either. Can I join? Promise I won't talk to you unless you want to."

Gelise shrugged. "I don't care. I'm just surprised you would even sit by me."

"As long as you don't bite," Val said, folding up and joining her under the table.

He was so tall, he had to bend over to keep from bumping his head. They sat there, looking at the dancers and watching the people who came up to help themselves to food, identifying them only by their feet.

The drolls were easy to identify by their hairy toes and the slave workers from the Farm didn't wear shoes. But the various boots were harder to identify, and soon Gelise was laughing over getting a Rogue mixed up with a Traveler's legwear.

"Look, I'm sorry I gave you such a hard time," she said impulsively. Then she shyly looked away rather than meet his gaze. *She must look like a cross between a mutant and a worful*, she thought.

"That's all right, I understand." Valerian sensed how hard it was for this tough girl to make an apology. "I didn't think my father was alive and my own mother died after I was born. I never knew her. So I know how it feels to grow up alone. But I want to change all that. Build a society where families don't have to be torn apart like yours and mine were. Where you don't have to hide and you're free to go where you want."

"But how?" Gelise met his eyes and then looked away. "How can one person change all that?"

"Not one. All of us. This is a good start, don't you think? All of us together?" He nodded at the lineup of footwear in front of the table along with the drolls' bare toes. Gelise erupted into more giggles. When Valerian looked again, he saw deerskin boots with embroidered leaves on the cuffs. They belonged to Miri.

In a hurry to back out from under the table, he bumped his head, causing the bowl on the table containing Yop's blackberry wine to slosh back and forth. Miri looked under the table to see what caused the disturbance.

"You!" she said, seeing Valerian rubbing his head and Gelise laughing at him. "And her! Of all people!"

"Miri, wait! It isn't how it looks!" Valerian scrambled out from under the table. "Wait a minute, I can explain!"

But Miri was gone. Across the crowd, he met Riga's hard eyes. *You break her heart and I'll break your head,* was the message.

ↄⱷↄ

Over the course of the weeks that followed, Miri brushed off his efforts to explain. Finally she stopped avoiding him long enough to say, "You didn't have to hide, you know. Anyone could see she was trying to get your attention all along. I hope you'll be happy."

One morning she left for the farm with Pier and his friend Rufus who were anxious to spread the news that the Borgs were defeated. Pier left his daughter Nadja with Qin and Aya who had started a school in the Hollow. Zak went along with them as well as Basi and some of the Rogues. Now that the river was calm, they could transport some food to the stricken city. "And find some loot for themselves, of course," Basi said to his men.

Finally, in despair, Val decided then to go back to Megacity with Androz and Mediah. What was there here worth staying for, now that Miri was gone? It felt like half of him were missing. The trouble was he didn't know which half.

ↄⱷↄ

In the rubble of the prison, Riksbury was pinned down by a large piece of cement. He felt his strength ebbing away when he suddenly heard voices. With his last ounce of strength, he managed to croak, "Help!"

"Over there," someone said. "See that wheel sticking out from that pile of rubble? Riksbury, is that you? It's me, Sargon."

"Sargon, help me," came the pitiful cry.

The commander of the Grays gave what passed for him as a laugh. "As you well know, Councilman, I don't help nobody for nothing. What's it worth to you not to lie here and die like a sewer rat, eh?"

"Anything you want, Sargon. Just help me," Riksbury sobbed in desperation.

"All right then, I want full control of everything the farm produces plus full control of the Pleasurable Delights which includes Swaug and Happy Pills."

The reply was a desperate whine. "Yes, yes. Now, get me out of here, please, Sargon."

"What am I asking you for? You're on the way to the Dumpster!" Sargon gave a loud snort. "So long, Riksbury. Come on, lads, let's see what else we can use."

CHAPTER 19

THE REBELLION

When Miri and the others arrived at the Farm, they found the workers fighting among themselves as to who should be in charge. The sight of their returning comrades calmed the workers down for a while, and they greeted the news that the Borgs were defeated with a cheer. But soon, the arguing resumed until Pier took over.

Pier took charge. "Enough of fighting over who does what! The fact is, nothing is getting done and the crops need picking and the cows need milking. When that's done, we'll meet back in the Control Room—correction, the office—to discuss, not fight, over how we're going to run this place." The workers fell silent. Pier looked around. "If this is going to work, we're going to have to work with each other. We'll vote on everything."

"Just like the Triumvirate Council?" somebody said. There snickers from the crowd.

"Unless you're so used to taking orders, you can't think for yourselves," said Pier.

"We'll vote then," said another worker. "Let's get to work. All in favor, say aye. Otherwise, keep your mouth shut."

"I see we've got a lot to learn," Pier said under his breath.

Miri's job was to organize the women and the few children among them. She still carried her adl-adl in its sling and the children were curious about it. "I'll show you what it does if you show me a cow. I've never seen a cow before. Or a chicken for that matter."

The children laughed out loud and then covered their mouths as if they had done something wrong.

"It's all right," Miri said. "I used to be afraid to laugh, too. But now we can laugh all we want. And play, too! Come on, let's play a game. Hide and seek. Who wants to be first?"

When it came Miri's turn, she hid in a cow shed until the alarmed cow bellowed loudly right behind her. She burst out of the shed, reaching for her adl-adl. The children laughed so hard their mothers came running to see what was wrong.

"They're only laughing at me," Miri said. "Because that great horned beast roared at me. I hope the chickens aren't that big and noisy." The women burst into laughter along with the children. "I see I've got a lot to learn," Miri said with a sigh.

One woman put her arm around Miri's shoulders. "And we've got a lot to learn about your world, too. Let's help each other."

Something about her voice was familiar and, though years of hard work had lined her face, the woman's blue eyes were still bright, her smile just as wide. Strands of copper hair escaped from under her work cap, exactly the same color as her sister Qin's.

They looked at each other with dawning recognition, afraid to trust what they saw. "Do you have a younger sister, girl?"

Miri nodded. "Three years younger with hair the color of yours."

The woman's eyes filled with tears. "I had two little girls once. Those monsters took them away when they captured our town. I've stayed alive, just hoping I'd see them again…" Her voice wandered off into tears.

"Mother? Could it be you?" Miri's fingers stroked the woman's face. The same nose, the same dimples on either side of her mouth. "Did you used to sing me a song at bedtime? Something like 'Sweet and low, sweet and low, wind of the western sea'?"

The women and children formed a circle around the pair more out of fear than curiosity. They were used to shielding their own from the eyes of the Guards.

Her mother could only nod and hold her daughter tight. It was the first time both women allowed herself to cry in years.

❧❧

In his underground laboratory, Spencer was putting Blu back together with spare parts from the robotic Borgs left in the ditch. When Blu was complete, he lit up at once. Rolling his mismatched eyes, he blurted, "Large group approaching on foot through the woods."

Androz was watching Spencer work. "Can't be Borgs. Are you sure that old tin can works?"

"I resent being called a tin can," objected Blu, rolling his eyes. "Especially by renegade generals."

Dr. Spencer wasted no time settling an argument. "Blu, go get Thur and Riga. Tell them to scout the trail leading from the river. Androz, we'd better get Yop to call a meeting."

"You'd make a good general, you know that, Spencer?" Androz chuckled. He was enjoying himself in this accidental getaway without the creature comforts. But he knew Mediah yearned to get back to the city and get things under control. Her control. He decided to let her wait some more. Waiting was what Mediah hated the most.

But controlling Megacity was not foremost on Mediah's mind. It was Valerian, whose unhappiness was like a wall between them. She had seen his pursuit of Miri and, while she was glad the girl was gone, she hated for him to be so unhappy. She didn't know why. Unhappiness was such a human thing.

But the more she was around humans, the more her own feelings identified with theirs. *It's frightening*, she thought. She longed to get back to the city, surrounded by things that always obeyed her. Control of oneself and one's surroundings, that was what she wanted. For Valerian, too. Not hankering after some slip of a human with hair like a cascade of dripping honey.

She found him alone working on some equipment that had been damaged in the attack of the Borgs. "Don't waste your time trying to fix that old junk. Wait until we get back to the city. Androz will get you ten new ones."

Valerian looked up with a smile. "Mediah, you're looking well."

"Good repair job, that's all. Good thing my makeup kit was strapped to my waist."

Valerian shook his head. "All the same, that was a pretty narrow escape."

"If that girl hadn't tried to kill us, you mean."

"She thought you were responsible for her parents being taken from her. Were you?" Val searched Mediah's face for answers.

"That was well before my appointment to the council, Valerian." She fiddled with her artificial hair, a sure sign that she was feeling guilty, Valerian thought.

He persisted. "But you did use your influence to save me. Why was that?"

Mediah wished for that control again so she could avoid uncomfortable questions. "Because you are my son," she said, not knowing any other answer. "I couldn't let you die. Not then, not now. So I hid you. Made it look like you were just a mutant child I'd saved."

"What?" He shook his head as if denial could clear up his confusion. "But you adopted me after my real mother died. Father said so. Don't tell me he lied to me."

Mediah found herself blurting out the truth to the young man looking to her for answers. "If he did, he did it to keep you safe. I'm your real mother, Valerian. Elizabeth Spencer was already dead when you were born. Your father kept it secret because, if they'd known, they would have sent all of us to the Recycle Dumpster."

Valerian couldn't believe his ears. "But I didn't think…you're a mutant, aren't you? I didn't think they were able to…"

"Reproduce?" She said the word he was hesitant to say.

He didn't want to conjure a mental image of his father and his guardian together.

"We thought so, too, your father and I. But I was the result of a laboratory experiment, you see. One of my biological parents must have been human. I never knew who they were so I'm only guessing. But Edward was so lonely after his wife died, he needed some comfort. And the rest, as they say, is history. Oh, these feelings are so confusing!"

Valerian stood up, letting the equipment fall from his hands. "Now, I don't know what to believe. I'm so confused, I'm sorry. Sorry," he said again, seeing the disappointment on her face, "but I must be excused." He left her sitting there, and went out in the forest to think.

☙❧

Gelise was traveling among the treetop branches before Riga and Thur even left the Hollow. Lingering in the passageway hoping to catch a glimpse of Thur, she had overheard Blu delivering the message to the two warriors.

Now, she saw a makeshift bridge of rafts and boats crossing the river. Following the trail leading into the forest from the river, she saw a group of figures in gray hoods. They looked menacing, armed with all sorts of weapons—lazorizers, clubs, swords, and spears. It was clear they were intending to fight. She was back at the Hollow with the news just after Riga and Thur had left.

The people had already crowded into the Parliament meeting room, their usual numbers swelled by Travelers, a farmer or two who had reunited with members of their families, and one droll, Tookie's mother, who took quite a bit of space. No one complained, however.

Everyone speculated on who the invaders might be. "Gray Hoods, I'll bet anything," Androz said. "Naturally, I expected Sargon to take advantage of the situation. I wonder who they're going after."

"I can tell you that." Basi didn't bother with invitations. He joined the meeting with some of his Rogues, a rough-looking bunch who constantly flirted with the women of the Hollow. "The farmers who were here. The Hoods do a good business with the farm and they aren't going to take interfering with that business by a bunch of slaves. They aim to get their own back if it takes knocking a few heads together."

A farmer stood up. "Isn't there a way to contact the farm? To warn Pier and Rufus that the Hoods are coming to take them over?"

"Not without tipping off Sargon, unfortunately," Dr. Spencer said.

"Then I'm going back to the farm to help the others," the farmer said. "Anybody who wants to join me, you very welcome."

Tookie did a fast translation for her mother. "My mother says they have three of those men back at the caves. I've seen them. They're wearing gray hoods. Maybe they can be some use because she says they are no use at all to drolls. Always whining about something. She says maybe you could trade them for something useful."

By the time Thur and Riga returned, the group had gone to the defense of the rebels of the farm. In spite of Mediah's protests, Valerian went with them, determined to prove to Miri he would risk his life for her.

As Sargon's men approached the farm, Gelise stayed out of sight in the trees above them. She thought if she could get ahead of them without being spotted, she would have a good chance of dropping down into the river just as Thur had done. That way, she reasoned, the Grays would be caught between the defenders of the farm and the army from the Hollow.

She didn't count on the geese.

The farm was operated as a natural science museum by the Triumvirate to house not only examples of the human species but also rare animals and birds, like cows, chickens, and the noisiest, most cantankerous of all birds, geese.

There were a flock of geese down by the river, pecking at water insects and occasionally taking a swim. Gelise plunged down right in front of them, sending up a small tidal wave of water that sent them into a squawking, flapping mob of hysteria.

That got everyone's attention including Sargon's. "Blimey," he swore, "go see what that noise is, will ya? It's enough to wake the dead!" His men fanned out in both directions to see what the commotion was.

A group of workers rushed out to the river armed with weapons taken from the Guards. They were taking aim at Gelise when Miri stopped them. Still, one lazorizer carried by a young boy. went off accidently. Gelise's inert body disappeared below the surface of the water, and was carried away by the swift current.

It took some harsh words from Thur to convince Riga that traveling by the Forever Road was faster than traveling by foot through the forest. But, in the end, Riga followed Thur over the series of ropes and pulleys that Gelise had showed him, though the mutant looked decidedly pale blue. Mutants didn't like to leave the ground and Thur had to reassure Riga constantly that he wouldn't fall and break his neck. However, Riga didn't look convinced, always looking down, even though Thur had told him not to.

Just as they approached the river bend, Thur from high up in the branches spotted something in the river. "Riga, can you see what that is, floating down the river? You've got that zoom lens in your eye."

Riga climbed up to where Thur was sitting, and looked in the direction Thur was pointing. "Well, can you see it, Riga? It's just passed the river bend now."

The mutant warrior was at a loss for words, climbing down to a level where he felt safe.

Thur climbed down beside him. "You look sick, friend. What is it? Height sickness?"

Riga remained silent a long time. Then he said, "It was that girl with the rude mouth. She looked so peaceful, so quiet as if all the hate was gone."

"Gelise?" Thur's mouth formed her name, not his voice.

"That's the one." Riga nodded. "She looked dead, and, if she's in the river, she's gone down to the Churn, Thur. Even if we ran down there, we couldn't save her."

They sat up in the tree, Thur utterly paralyzed by grief, and Riga wondering when the boy he had always guarded had turned into a man. Now looking at Thur's face glistening with tears, Riga recognized a man's grief, something he had never felt.

After a long time remembering the first time he had traveled the Forever Road with her, Thur said, "Come on, Riga. Let's go get find her killers and take them out."

To his surprise, Riga just shook his head. "They have to come this way to get back to Megacity. Go back to the Hollow and rest. There other wounds in war than are just on your body. The ones that hit your heart are the worst. And you've had a bad one. Go home, Thur."

"Since when did you learn about the human heart, Riga? Do mutants even have a heart?" The moment the words were out of his mouth, Thur regretted them.

Riga looked away, hiding the look of pain that crossed his blue face. "Go home, I said. I swore to protect you and I will. So, go home, boy. Your father, if he were still alive, would be proud of you." Then he swung down to the ground below and, before he disappeared into the forest, Riga called up to Thur, "You are a man now. Go claim the title of Thane of Galen."

"Thane of Galen? But how am I going to do that?" Thur almost fell out of the tree, he was so surprised.

As Riga walked away, he called back, "Don't worry, they will claim you."

Dumbfounded, Thur watched his mentor navigating through the woods as if he was raised there instead of the hard streets of Megacity. With what seemed a million questions to ask Riga, Thur climbed down and headed back to the Hollow. When Riga returned, he would ask the mutant just what he meant by "the title" even though he had never mentioned Thur's father before now. Up until now, Thur had secretly thought of Riga as his father.

Now, his mentor's parting words rang in Thur's ears with each step as he made his way through the carpet of leaves.

He paused to sit down on a rock and get something out of his boot that was scratching his leg. It turned out to be a spiny chestnut burr and he tossed it away into the bushes. Then he noticed the giant trees that were scattered all around the area. He was getting up to leave when another burr hit him in the head. Thur looked up at the tree towering above him, nearly fifty feet high. Its branches housed a city of wildlife, spreading in every direction. It was an amazing sight and he was staring at it in awe when he noticed curious markings into its massive trunk.

Then he looked down at the large stone he had been sitting on just a moment ago. Although they were nearly covered by moss and lichen, Thur made out the same markings carved in it. Something about the shape of the larger carving looked familiar. It resembled an old shield, the kind made of metal that the old Traveler had carried across the river. The outline of the shield was divided into four sections, each with an object crudely carved in it. He made certain he could reproduce each of the objects before leaving for the Hollow. If the old man was still there, he would ask the Traveler what they meant. Otherwise, Riga might be able to tell him when he got back. Riga knew everything about The Time Before The Lost Times. Thur had sometimes entertained the family stories about cowboys and trains which ran on something called tracks and sweets like candy, which mysteriously melted away in your mouth.

With a sudden feeling of dread at what his future held, Thur hurried back to the Hollow.

Across the river from the farm, the Grays spread out along the river bank, waiting for a signal to attack across their inflatable bridges. But Sargon hesitated, sensing there was something different about the slaves—a defiance or maybe it was only the fact they were carrying weapons that made him hesitate.

He tried diplomacy first. "Hey, Pier, Rufus, is that you mud-slingers?"

Rufus answered, his voice ringing across the river. "Yeah, Sargon. It's us. We don't want trouble, but we don't want you Hoods back over here, either. This farm belongs to the people who worked on the land and made it prosper. Not you lot who want that prosperity for yourselves and let others starve. So back off and let us be."

Sargon then took a different tack. "Now, Rufus, let's make a deal here. We can both get rich if you take the deal I'm gonna offer you. If you don't, I'm gonna wipe you suckers out."

The answer was loud and clear. "No deals. Forget it, Sargon. I know what kind of deals you offer. Ones that make only you get rich and keep our kind as your slaves."

"So, that's how it is, Rufus?" He was dragging out the conversation until all his men took their places along the riverbank. "You're saying you're willing to die for that piece of dirt you call the farm?

"That's how it is, Sargon," Rufus called back across the water. "You try to take over again, and somebody's going to get hurt."

Miri was moving up behind the men while the women herded the children back to the office to safety. "Keep him talking," she whispered, "while I get a good shot at him."

"I'm warning you, don't try anything, Sargon," Pier shouted defiantly. "You'll regret it if you do."

Sargon spat in the river between them. "That's rich.

You dirtbags are threatening me. What make you think you got the balls, huh? You're just pieces of human garbage, that's all you are. Let's face it, you'd be down there in the dirt making the pretty flowers grow if I hadn't found a use for you."

Valerian who had scouted ahead of the others, took in the whole situation. Using the standoff between Pier, Rufus, and Sargon as a distraction, the Grays were sneaking along the river bank to get their inflatable bridge in place. The farmers were lined up on the other riverbank with whatever weapons they could lay their hands on. He didn't see Miri crouching behind the row of farmers standing shoulder to shoulder ready to do battle.

"Hey, Sargon," Valerian shouted, standing in the clearing. "You going to stand there talking while your men do all the fighting?"

Sargon whipped around to see who was taunting him and Miri hit him squarely in the back of the head with a big stone whistling from her adl-adl. The Grays seeing their leader fall and their treachery discovered, dropped their inflatable bridge and headed for the woods. They ran straight into Riga and the rest of the farmers coming back from the Hollow accompanied by five drolls and Tookie's mother. The drolls' three captive Grays crawled on their hands and knees behind their droll masters, carrying supplies like pack animals.

"Take us with you," the captives called to their fellow Hoods, but their piteous cries were ignored by their fleeing comrades. However, the drolls, having finally found a use for them, gathered them up like so many wild flowers and dragged them back to their caves.

Between Valerian, Zak, and Riga, they cleaned up the rest of Sargon's men, throwing them into the river which carried them swiftly along. "That's for Gelise,"

Riga shouted as the last one was cast into the rushing water. "Enjoy the ride."

But Valerian had been wounded in the battle, which he tried to conceal by lagging behind the rest of the defenders who started back to the Hollow, taking their wounded with them. Finally, he had to sit down under a tree to inspect the damage. Taking his breastplate away, he saw a gush of blood coming from a deep wound in his chest where a Gray 's lazorizer had split the flesh and bitten deep into the bone.

He looked for something to bind the wound with but there was nothing except his tunic. He succeeded in ripping a piece of cloth from that and stuffing it into the wound, replacing the breastplate to keep it in place. Getting to his feet, he made his way through the forest following the trail of the others.

Mediah noticed he wasn't among the first victorious group returning to the Hollow and alerted Shadow who was working on a new machine.

"He must have stayed behind to see Miri got back safely. Now that Sargon is gone, I'll see if his sensor belt is working," Dr. Spencer said. "He had it on when he left."

But Sargon wasn't gone. He stirred in the mud coating the riverbank where he had fallen, a fierce pain shooting through his head. There was a gash on his forehead and another in the back of his head where Miri's adl-adl had hit home. He'd kill that girl if he ever got hold of her! Because he was a drumman, there was no blood, only a kind of ooze that attracted all the flies that weren't feasting on the other bodies. With a groan, Sargon hoisted himself to a sitting position and looked around. The first thing he saw was Valerian propped against a tree with his eyes closed. He looked dead.

"Well, if it isn't Lover Boy." Despite his pain, Sargon's face withed into a sneer. Just then a light flashed on and off on Valerian's belt. "What's that, I wonder? Are you set to explode in case you got killed or what?" Sargon got to his feet, still watching the pulsating light on Valerian's belt. "Wait a minute, that's a some kind of a signal. Is Mama wondering where her little boy is? Does she want him to call home? Well, I'll be you and you, Lover Boy, be old Sargon for a while. How's that?"

Taking off the gray hood that marked him as part of the Gray clan, Sargon put it on the unconscious Valerian. He put on Val's uniform and belt, shoving his lazorizer in the belt. Though he resisted until the last minute, he eased Val's helmet over his aching head, cursing as he did so. Giving Val one last kick in the side, he said," So long, sucker. You should have stayed in the Borg Guard." Leaving Val lying where he had fallen, Sargon marched toward the Hollow.

❧❧❧

They had marched about halfway back when Riga noticed Valerian wasn't following them. "You go on," he told the others. "I'll go back and see what's holding Valerian up."

"Sure you don't want some company?" asked Zak. "He might have run into some of Sargon's men who were hiding in the bushes."

Riga regarded the mud-caked farmers. They all looked weary and tired, even the young ones. "No, go on to the Hollow. You look like you could use some cheering up. I'll be right along."

Heading toward the farm upriver, Riga could see Val coming from a distance. "Val!" he shouted. "What kept you so long? You all right? Is Miri with you?"

Riga knew there something wrong when Val kept his

head down, fumbling with something on his belt. But before he could determine what was not right about the figure moving through the trees, a shot hit him directly in the heart. Riga, the warrior, fell among the tall ferns, looking up at the sky which was the color of his face.

Sargon kept going with a smile, imagining the look of Mediah's face when she realized he'd tricked her into thinking he was Valerian, her darling protégé.

⌇⌇⌇

Miri and some of the other farmers crossed the river using the Grays' own makeshift bridge to make certain there weren't of any of Sargon's men around to make trouble. After making sure the area was free of Grays, she found what appeared to the leader himself lying against a tree, the hood pulled down over his face.

"That's not Sargon," said one of the men. "He's not that young or buff. I don't know who he is but he's not one of them Hoods. They're all as scrawny as rats."

But there was something about the man that looked very familiar. The man she had hit from across the river was much older and smaller. After making sure the man wasn't armed, she dropped to her knees and pulled back his hood.

"Valerian!" At the sound of her voice, he opened his eyes briefly. Then he closed them, but with a faint smile on his lips.

Gently, Miri probed for the wound and found the gaping hole in his chest. Without looking up, she said to the men with her, "This is Dr. Spencer's son, Valerian. He's been hit with a lazorizer and has lost a lot of blood. Help me get him back across the river."

Meanwhile, Mediah paced the floor while Dr. Spencer fooled around with various machine until his whole laboratory seemed to be flashing and humming. Finally, he said, "His belt has a locator and I've activated it."

"And Valerian?" Mediah stopped pacing. "Where is he?"

"Coming this way, I'm happy to tell you. In fact he'll be here any minute," Spencer said.

"I'm going to meet him," she said and was out the door before anyone could stop her.

"There goes the world's most headstrong woman. I guess I'd better go with her." With a sigh, Androz got up from his comfortable chair. "You know, I could get used to doing nothing all day. Makes a change."

They passed Thur coming along the main path through the woods. When they asked him about Val, Thur shook his head. "Val? Riga's gone back after him. They'll be along any minute. I'll stay if you want me to."

But Androz sent him on his way with a wink. "You'd better clean up before the girls see you or they might run the other way."

Mediah wasn't so sure Thur was right. "Valerian is usually the first of his unit to return, right, Androz? There's something wrong. I know there is."

Just then, they saw a figure approaching through the woods. The man had on a Borg Guard's helmet, tunic, and belt. "That's Val's kit he's wearing," said Androz, "but I'd just about swear that isn't Val."

"It isn't." Mediah shielded her eyes against the setting sun. "I'd know my son anywhere. That's Sargon! Come on, shoot him, Androz!"

But Sargon heard them over the radio on his belt and fired a warning shot with his lazorizer over their heads. "Unless you don't want to end up like burnt toast, you two will stay right where you are."

"He's bluffing! He's out of range," growled Androz under his breath. "Let's make a run for it!"

But Mediah just folded her arms and stood her ground. "I know Sargon. He's got a deal we can't refuse. And it's about Valerian, it has to be, for him to be that confident."

"Well, I don't deal, baby. I'm out of here." Androz broke into a run, zigzagging through the trees while Sargon fired wildly around him.

When he saw Mediah, his mouth twisted in a sneer. "So your boyfriend deserted you. Now, what's was his is mine."

"Put away your weapon, Sargon," Mediah said as he approached her. "What do you want and what have you done with Valerian?"

"Oh, come on now, Mediah." Sargon stuffed the lazorizer into Valerian's belt. "What do you think happened to him? We just decided to swap clothes for the day for a joke? He's gone. Lover Boy is dead or close to it."

Her eyes glittered fire. "You killed him?"

Sargon's grizzled face assumed a mask of innocence. "No, I didn't. See this wound on my head? I was left for dead by those zoo animals that took over the farm. When I came to, I saw this Borg Guard lying there so I took his uniform. He wasn't going to need it anymore and I figured I could get back to the city dressed as a Guard. If there is a city left."

Mediah closed her eyes as the trees spun around her. Valerian was dead. She would find out who killed him. If it was Sargon, he would pay. Right now, she needed him.

When she opened her eyes again, he was watching her. "Blimee, you had me scared for a minute. I thought you'd turned all human on me."

"So what's the deal, Sargon? What do you want from me?"

"You want to go back to the city? I want to go back

to the city. You'll control the Mother Boards again, and I'll start making Swaug again. Same deal as before, except we'll get in on the ground floor this time. No humans to mess things up."

"And food?" Mediah said. "The people will need food from the farm and you, of course, will rake off huge profits, now that the Happy Pills are gone. Together, we'll make a great team. But what about Riksbury? What if he manages to wiggle out of prison.?

"Don't worry about that old drumman. Last time I saw him, he was buried in a box of rocks. Let's get back to the city. These big weeds," Sargon said, looking up at the towering trees around them, "give me the creeps."

As they hurried toward the river, Mediah suddenly thought about Androz. "But who is going to control the Borg Guard now that Androz has deserted to the other side?"

Sargon became cockier by the minute. He even started walking with a swagger that little men adopt, Mediah observed. "I've got the uniform and it kind of suits me, don't you think? Anyway, I'll make a better imperator than that fat old has-been any day. With them at my command, you'd better believe I'll mop up on anybody who stands in our way, including those human hedgehogs in the Hollow."

They were approaching the river and, if Sargon was moved by what he saw there, he didn't show it. Mediah, on the other hand, almost fled back into the forest, except Sargon's iron grip on her arm stopped her. A seething, desolate crowd of people lined the banks of the river on both sides, making any kind of shelter they could find out of debris to keep out of the cold, gray rain the smoldering ashes of Megacity produced.

In spite of their misery, curious eyes turned in their direction. "Take off your hair," Sargon muttered.

Mediah looked at him in horror. "I certainly will not!" she said indignantly.

But before she could protest further, Sargon ripped her wig off, leaving her bald as a Fluglitz egg. He gave her a poisoned smile. "Now, except for the outfit, you look just like one of them. I'm the Borg Guard and you're my prisoner, get it? Now, come on," the drumman said. "We can't let this trash stop us from getting across the river. Keep your eyes peeled for a boat."

Slowly, they walked through the desperate crowd, Sargon with his lazorizer out in case of trouble. Still, jeers and shouts of, "Get that Borgie!" could be heard on every side.

"Where're taking that poor bloke, Borgie? There ain't no more prisons," somebody called from the crowd around them.

"Yeah, let the mutie go. He ain't gonna be no more use to you, motorhead," demanded another voice.

In spite of their misery, the refugees laughed. "Yeah, motorhead! Borgiebrain!"

Sargon pointed his weapon at the crowd, and the mutterings were reduced to curses. "I'm in command, now. Unless you want to get wiped out before your recycle number comes up, you'll pipe down and go back to eating mud. Or if you want some real food and Swaug, you'll help me get across that river and get something organized."

The cheering stopped, except far in the back of the crowd, someone shouted, "Don't believe him! He'll organize the Guard to come and take us all back to that hellhole of a city. Better die free and breathe real air instead of being recycled!"

"Who said that?" Sargon looked in the direction of the speaker but all he saw were the hard faces around him.

Standing far back at the edge of the crowd, Zak smiled. He knew his father had recognized the sound of his voice.

When Sargon and Mediah reached the riverbank, they found a small wooden row boat with an antique motor on the back. A mutant was sitting nearby, heedless of the rain on his slick head.

"It don't run," the mutant said. "No fuel. It runs on fuel, you know."

"Yes, but it has two paddles made of wood." Mediah gave him her best smile. "Have you seen them anywhere?"

The mutant gestured toward the forest behind them. "If you want to chop down trees in the Trezarium, go right ahead. That's the only place you'll find wood. Anything else is being burned for fires to keep warm."

But Sargon spotted a curl of smoke coming from behind a tent. He went over and snatched a wooden paddle before the flames curled around it. The mutant cringed as Sargon marched back, brandishing the smoking piece of wood overhead. "Just for lying, you get to row us over to the city or your recycle number is up, fool."

As they got into the boat, Mediah glanced back at the woods behind her. She got a glimpse of crimson before it disappeared behind a tree, but she recognized it as Androzarian's cloak. Farther in up the same tree, she saw branches shaking. The people of the Hollow were not far behind.

⌘

All the people at the Hollow had just helped Aya, Qin, and Thur bury Riga beside the chestnut tree deep in the woods. As they had had lowered the warrior into his last resting place, they had started singing, a sweet, sad sound Thur had never heard before. It tore his heart open, letting all the grief and loss spill out in his tears. He knelt beside the grave and put Riga's shield over his body. Comforting hands pressed his shoulders as they covered the grave with earth. Finally, Aya led the way back to the Hollow, leaning on Dr. Spencer and Qin for support. One by one, everyone left Thur alone, sitting beside the grave with his head in his hands.

"If I had been with you, this wouldn't have happened, Riga," he kept whispering over and over, in a voice raw with tears.

"Weep, boy," someone said. "The scops have a poem that goes, 'When he who is the seed becomes the leaf, he will know both loss and grief, when he gathers kith and kin, 'tis he who'll be Thane of Galen.'"

Looking up, Thur saw the old Traveler who had crossed the river with them, carrying his obsolete weapons to the Warriors.

"So say the scops, so it will always be," he added, pounding a thick wooden staff on the ground to emphasize the words as much as to get Thur's attention.

"Who are these scops, anyway? And how do they know so much?"

The old man's eyes glowed with mystery. "Ah, the scops, now. Those are the wisest men of the Clan. Poets, mostly. They're like the River Rye, flowing through the hearts of the people. The passers-on of history, of the legends and the language." Seeing that he had Thur's full attention, the Traveler took a step a step closer. "I know the mutant was your friend. You will lose more friends before this is over. But you will gain many more. There is a time for weeping, but there will be a time for rejoicing, too." He leaned on the staff, offering Thur his hand. "Come on, these woods are dangerous enough and we've got work to do. Warrior's work." The old man got to his feet wearily. "My name is Gof of Galen. I will be your guide now."

"Wait!" Thur wiped his face and pointed to the markings on the chestnut tree above them. "Do you know what those carvings mean?"

Without even looking at the tree, the old Traveler nodded. "It says, 'Here lies the Thane of Galen, killed at the Battle of Sumi. Long live his tribe.' The mutant Riga had sworn fealty to your father. That's why they allowed him to be buried here."

"What do you mean, 'they'? I wanted Riga buried here," Thur snapped, thumping his chest for emphasis.

Gof nodded. "That's who I mean," the man said mysteriously. "Come on, young Laird of Galen. Follow me back to Yop's place. And keep your weapon drawn. Leave weepin' for the women. I'm sure they'll have plenty to do when all is done."

Without another word or shedding one more tear, Thur got up and followed his new friend back to the Hollow.

⋙⋘

Carrying a tray, Miri tiptoed into the little room where Valerian had been recovering from his wound. It had been nearly a week since she had found him propped against a tree unconscious and bleeding. The last thing she expected was to see the young soldier standing fully dressed by the window.

"I don't think there's anything more beautiful than the sunrise," he said, without taking his eyes off the sky. "Except you, Miri. Funny, I never thought about beauty before now. Now, I see it's all around me."

She nearly dropped the tray. "Val! You shouldn't be out of bed already! The wound could open again and the healer said—"

"Watch out! The tray!"

He turned to help her steady the tray and grasped her hand. They were standing so close, their hands clasped on the tray, he obeyed the impulse to kiss her lips. He'd never kissed before so he just obeyed instinct but, to his surprise, Miri kissed him back even harder. Then she gave him a shove that sent him falling backward on the bed.

"You're not going anywhere, not until the healer gives you permission. Get that through your hard head, Mr. Val. Now, eat your breakfast like a good Borgie!" She put the tray down on a small table.

Val sat up on the bed, a hundred different emotions tumbling around in his head. He looked up at Miri, wondering if what he felt was love, the emotion humans always talked about. "You know, you're getting to sound more like Aya every day. Except you're more beautiful."

"Well, I'm glad you think so." Miri couldn't help teasing back. "At least Aya kept us safe from the likes of you, didn't she? Just kidding, Val. I know you couldn't help where you landed. None of us could. I'm just glad we all survived."

She looked so beautiful with the sun in her hair, his mind suddenly focused. Val stood up again and, taking Miri in his arms, kissed her even harder. "Then I have to make sure we will continue to survive in the future, darling Miri."

She pulled away to look up into his face. "How?" she asked. "How will you do that when you're already hurt?"

"A group is ready to go into Megacity this morning to see what needs to be done. We'll meet the people from the Hollow there and set up a camp to feed the people left there. General Androz will lead us. He intends to find Sargon and Mediah."

"And together, they will start a new Triumvirate, don't you see that?" Miri took a step back, looking up into his intense blue eyes. "Do you intend to join them? If you do, that will part us forever. I never want to see that place again. It has been my prison since I was born and I'm free of it here. Besides, my family is here. Aya, my sister Qin, and I've just found my real mother. I'm sure none of them wants to go back either."

Val felt a new emotion, as if he were being torn to pieces by her words and the resolve in Miri's eyes. He struggled for the words to wrap that emotion in. "I want to be with you, Miri. Anywhere you are. Promise me you'll be waiting when I get back. I never knew what love was until I saw you. No, I heard your sweet voice first and then I saw the girl that matched it. Now I know it's more powerful than I could imagine. It's like a force that guides you to do things you never thought you could or would."

They were both startled by a knock on the door. Pier's voice called, "Ready, Val? We're leaving."

"Coming, Pier." To Miri, Val said, "I'll be back. Wait for me." He grabbed her hand and kissed it. "Please!"

"Oh, I'll see you sooner than you think," she said with a brave smile and another kiss. Valerian left the room and Miri sank onto the bed, bursting into tears. *That's the last time I'll ever see him,* she thought.

ↄ৩ⅇ৩

The scene on the other side of the river was even more desolate than Mediah could have imagined. Packs of armed mutants and drummans roamed the streets, looking for anything they could steal. Robots had collapsed in the street when the Brain had exploded, and were now being torn apart by worfels who had swarmed across the river.

The human survivors huddled in dark buildings, too afraid to emerge.

Mediah was actually glad to have Sargon with her. He didn't hesitate to blast anything that got in his way. Once a worfel lunged at him, grabbing his arm holding the lazorizer.

He dispatched the wild dog with a kick in the belly then blasted the animal, sending the rest of the pack scurrying for cover. Mediah saw the animal's teeth had torn open his arm, but being a drumman, no blood poured from the wound. *There are some advantages to being a mutant*, she thought.

Her office wasn't far from the Flyover. They had to break into the building and race up the steps, dodging crowds of huddled people and pitiful appeals for help, until they reached her office. Immediately, Mediah rummaged in drawers for her spare wigs. Sargon, meanwhile, was trying any form of communication he could find until at last, he located one of his men.

"They've rigged up a vehicle," he said over his shoulder. "They're coming to get us, so get ready." When he heard nothing, he looked back at an empty room. Mediah was gone.

She was hurrying down the stairs, distributing all the foods, drinks, and blankets she could carry. "There's more up in my rooms on the third floor. But make sure you wait until the Borg is gone. He's armed and won't think twice about blasting you to bits."

"Don't worry, we'll take care of him," a familiar voice said out of the darkness. She didn't stop to look around, but hurried into the dark, dangerous street. Sardon's men were just coming around the corner, driving a street cleaning machine. It crunched over anything in its path—worfels, beggars, bandits—or blasted them with sewer water which turned them to ice statues. Mediah hid in a doorway as the juggernaut passed, shuddering at the carnage it caused but grateful that it cleared the streets.

Since her robocar was at the Aeroplex, she had a long walk ahead of her. She had packed a small lazor pistol as well as a stiknife, just in case someone got too close. But thanks to the patrolling Gray Hoods, the streets around the Aeroplex were quiet. She found the robocar where she had parked it, but the locks wouldn't work. Finally, Mediah shot the stiknife into the lock to open the door and got in the little car. The familiar smell was so comforting, she rested her head against the upright seat. Her legs ached from so much walking and she was aware of a nagging feeling in her stomach that must be hunger. Her head ached from being exposed to the dripping cold. Even though she had never felt so awful in her life, Mediah fell asleep.

She was wakened abruptly by a knock on the window. A peculiar old man with a long white beard was peering in the window at her.

"Are you all right, my dear?" he asked. "Can I help you?"

The idea that this old fossil could be of any use whatsoever to her made Mediah laugh out loud. Lowering the window, she said, "No, I'm all right. Is there anything I can do for you?"

The old fossil laughed, displaying few teeth. "Oh, I can really take care of myself. I'm responsible for all this mess, you see, so I really have to clean it up."

"And how will you do that?" *I ought to humor him,* she thought. *He's probably lost his mind, what little was left of it.*

"By starting with you, my dear Mediah, if you will just give me a ride to wherever you're going, that is."

Alarmed that this toothless wretch knew her name, she cringed. "How do you know my name?"

"Oh, I knew you as a child. In fact, I was a friend of your father's. I am Evan Mercator."

"Mercator? But I thought—how did you, I mean—" she stammered.

"Escape?" Suddenly, voices behind them meant the Gray Hoods guarding the Aeroplex were on the move.

"There he is! Get Mercator!" someone shouted. "And that's the woman! After her!"

"Get in," Mediah ordered. "I can't let them find me. Or you, for that matter. You're my secret weapon, Mercator," she said as he climbed into the seat next to her.

"And you, my dear, are mine." Mercator buckled his harness strap. "This little machine has a manual system, I believe, although you probably don't know how to use it." He pressed a switch on the console. "Let's just hope the thermonuclear battery has a few more years on it."

"But I don't think the tube will open." She looked anxiously at the Gray Hoods running toward them. "It's computerized, remember?"

"No matter, just put it in reverse and follow the exit signs. Although it doesn't go very high, this little beauty is lazor-proof and anything-else proof. Only, I suggest you start engines forthwith, my dear," said Mercator, "because we, on the other hand, are neither. Sargon's thugs look like they mean to do us harm," he added, nodding at the armed mob running toward them.

Mediah started the robocar engine and hit the Reverse button. They were jerked backward at nearly light-speed, crashing through the launch tube like someone spitting out a peach seed. At Mercator's command, the robocar spun around and headed for the exit, two floors below. Sargon's men hit the floor as the vehicle elevated over them, its backwash setting their hoods on fire and melting their lazorizers in their hands to molten junk.

As Mediah followed the exit corridor, until it spiraled out to the street, they passed clusters of thugs and bandits who were carrying pieces of equipment looted from the Aeroplex. When the robocar appeared in the narrow corridor, the looters dropped whatever they were carrying and ran toward the street. But the robocar overtook them, melting the equipment and singeing those in the way.

Once out on the street, they encountered Sargon's streetcleaner-turned-tank head-on.

"Look out! That thing is armed with a lazor cannon," Mercator cried.

Suddenly, there was a roar overhead, and an even stranger vehicle landed on the roof of the street-cleaning tank.

"A Jetster," Mercator shouted. "I haven't seen one of those since I was a boy. Used to ride one myself." Astride the Jetster was an even stranger figure wearing a helmet and clad in leather. There were more like him landing in the streets around them. Mercator whooped. "The Noble Warriors are back! Now we'll see some action!"

While they watched, openmouthed, the warrior torched the tank's turret. It fused shut, locking the occupants inside.

"That's one can of worms that won't get opened for a while," Mercator said with a chuckle. "Nice work. Couldn't have done better myself."

Mediah put the throttle full forward and eased the robocar into the air. After being locked in a cell for ten years, Mercator was enjoying the action. "Now, where're you headed, if I may be so bold to ask?"

She neatly avoided a warrior on a careening Jetster. "To my suite in the Tower Two building. I'm sure it's as safe as anything in Megacity right now. And besides, I can control the Mother Boards from there."

Mercator gripped the seat of the flying car as they

went zipping between two buildings. "Why on Earth would you waste valuable time doing that? Isn't it clear this rabble intends to destroy everything related to the Triumvirate's rule, including the Mother Boards?"

Her answering smile surprised him. "Because I think the Mother Boards will give them hope. After all, it's the power of suggestion that made them such a force in the first place."

He looked at the woman at the controls. *She has not a hair on her head*, he thought, but, in the flashing lights from explosions all around them, she was the most beautiful woman he had ever seen. Of course, he'd been locked in a cell for ten years. "And what would you promise them to hope for?" he probed in a gentle voice that barely rose above the chaos around them. "There is no food, no shelter from this miserable weather that we have created. No water, no lights. Tell me, what would you have them to hope for?"

"For the future," Mediah said. "I don't know how, but there's got to be a future for us."

"Halleluiah." Mercator sighed. "That's exactly what I wanted to hear you say."

Mediah smiled. "What was that peculiar thing you said just now? I've never heard it before. Hallelusomething?"

"Halleluiah. That was something people said during The Lost Times. My parents used to say it when something good happened. Whoa, why are you descending so sharply?" he said as Mediah nosed the robocar down to the ground. "We're going to hit that towering building!"

"Because I live here," she said, laughing, as the robocar scooted under the building. "Don't be such a sissy, Mercator."

"Now that's an expression I haven't heard in a long time," he said, bracing himself against the console. "My brother Edward used to say that to me even though I was the oldest."

"He still does." Mediah expertly sent the robocar into its parking slot beneath the hydraulic tube. "He's right, too. You are a sissy."

"What?' My brother is still alive? How do you know?"

"Because I've seen him." It was her turn to impress the famous scientist.

"Halleluiah," Mercator whispered, closing his eyes.

For a moment, Mediah wondered if he meant the "halleluiah" for arriving safely or for the news that his brother was alive.

The tube didn't work to bring the robocar up to Mediah's suite. She was just about to start climbing the stairs when Mercator opened the switch box and crossed a few wires.

"Hop in," he told her. "It should work now."

Mediah heard the familiar whir of the hydraulic tube as soon as she closed the car door. "You're a genius, Mercator!"

"Tell me something I don't know," the old man groaned as he got back in beside her. "Does this thing go straight up?"

"Your brother's alive," she said as the car shot up the tube. "And yes. It does. That's two." They came to an abrupt stop with Mercator sitting on the floor. "Remind me to get the robomechanic to work on that last bit," she said, helping him up. "It's a bit rough."

Her flat was just as she left it mainly because the door to the stairs wouldn't open to anyone who didn't live in the towers. "I'm sure the downstairs floor is filled with refugees," Mediah said, looking around. "I have to find a way to let them have some food without letting them know I'm up here."

"What a beautiful abode," Mercator said admiringly, slowly going from room to room. When he got to the room that housed the pool, he gasped. "All this water for one person! You have done well for yourself, my dear. Your father was a fine man and a great scientist as well. You were one of our first successes at joining a human with a mutant. And look how well you turned out. Brilliant, beautiful, and, if I may add, able to bring this city back to a functioning society. With my help, of course."

Bustling around the kitchen, throwing packages of food into boxes, she stopped and smiled. "You don't have a shortage of ego, Mercator, I'll say that for you. You really believe anything is possible, don't you?"

"Even when I was imprisoned in a dark cell, I always believed in the future, my dear. A future where humankind will once again take their rightful place. For the present, I'd like to take a bath, if that's possible."

"Certainly, get in the pool and I'll get you some clean clothes from the wardrobe Androzarian leaves here."

At the mention of the commander of the Borg Academy, Mercator's thin frame began to tremble. He looked too weak to stand and Mediah thought he was going to fall. She rushed to help him to a seat and gave him some Swaug to steady his nerves.

"That was another thing I didn't know. That you and he were…acquainted," he said weakly.

"'Were' is right," she said with disdain. "He's no longer an acquaintance and never will be again. He let Sargon capture me and exposed me to all kinds of humiliation and danger. Now how about that bath?"

The old man was accustomed to bathing in a tea cup full of water once a month. Finding the room-sized pool overwhelming, he bathed in the wash basin while Mediah luxuriated in the pool. After they had something to eat, she made Mercator some tea and began emptying the cabinets when the whole building shook from the explosion around them.

"Oh, dear, I'm afraid they've got the lazor cannons working again."

Another loud crash sent the top of the far tower flying off. "We'll be next," Mediah shouted above the noise. "Here take the food to the elevator and send it to the bottom floor. I've got something to do."

She rushed to her computer station and typed *The Future is Yours*, then pressed the Send key. "Damn! The computers that control the Mother Boards are down. Now, I can't send my message!"

They both ducked as another volley from the lazor cannons splintered the building next to them.

Mercator took something from his jacket pocket. He pointed at Mediah's computer and clicked a button. "There, it's gone. And we should be, too."

As they hurried to the tube, Mediah asked, "Was that what it looked like? A simple door opener?"

"Just a little gadget I picked up along the way," Mercator said modestly. "In the Borg Academy control room. Seems like your Androzarian was preparing for the future."

They were on their way down to the robocar when another blast tore the roof off the Tower Two. With it went Mediah's entire luxury suite. The magnificent pool rained perfumed water down on the filthy streets below, washing years of soot away.

When the cannons were quiet, the survivors ventured out to the street, marveling at the sparkling white pavement and the beautiful debris scattered there. Above them, framed against an ever-widening patch of blue sky, the Mother Boards carried Mediah's last message: *The Future Is Yours*. The people renamed the street The Halleluiah Road after an old word somebody remembered.

In the parking slots for the robocars, two Borg Guards were waiting. When Mediah saw them, she turned to run into the building, but Mercator stopped her. "Don't worry yourself, my dear. Let's see what they want first. I much prefer negotiation to getting zapped."

"My good fellows," he said, taking a step forward. "Can I be of service?"

"Are you E. Mercator, the famous scientist?" said the biggest Guard.

The old man straightened to his full height. "I am. And who sent you to inquire?"

"My master, Councilman Riksbury. And who is this lady?"

"I am Councilperson Mediah," she said. "Why do you ask?"

The two Guards consulted, and the biggest one said, "Then you will accompany us. Councilman Riksbury also wants to talk to you."

"Oh, I'll bet he does," Mercator said. "And we want to talk to him."

"Are you crazy? It's a trap," Mediah whispered.

But Mercator patted her arm consolingly. "You are so correct, my dear. But the trap is also set for Riksbury."

"I don't get it."

"You'll see. Lead on, my good man. Lead on," Mercator said with a wink at Mediah. "Mustn't keep such an important personage waiting, now can we?"

✂✄✂

The people of the Hollow marched out of the woods and down among the refugees on the riverbank. They distributed food and warm clothes as they went until there was a mob following them as they walked down to the river. But the hungry people scattered in fright when they saw the drolls coming out of the woods.

"Don't mind them," shouted Yop. "They're just bringing more food, including blackberry pies."

"What are blackberries? Some kind of poison?" shouted one skeptic.

"We're not trying to recycle you," Yop replied. "We want to get you ready to fight. So taste 'em and see."

The idea of food to gather an army was Aya's plan. "An army marches on its stomach," she said. "so let's fill 'em up so they can fight."

"Brilliant! Why didn't I think of that?" Yop's round face lit up with a big smile. "Anybody that tastes your blackberry pie will want to fight to get more."

Now, Aya's wisdom worked wonders, as the hungry people slowly gathered around piles of bread, nuts, dried fruit, venison, and pies of every kind. Joining in the feast were Basi's River Rogues and some Travelers. Among them, Yop spotted some Gray Hoods. "You've got a nerve," he said. "Eating our food after your leader killed his way to safety across the river. You had better get out of here and join him."

"We're getting ready to join his son Zak, not the old man," said one around a mouthful of food. "Zak wants to go straight and so do we. If you want to come with us, we'll take you to him." The man took another bite of pie. "This stuff beats Happy Pills any day."

Androz joined them. "How do we know it isn't a trap? Let's face it, you guys aren't known for your honesty."

"Because he's got Councilperson Mediah with him, that's why. And Zak is meeting Valerian and his men in the city. That's where they're joining up. In fact—" He took a small object out of his pocket and glanced at it. "—they've just met up. Okay, boys, let's go."

Grays, Travelers, and Rogues stuffed as much food into their clothes as they could and set off across the makeshift bridge constructed from the pontoons and rafts the people had been using for shelter.

"Hallo, wait," Yop shouted, "we're coming with you!"

Thur watched as Yop's people marched to the bridge and stopped there as the portly leader put one foot on the makeshift bridge. It immediately sank to the level of the water.

The refugees gathered around him. "You'll never make it across, Uncle. Best stay out of the city anyhow," shouted one scruffy fellow. "You don't look like much of a fighter."

"Or much of a swimmer, either."

That brought laughter from the bedraggled crowd. For all they'd lost, they had gained one priceless moment, though at poor Yop's expense.

However, Yop was not discouraged easily. "Has anyone of you river washups got a boat to row me and a few lads over to the other shore?"

"Not one that's big enough to hold you, let alone what poor fools row you over," said one ragged woman. "Why don't you stay here where you're needed?"

"That's right, who's going to defend us? Do your fighting here, Uncle. And meanwhile, fix us supper." At that, the people from the Hollow joined the refugees in laughter.

In the end, Yop had to back down. Disgraced in front of his people, he slunk through the crowd to where Thur stood with Skye and Loki. Gof of Galen stood not far away, leaning on his staff.

"Come on, Mayor Yop, let's go back to the Hollow." Thur put his arm around Yop's shoulders. "Let's leave the ungrateful trash to fend for themselves since they don't appreciate a kindness or the man who took it upon himself to feed them."

As they walked deeper into the forest, Loki looked over their shoulder. The drolls were behind them, making no secret of their disgust for humans. "Look, some are tagging along after the drolls."

"Probably because they want some food. Tell them to go back to the city," Skye said. "And stay there."

"Now, now, boys," Yop said. "They're good people, just a bit prickly, that's all." The farther they went into the forest, Yop picked up the pace, happy to be at home. "Like chestnut burrs. Just tossed away because they're a nuisance. But, if you look inside, you see the seeds of our next civilization, right, Thur, my lad?"

જ૭જ૭

Crouched in his chair, Riksbury looked even smaller and more sinister than ever, Mediah thought as they were ushered into what the Guards called "the commander's office."

In fact, it was the only building left standing in the once spacious citadel—the prison. The rest of the fortress that had been the Academy was in ruins.

"Ah, Riksbury, I see you've made yourself quite at home in my old cell." E. Mercator looked around almost fondly. "Here's where I spent ten good years of my life."

"Constructing our downfall, you mean." Riksbury looked around at the walls as if he had suddenly noticed them. They were covered with mathematical calculations and notes which the former councilman couldn't read. "I suppose these are the formulas by which you destroyed the Brain."

"How observant of you, Councilman," Mercator said, knowing that Riksbury didn't have any idea what the sqiggles meant. "And I can put it back even better than before if you would allow me."

Riksbury's lips writhed like a serpent. "I hoped we could make a deal, my old friend. Glad to see you looking so well. And you, Mediah. You've gone quite brown in the sun."

"And you look more like a toad than ever, Riksbury. An odious, ugly reptile. Your cannons are blowing away the only shelter the people have left! I wouldn't expect you to have a heart, being a drumman, but I would at least think you'd want to save the city."

Riksbury made a disgusted sound. "And give the riff-raff a place to hide? I'm just cleaning up the mess, Mediah, since there's no one else around to do it. Oh, and by the way, that includes the Trezarium where it seems you've been hiding out with those prehistoric relics, the people of the Hollow. Even as we speak, my laser cannons are pointed in their direction and, at my comman—"

"Since when are you in command, Riksbury?" Looking like the survivor of a shipwreck, Sargon came through the door. "There you are," he said grabbing Mediah's arm and twisting it behind her back, "you little bitch! I'll settle with you later. Right now—"

He didn't finish the sentence. Mercator clicked a small object in his hand and Sargon froze in mid-step. Mediah jerked her arm free of his stiff fingers.

"Guards," Riksbury shouted in panic.

The two Borgs who were standing by the doorway started to come into the room but when Mercator pointed the gadget at them and clicked, they stopped as if they were frozen solid. Next was Riksbury's turn, but the old drumman had a lazorizer in his shaking hands. He fired at Mercator but the scientist clicked simultaneously and the blast halted in midair.

Then the scientist took hold of Mediah's arm.

"Come, my dear, let us 'scram,' as the old folks used to say. This immobilizer only lasts for a few minutes. I have to perfect it later. Meanwhile, we're out of here!"

With one hand, Mediah pushed the frozen Guards over, sending the two robots crashing to the floor. She and Mercator were hurrying down the hallway when Valerian and Zak, followed by a mob of people carrying a variety of weapons, burst into the building.

Mediah ran directly to Valerian. "Quickly, they're all down there," she said, pointing to the room she had just left. "Riksbury and Sargon, and Riksbury's armed with a lazorizer. Be careful!"

"I'm glad you're all right." Val pulled Mediah aside as the mob boiled passed them, freeing prisoners as they went. "Here," he called to a man passing by, "take her to safety. She's my mother. Take good care of her." To Mediah, he said, "Go with him. He'll take you to General Androz who is securing the control room. I'll see you later."

"And Mercator, too. Without him, I'd still be Sargon's prisoner. Meet your uncle," she said, taking Mercator's hand and pulling him beside her.

But the old scientist shook himself free of her grip. "Tush, tush, woman, can't you see this is no time for introductions? Let the lad get on with conquering or whatever it is that he's got to do. Plenty of time for that later. Lead on, my good man. Time's a wasting."

By the time Valerian got to the room, Riksbury was tied up and stuffed in his own paper shredder by Rufus and other two stout farmers who wanted to shred up the former councilman right then and there.

But Rufus stopped them. "No one has lost more than I have. He sent my parents to the Dumpster," said Rufus. "And my wife and kids were taken away when he sent me to work on the farm. I'll never see them again, but we must do things the right way."

One of the Borgs stirred and sat up, pushing the visor of his helmet back. "Daddy?" he said, "is that really you?"

Rufus stared in amazement. "Dax?"

Going to the dazed Guard and taking off his helmet, Val said, "It's Dax, all right. We were in the Academy together." Helping the young man to his feet, he said, "You have a little sister, doesn't he, Rufus? But if you want to meet her, you'd better take off that uniform. There's a whole lot of angry people out there in the city just looking for Borgs."

Their reunion was drowned out by the whine of the paper shredder starting up as Councilman Riksbury was recycled. At the same moment, Riksbury's lazorizer blast, freed from its immobilized state, dropped down on the shredder, blasting it to bits.

"Well, I guess Riksbury finally got his own office," Val commented, surveying the splattered walls.

Going down the crowded hall, he was about to rejoin Androz when a familiar voice called out his name.

"Val, look out!"

He turned around to see Miri struggling with Sargon, trying to fight him off.

"Well, if it isn't Lover Boy," Sargon snarled. He jabbed a lazorizer into her side. "I won't hesitate to pull this trigger on your girlfriend here so I wouldn't make a move if I were you."

"What do want to let her go?" Valerian said coolly, not letting his voice show his fear for Miri. "I know you want something, Sargon. You always do."

"Just safe passage for me and my friend Riksbury on a Jetstar to…let's say, that stinking place called the farm"

"Riksbury is busy cleaning out his office," Val replied dryly. "And the farm is under new management. Choose someplace else."

"How about coming with us, Father?"

Sargon whirled around to see his son, Zak, standing in the corridor with all the Grays behind him.

"Zak! It's about time you showed up! What took you so long? Stealing, I'll bet."

Taking advantage of his distraction, Miri kicked the lazorizer out of Sargon's hand, sending it spinning down the hall toward Valerian. Then she socked Sargon so hard in the face, he fell against the wall and slid to the floor. "That's for Val! And that's for me, you creep!" she said, giving another kick where it hurt most.

"Better take your father away before she does him any more damage," Val said to Zak.

"Wait," Miri said, "don't you want your belt? Sargon's still got it on."

"Let him keep it. It works both ways. We'll always know where he is." Seeing her standing there, her bright hair tumbling loose down over her shoulders, Val couldn't help putting his arms around her. "I'll have my dad make us a matching pair. That way I'll know where you are every moment. How did you even get here?"

"I just couldn't let you go alone." Miri snuggled against him. "After you left the farm, I just had to follow you."

"Actually, she came with me," Zak said, joining them.

Together, they watched Sargon limping away supported by his former gang members. "She comes in real handy in a fight."

Val couldn't help noticing the way Zak looked at Miri. He recognized the feeling too well.

"How do you know he won't try to take control again?" Miri asked, still encircled in Val's arms.

Zak shrugged the suggestion way. "Oh, Sargon'll try to get his cut of the action. Making fake Swaug, peddling Happy Pills that taste like candy, but I think Yop has other plans to keep him busy. Let's just say it involves making pies for Tookie's mother."

"I can't wait to see that," Val said, laughing. "I almost feel sorry for him."

"Yeah, almost," Zak replied bitterly. "Don't forget, he made a lot of a lot of money getting a lot of suckers hooked on Swaug and Happy Pills. Speaking of the former people of power, Mediah has big plans for you, I'll bet."

"I only want the old warrior tribes to come back and be represented in whatever she and Androz are planning. You could play a big part in the new government, too, Zak. That is, if you want to. Slitz!" Val glanced at his wristband where a red light was flashing. "That's Androz wondering where I am! I said I'd meet him at the command post in half an hour. It's way passed that now." Val looked down at Miri who was inspecting her bruised knuckles. "Coming, Miri?"

Taking a step back from him, Miri hesitated and then shook her head. "No, Val. I'm going back to the Hollow with Yop. I told you I hate this place." She looked around at the cracked, gray walls, and the emaciated former prisoners shuffling aimlessly around as if they didn't have any place to go. "It looks too much like a sewer with all the rats around. No, I want to live in a place where I can see the sky. Anyway, I've got to make sure Aya and Qin are all right. And get to know my real mother. I found her at the farm and I know she's worried."

"In that case, since Val is in such a hurry, I'll take you back across the river if you're ready to go. Got to rally my troops, as they say." Zak had a look of triumph in his dark eyes as he took Miri by the arm. "Can't leave the Hoods on their own too long. They might cook up something illegal to do. It's anybody's game right now. No Guard to enforce the laws."

"But I thought we were going to clean this place up together, Zak." Val looked surprised and hurt by the sudden betrayal, as if the notion that people could change their minds was completely new to him. "Establish some kind of government."

"Don't get your tail in a twist," Zak called over his shoulder. "I'll be back. And forth," he added gleefully. "Getting the Hoods together is like herding cats. They all think they can do their own thing."

The look on Val's face almost changed Miri's mind. She hesitated, locked in place by his expression of longing and pain. If his love for her was as strong as he vowed, then he would surely choose her over the power offered to him by Mediah.

"Look, Val," she said gently, "we both have obligations that take us in different directions. I'll see you when you get back to the Hollow." As Zak led her away down the prison corridor, she looked back to see him still standing there, watching her go.

"That guy's got to learn to roll with the punches. He's like a robot. Gets an idea in his head and that's it." Zak snapped his fingers. "He's programmed to just follow orders!"

"I guess that's what comes from being around robots all your life," Miri said defensively. She turned to look back again, but Val was gone. "You expect people to be just as dependable. But, unfortunately, that isn't the case."

"You mean, as opposed to growing up around Sargon and the Hoods, don't you? Dependable was not in my vocabulary. But it could be, if—" Out of the corner of his eye, Zak looked at the golden-haired girl beside him.

"If the right person could teach me what it means."

But Miri didn't even hear him. She was still seeing Val's face as they had left him.

Watching her leave, it seemed to Val that Miri took all the light with her.

ʘʓʘʓ

In the dark days that followed, he was swept up in the power struggle for dominance between the warrior tribes, the Grays, and the last remnants of the Guard backed by Imperator Androzarian.

While publically throwing her support behind Androzarian, Mediah was quietly building her own popularity among the residents of Megacity. Already hailed as one of the leaders of the Great Human Revolution, she continued to gather support in the poorer quarters of the city by making food and shelter available to the displaced inhabitants of the Flyover. All the while, Mediah spread the word about the popular elections that Androzarian had promised in the coming months when the situation was stabilized. She fully intended Valerian should be on the ballot for governor and was doing all she could to make certain everyone she came in contact with would vote for him.

Caught between Androzarian and Mediah as their rivalry grew, Val found himself shuttling between the two trying to make peace. In his few leisure moments, he tried to contact Miri. But she had gone to stay with her mother at the farm where Qin had gotten the job of setting up a school. There was no direct line of communication with the farm, and there wouldn't be until the new government was formed. Once a week, the farmers brought truckloads of food to the Academy, to be distributed among the few residents of Megacity.

Val always searched for Miri among the line of trucks, hoping she might be among them. She never was and, when he asked one of the farmers about her, the man shrugged. "Miri? She's real busy with the school and all. 'Least, that's what she says—too busy with that son of a Gray, Zak, more like. Anyway, she says she'd too busy to come to the city. Shall I tell her who's asking?"

"Never mind that." Thrown into confusion at the mention of Miri and Zak, Val reverted to Borg Guard 80047. "I'll take some those orange things with no bugs, please."

"They comes with bugs and dirt out of the ground, not all ground up in your nutrition pills, Borgie."

To Val's amazement, the farmer burst into laughter. He was about to say laughter wasn't allowed on city streets, and then he realized that it was. A crowd gathered around them wanting to hear the joke and when they heard the farmer's story about bugs and dirt, a huge roar of laughter went around the market.

That was the last time Val inquired about Miri at the market. He decided to go out to the farm to see for himself if Miri preferred Zak to him. He couldn't believe Miri capable of such duplicity, but then, he had no idea how love worked. It was like walking on glass. One wrong step and it broke into a million pieces, never to be put together again. He used an inspection tour of the defenses along the river as an excuse. He had to see Miri again. If she still loved him, he wasn't going to leave her alone anymore. If he couldn't be with her, then Mediah and Androz would have to settle their differences by themselves. He was just afraid that as power hungry as they both were, they would resort to war to get the upper hand.

When he told Androz he was leaving on an inspection tour, the general burst into a hearty laugh. "Well, I wondered when you were going to get around to seeing that girl again. Don't let your mother know, or she'll come up with something to keep you in the city. Take a couple of Guards along, though. There's still a lot of bandits out there."

Without the Triumvirate's rigid standards, barring humans from the Academy, Androz had allowed anyone to enroll, including humans and mutants.

Val chose a couple of human Guards he knew well and set out along the river in two official robocars belonging to the Academy. They flew a little above the rutted road, avoiding holes that would have swallowed up the entire car.

As he neared the farm, he was surprised by how much progress he saw along the way. Instead of going through the formidable Churn, the Rye River now ran smoothly through the broad fields, irrigating small farms with neat houses and barns. The eternal clouds over the city had lifted, revealing the few tall buildings that still stood in brilliant flashes of sunlight. Flights of birds soared up as the three robocars passed, keeping close to the ground.

They entered a makeshift camp that had sprung up in the months after the siege, full of shelters made of whatever the refuges could find. Walls were rubble, and pieces of metal served as roofs to keep the damp out. Since the road narrowed, the two Guards dropped back behind Val as he led the way, slowing down, so as to avoid people crossing the road. They were just about to the other side of the settlement when they nearly ran into a barricade of cement blocks. Val tried to lift the robocar above it but just then a rope with a boat hook tied to the end caught his vehicle, bouncing it back into the vehicle behind him.

The crash jarred him into losing consciousness for a

minute or two. In that brief interval, a gang of Grays rushed to the wreck and pulled him out of the vehicle.

"Don't hurt him, boys," shouted a familiar voice. "We want him in one piece so his mommy'll give anything to get him back." It was Sargon, his grizzled face sneering from his gray hood as he thrust his face close to Val's.

"Don't count on it," Val spat back. "General Androzarian will hunt you down for this, Sargon, like a dog hunting a rat."

"Guess again, Lover Boy. See that robocar behind you, the one with your two friends in it?" It was then Val saw that the second robocar was empty. "They bailed back in the village. The car's been on auto pilot ever since. See, you can't trust nobody, even people you think are your friends. Don't it hurt, though?" Sargon pressed his face closed to Val, so close Val could smell the Swaug on the crime king's breath. "And that rat of a son of mine has gone off with your girlfriend, ain't that sad?"

"I don't believe you, Sargon. You wouldn't know the truth if it hit you between the eyes."

In reply, Sargon pressed a button on his belt. Val recognized it as his own that he had given Miri. Androz's familiar voice boomed out across the quiet countryside. "When you've got him, just keep him there, Sargon. Then we'll see what Mediah will give for him. Once we have her in a corner, she'll bargain, that's for sure. Afterward, just dispose of him. Tie a couple a cement blocks to him and chuck him in the river. The other two won't talk. I'll buy their silence with promotions. Then you can operate freely. Take whatever you want, it's yours, just as long as I'll be in charge."

"That's your boss, sonny." Sargon's beady eyes had a deadly light in them. "And you thought you and your ma was going to reform Megacity. Only we want it exactly the way it was before you decided to tear it up. Take him away, boys," was the last thing Val heard before Sargon hit him over the head.

Sargon was so engrossed in gloating over his captive, he and the men gathered around Valerian didn't notice two dark figures sneaking between the huts and running down to the river.

The people of the Hollow were just sitting down to a fine breakfast, which had turned into an equally sumptuous lunch when the first drone came over, dropping a torch bomb. Nearby trees became fiery candles and the tunnels of the Hollow below ground were filled with smoke.

Luckily, the residents, including the children, loved to eat and were in the dining room when the drone struck. The emergency doors were closed and Dr. Spencer had to take a back passage filled with pots and pans from the kitchen back to his laboratory. When he got there, he raised his telescope to see four more drones approaching, all carrying torch bombs. He trained his demagnetizer on them and fired, but this time, it didn't work. The drones kept coming.

Then he recalled telling Androzarian how it worked. In a split second, he moved to another machine, one that wasn't quite finished. There were wires sticking out all over and he wasn't sure it would work. But if not, one more torch bomb would finish Yop's Hollow and most of the people in it.

He pressed a red button and there was a blinding flash. The last thing he remembered was sailing through the air. When he woke up, Spencer was against the opposite wall, gasping for air. Yop's big red face was all he saw.

"You okay, Doc?"

"That is an illogical question, Yop. Would I be lying

on the floor if I were okay? Help me get to my feet, will you? I want to assess the damage."

"There ain't nothing much to assess," said Yop. "Few trees burnt to matchsticks. Nobody's hurt. C'mon let's celebrate."

Spencer shook his head to clear it. He couldn't believe his ears. "But the other four drones. Didn't they drop their torch bombs?"

"Just went poof, they did! Like fireworks in the night 'cept it was broad daylight. Didn't you see them? Must've malfunctioned or whatever them things do when they don't work." Yop looked at the scientist and his nut-brown eyes slowly widened. "You mean, them exploding was your doing? Dingy-dong-dang and little string beans, Doc. You're a genius! Imagine you down here under the ground and them flying up there like buzzards. And you just—poof, poof, poof. Just like that. Lemme go tell everybody so we can celebrate! Break out the elderberry wine." Yop went away, saying "poof" with every stride down the passageway.

Spencer just sat down in a chair and looked at the second machine. It was the anti-demagnetizer he was working on with Val before Androz and Mediah had arrived. He had put it aside when they arrived and only discussed the first invention with Androz. He had thought the general was not scientifically advanced enough to understand how it operated, and could have kicked himself for underestimating him.

Probably Androz had just told someone the basics, probably someone like Mercator who as far as he knew was still imprisoned at the Academy.

Where was Val? Mediah had said she would send him back as soon as it was safe, but it had been months since then and still no Val.

There was a knock on the door and Thur looked in.

"I think you ought to come see who has arrived with news."

"Valerian? Is it my son?"

Thur shook his head, his expression grim. "Afraid not. Come see for yourself."

Standing at attention when Spencer came into the dining room were the two Guards who had been with Valerian. Their faces were blackened and they were wearing dark cloaks over their bright uniforms. They said Androzarian had taken them aside and told them about the plot to seize Valerian.

"But he made it sound like it had been discovered," said the taller one named Dax. "Then we were told to bail when we got to the squatters' camp along the river. We thought Val had got the same orders we did, but he went ahead and was captured by Sargon."

"What are your names so I know who to thank for this unfortunate news?"

"My name is Dax. I believe you've met my father, Rufus. And this is Oti. We've known Val since first class at the Academy."

"Dax, Oti, I thank you for risking everything to come here and give me this news. So Androzarian is turning on Mediah and Val is caught in between those two ambitious persons. I was afraid this would happen. That's why the drones were unleashed against us just now. To eliminate us as a threat to Androz's takeover." Dr. Spencer clasped his hands behind his back, and began pacing around the dining room tables, shaking his head. The people seated at the tables watched as he went by them, their heads turning to watch him like flowers following the sun.

Thur stopped Spencer as he passed. "Then I say let's go rescue Val! Who's with me? Dax, Oti, will you show us where Sargon's camp is?"

The two Guards looked at each other and nodded.

"Oti will show where they captured Val. I have to go warn my father the Grays are planning on taking the farm back and enslaving all the workers."

But Oti was steadfast. "Yes, I'll go with you. Val is my friend and I hate what that scum might be doing to him."

Dr. Spencer winced and Annabeth jumped up, putting her tiny hand in his. "Come sit by me and tell me stories," she said, pulling him to a table.

Thur gathered Loki, Chez, and Skye around him in a huddle—while in a corner of the vast dining room, Gof watched, nodding his approval.

"Oh, don't look so pleased with yourself, you old vagabond," Aya snapped like a little dog nipping at his heels. "I've lost one son, now I might lose another, and you're sitting there, nodding like it's all a ball game. All in fun! You men think war is a game, all of you!"

"Calm yourself, old woman," Gof replied. "I've lost two bairns myself so you're none up on me. That boy's a born leader, he is. He'll do what his heart tells him to do and no other."

Thur left with Oti and the others, after dropping a kiss on Aya's cheek. "I'll be back and I'll bring Val back with me, you'll see, Aya. Don't look so sad. Remember, he saved us all, and we owe him our lives."

Aya nodded, clasping his hand. "Come back safe," was all she could choke out.

Then he turned to Gof who gave him a kind of salute, arm across the chest, fist against the heart. Thur imitated the same gesture, surprised at how right it felt. They finished with a nod of the head, as if they had agreed on something silently.

⋘⋙

Val woke up in the dark. Somewhere he could hear

water dripping and he smelled the river nearby. Then he heard a whisper.

"Shhh."

"Who's there?"

"For pity's sake, shut up!" He thought he recognized the voice. Then nimble fingers sawed at the thick ropes tying his wrists together.

"Thanks." This time he whispered.

When whoever it was moved around to untie his feet, he realized by the graceful way she moved, it was a girl. It wasn't Miri, however.

"Now follow me out of this hole." Holding his hand, she led Val to an opening through which he could smell fresh air. "You're so tall, you'll have to crawl on your belly like a snake, Val. Sorry about your uniform," she said with a subdued laugh. "But I'll have to get on my hands and knees like a pig. Ready?"

At her signal, they both wiggled out through the hole and stayed down in the mud, looking to see if was safe to get to their feet.

Then she grasped his hand. "Run!"

They ran between the buildings down to the river where there was a rowboat moored to a pylon.

"Get in and lie down." The girl cut the rope with her knife and got in, pulling a cover over their heads. "They teach you know how to swim at the Academy?"

"Of course," he said. Her face was inches from his in the dark. "Do I know you?"

"It's Gelise. From the Hollow? The one that always thought you were a spy for the Borgs."

"Gelise! But I thought you were—"

The girl beside was quiet for a few minutes. "I wish I was. See, after I was hit by a blast from a lazorizer, I was knocked unconscious and floated down the river. I guess I washed up on the city side. Anyway, that's where Sargon's men found me and pulled me out of the water like a piece of trash. Turns out that's the way they treated me. Like garbage." Gelise turned her face away from Val's eyes. "Anyway, we're going to row across—"

"Look out," a voice yelled. "Steer away, steer away, you idiot!"

The yelling was followed by a bone-rattling crash that splintered their rickety craft, throwing them both into the water. In the dark, Gelise swam to the other side.

When Val surfaced again, he found himself nearly face to face with Thur who was having trouble swimming in the frigid water. "Be still, I'll take you to shore," Val said.

"We were coming to rescue you. Now you're rescuing me. I can't win." Thur tried a few strokes but it was useless against the strong current. He relaxed, letting Val's powerful strokes take him back to shore.

"We? Who's we?"

Thur was amazed that Val could talk and swim at the same time. "Your Borgie friend Oti and a couple of boys from the Hollow. But you got free by yourself."

They reached the muddy bank and hauled themselves out of the water. "Not quite. Gelise freed me and got me out. Otherwise, they were planning to kill me,"

Thur shook the wet hair out of his eyes. "Wait a minute, Val. Did you just say Gelise?"

"I did and now, we'd better get out of here before the Grays come looking for me. I mean us."

The two ran along the river bank. It was dark except for a few fires burning in the squatters' camps. At one of those ramshackle settlements, they saw a little group huddled around some smoldering logs, dripping wet. They looked up as Val and Thur approached them, smiling and then bursting into laughter.

"We thought we'd lost you, you son of a Borgie!"

Val and Oti embraced, leaving Thur to shake hands with Skye and Loki. Gelise was standing alone at the edge of the shadows, watching them. Just as she was turning to leave, Thur caught her by the arm.

"Gelise! Is it really you?"

She recoiled as if he had burned her. "Don't! Don't touch me!" she screamed so loudly that the other men turned to look at them. Seeing all the men were looking at her, her eyes filled with angry tears and she ran away into the darkness.

Thur started to run after her. "Gelise, wait! I didn't mean to—"

Val stopped him with a word. "Don't. Not now, Thur. Let her calm down. She's had a bad time of it."

Thur looked baffled. "I was just going to tell her how happy I am that she's alive, that's all. Didn't mean to scare her. She's acting like she's afraid of me or something. What's wrong with her?"

"She'd better tell you herself," was all Val said. "Now, we'd better get out of here before the Grays come."

"Let them. We're ready for them." Oti got out his lazorizer. "And I'd also like to personally thank General Androzarian for setting us up. And you."

"Later, after we've made sure those at the Farm are safe from Sargon." Val went silent, thinking that what had happened to Gelise could happen to Miri and all the women at the farm. "Oti, when did Dax leave for the farm?"

"About four hours ago, give or take a half hour. He had to walk, after all."

"If I know Dax, he ran most of the way. He was always the fastest one in the Academy, for sure. We're not going to get there nearly as fast, especially with the Grays' camp between us and the farm." Val was shaking his head when Gelise came to the edge of the firelight. It was only then Val saw the bruises and that both eyes were blackened and swollen.

Before Val could stop him, Thur said, "Gelise, who did that to you?"

But the girl ignored him, raising her chin defiantly. "I'll show you how to get to the farm faster than you can walk. And safer, too."

"Then let's go!" they all said. All except Thur until Val nudged him.

Thur looked away, hiding the tears in his eyes. "But I'm going to come back for whoever did that to you, Gelise."

They were halfway across the makeshift bridge that had been put together from wreckage salvaged from the river when a blast from a lazorizer shot the raft out from under Skye. The water rushed through, creating a gap that sent the boy plunging into the river. Val, who was behind him, managed to grasp hold of his shirt before he was swept away.

On the other side, Oti grabbed Skye's arm and hauled him up on the wooden boat which held them both until Loki could pass the boy to Thur and hurry across to the other side. Val leaped to the boat just as the shattered raft sank, but the boat, too, began to drift away in the current. Thur, who, had reached the opposite shore, deposited Skye on the ground to choke up river water. Turning around to see if Loki and Val were safely across, he saw Val taking fire from across the river while struggling to make the next section of the bridge. Thur rushed back to help and locked hands with Val just as the boat overturned in the fast current. Val managed to pull himself up and on his feet.

"Run!" he shouted. "This whole thing is breaking up!"

They both managed to reach solid ground as all but
the pylons of the old bridge washed away. "That's the
second time you've rescued me. Thank you, Thur."

"No, I ran into you on the river. You pulled me to
shore, remember? And it was Gelise who rescued you
from Sargon's camp, not me. And you rescued Skye so it
just proves Yop is right. If we stick together, we can do
great things."

It was Val's turn to laugh. "How is the old fellow?
We could use some of his famous hospitality about now."

"Your wish is my command," said a booming voice
behind him. "Welcome back to Trezarium, Valerian
Spencer."

Yop's rotund figure emerged from the shadows, followed by men armed with all sorts of equipment—clubs
to lazorizers, oak shields to the light shields capable of
repelling lazorizer fire. There were women among them,
carrying trays of food and cups of Yop's elderberry wine.
They also had a basket of clothes for the refugees with
them, from which Val and Skye were able to find some
dry things to change into.

"We couldn't let our boys take on Sargon by themselves, so we were coming to help," Yop said, indicating
the armed men behind him in the dark, with a sweep of
his hand. "Your friend Dax was here and delivered the
news of your capture. Those boys volunteered to rescue
you. Put us all to shame, they did. So some more went
with Dax since he was a stranger traveling through the
Trezarium at night. And the rest came with me."

Skye's Traveler father grabbed his son by the arm.
"Oh, no. you don't, my boy. You come with me and
leave these fools to fight their own battles. They don't
have anything to do with us. We Travelers don't need
nobody."

Skye looked at his father contemptuously. "These

fools, as you call them, have twice saved my life, once from starving to death and once from drowning. That's more good than you have done in your whole worthless life, Father. Yes, I am going with them to defend the people at the farm that you made a living stealing from. It's time I learned how to give back because you never taught me."

"And you are welcome to come along, my friend Skye." Val looked over at Thur and Oti who nodded. "Then let's go give them a hand. Gelise was just going to be our guide—"

Immediately, there was a chorus from the men gathered around them. "Gelise?"

"Yes," said Thur. "She's right there, behind you."

But Gelise had vanished into the trees.

"Maybe you saw her ghost," somebody called, but no one laughed.

The sky was beginning to glow in the east when Yop's army set out on the Forever Road through the trees in the Trezarium. Val and Oti caught on to the rhythm of catching the ropes swung back by the man in front of them.

"This is a lot more fun than a robocar," Oti called, finding his footing on a branch of a sturdy oak tree.

"Unless you land on a branch that won't hold you," the man yelled back.

He was interrupted by a loud crack as the branch gave way under Oti's feet. The Academy cadet let out a yell as he plunged down two more branches until he got his footing again. He looked back to see the rope he had advanced on dangling uselessly down, leaving the next man without a way through the trees. A girlish giggle echoed through the canopy of leaves somewhere overhead as though the trees were laughing at his clumsiness.

"Sorry," he said, but only got a cheerful "Not to worry, mate" in reply.

The man scrambled down the tree like a squirrel and was back up again with the rope between his teeth in seconds. "If I had done something like that at the Academy, they would have called me a Reject and sent me to the Flyover," Oti told Val when he caught up with him. "Humans are a lot more forgiving."

"Some are, some not," Val replied. "Like Skye said back at the river, it all depends on what you've been taught."

High up in another tree, watching proudly as Thur led the way with swift confidence, swinging through the trees, Gelise overheard the conversation. *Easy for you to say,* she thought.

Across the river, Miri and Qin were getting the lessons ready for their students. Most were just learning how to read and write, even the oldest ones who were nearly grown. The students were eager to learn the new skill and were especially in awe of their teachers who could read them about the history of humans.

In the middle of a lesson about the vast Roman Empire, a little girl raised her hand. "You mean we weren't always slaves, miss?"

Qin looked at Miri who was thinking the same thing. They had never been slaves, thanks to Aya, and so they were appalled at the idea. But this child seemed to think it was every human's future—her future.

"No, not if you learn to read and write." Qin's voice shook with tears. "Then you won't be anybody's slave. You will always be free."

"And you will have skills that no one else in Megacity has," Miri added. "They counted on computers to tell them everything, even if it was wrong. So let's get to work now or some of you will run out of time."

The hardest thing for the sisters to do, besides borrowing all the books from Yop's Hollow, was trying to convince the fathers to spare their children from working in the fields. "Just four hours a day, two in the morning and two in the late afternoon," they pleaded. "That will be enough to give them a start."

"But what good will learning to read and write do if all they need to learn is farming?" Rufus shook his head. "And the girls need to learn cooking and cooing, that's what. No one wants a wife that can't cook. No offense intended but you can't expect a man to eat them books, now can you?"

"Just a minute." Pier held up one hand as if to stop Rufus's objections. "My Nadja happens to be smart as a whip. She knows a lot more than you or me, that's for sure. I don't want her to grow up like we did, just knowing farming. Look at these girls here." He indicated Miri and Qin, who had spectacles made out of two magnifying glasses Dr. Spencer had welded together for her. Miri called her Owl Woman. "They know how to read and write as well as defend themselves. And this one," he gestured at Qin, "came up with idea for that Ha-Ha thing that helped us defeat the Borgs. Now that's something I never would have thought of, would you? My point is, they know how to think for themselves not have somebody tell them what to do. That's what I want for my Nadja." Pier jerked his head in the direction of the girls. "To be like them."

Miri and Qin looked at him in amazement. Nobody had ever told them they were special, not even Aya, who treated all her children as equals. "Would you mind saying that to the other parents, Pier?" Qin asked.

And Pier did just that, holding the first meeting of what was to become The Rye River School.

School was just beginning the morning the Grays invaded. With the guides from the Hollow, Dax arrived with his warning that Sargon was on his way. But the wily drumman was already sneaking across the fields with his pack of Grays, moving like worfels, toward the men working there. Rufus was in the chicken shed, overseeing the collection and cleaning of the eggs when he felt the barrel of a lazorizer in his back.

"Don't move, fatty or you're dead," a Gray growled in his ear.

He was marched outside where he could see through the foggy morning air his son Dax coming across the field to greet him.

"Stop, son," he shouted.

Then a blow on Rufus's head sent him to the ground unconscious. However, the warning was out and the farmers just reporting for work fled back to the safety of the buildings. With the honed reflexes of an Academy cadet, Dax dropped and rolled down into a shallow drainage ditch as the Grays came running across the field, weapons drawn. He caught the foot of first Gray jumping the ditch bringing him down and grabbing his weapon. A blow to the head finished the job as the next Gray jumped the ditch.

Qin was in the middle of a reading lesson when one of the Grays burst through the door. "Well, this is a pretty sight, this is. All the little chicks left on their own. Line up, you little dirtballs or I'll put an end to youze!" he bawled at the top of his lungs, waving his lazorizer around.

Qin calmly closed her book and the students did the same. She turned her owl glasses on the Gray. "You don't have to shout, we're not deaf. Do as he says, students. Line up."

A little boy raised his hand. "I have to go pee, Miss Qin. Bad."

Qin looked at the Gray who looked confused. "What's he want?" he asked

The children giggled as Qin explained.

The Gray shook his head. "I don't know about that stuff. I'm a mutie, myself. Go on with you, then, boy. Mind you come right back."

The child ran back to the book room where Miri was stacking new books. He held his finger to his lips and whispered, "Grays!"

Together they climbed out a back window only to see the rest of the children and Qin, with a Gray behind them, marching across the fields toward the office. Coming up behind the school building, Dax and the rest of the men from the Hollow took Miri by surprise. With swift reflexes, she caught Dax in the chest with a powerful kick, knocking him flat.

"Hey, we're the good guys!" One of the men with Dax helped him get to his feet. "We were coming to warn you about Sargon, but I see we're too late."

"Sorry." Miri managed to look apologetic. "Reflex action, I guess."

"Val better not to move too fast, then." Dax gestured at the vanishing class Qin was herding into the office, with Sargon right behind her. "Where's he taking them?"

Miri explained the layout of the farm buildings. "It's the only one that's fortified, I'm afraid. I heard you mention Val. I don't suppose he came with you, did he?"

Briefly, Dax explained how General Androzarian arranged the ambush, and ordered him and Oti to go along with it. "I always thought he couldn't be trusted. Now, I know why."

"We going to stand here all day chewing the fat or are we going to do something?"

The men looked around to see who was speaking. It was Thur, at the head of a dozen more men.

Before anyone react, Dax grabbed Miri by the hand. "Drones! Get inside, everybody! Fast!"

"That's a Jetstar with them. You never could tell a Jetstar from a drone, you robo half-wit." It was Oti. In the schoolhouse, the two friends gave each other back slaps. "We thought you could use some help."

Miri threaded her way through the crowd to give Thur a hug. "Sargon's got Qin and the children in the office. I'm so afraid of what he'll do."

Thur extracted himself from her embrace. "We're going to give him a little surprise party like the one he gave Val. We're crashing in."

Crouched in the small wooden school building, Dax and Oti watched through the window as the squadron came into view. Oti's prediction was right, it was a Jetstar flanked by at least a dozen drones, all carrying missiles.

"That's not General Androzarian's Star! That's Mediah's insignia!"

Everyone looked up from the floor to see who the speaker was, but Miri knew the voice instantly. "Val? Where are you?"

"He's gone," Thur said.

"What?" Miri looked at him in disbelief. "Was he with you all the time? Why didn't he say anything? Why didn't any of you let me know he was here?"

Thur and Oti just looked at her and then at each other. But Dax said, "I guess he wanted to test my loyalty. To see if I was in on Androzarian's plot all the time." From their silence, it was clear questions about Dax's loyalty had been on everyone's mind.

Mediah's Jetstar sat straight down on the open field. As she stepped out, a dirty man dressed in animal skins ran up and she pulled out a miniature lazorizer. "Stay where you are, you animal, or you'll end up as fertilizer for one of your infernal trees."

Val stopped, holding up both hands. "Mediah, don't you recognize me? It's Val."

Mediah lowered her weapon and peered at him. "Val? I'm so relieved you're safe, though I should have known the likes of Androz and Sargon couldn't hold you prisoner for long." He was about to tell her Gelise had freed him, but she brushed aside any protests. "I'm surprised you recognized me, though." Her face was concealed behind a mask with a miniature oxygen container in the pocket of her immaculate white flight suit. A tail of long blonde curls attached to her helmet was draped coquettishly over one shoulder.

"As if you could go anywhere unrecognized, Mediah." It was Valerian's turn to smile. "Your insignia of office is everywhere, even on your flight suit."

"Oh, that," she said nonchalantly. "Well, you want people to know who's in charge, don't you?" Reaching inside the plane and taking out a flight bag, she tossed him a mask. "Here, get this on before—"

Lazor fire came from the buildings as Grays came running across the open field toward them. Calmly, Mediah clicked a small instrument in her hand and the drones, hovering overhead turned sharply toward the oncoming men.

Just as the Jetstar came under fire, the drones lowered their missiles and a soft mist settled on Grays who instantly dropped to the ground. The drones continued to spray the Farm buildings circling the office three times. They circled the farm buildings, spraying each one as they passed.

Val watched in horror as cows were transfixed in sleep. Chickens fell over where they stood. "What are you doing, Mother? There're children in there!"

Mediah smiled. "That's the first time you've called me 'mother.' And don't worry, it's only your Uncle Mercator's idea of non-violent pest control. It's a harmless sleeping gas. Takes the edge off things, you might say. But you had better get your friends out of those buildings before Sargon and his men wake up. Because I'm going to teach that son of a drumman a lesson he'll never forget."

As he jumped down from the Jetstar, Val's protective mask muffled his voice. "Promise you won't do anything until I get back!"

"I will promise only if you'll call me mother one more time." But Val didn't answer her. He was running toward the building where they had taken the children. Mediah smiled and sighed. "One day."

Seeing Val emerge charging toward the office, the others left the school and followed him across the fields. They circled Mediah's Jetstar, afraid she would give them the same treatment as the cows, though they had covered their faces with rags.

Mediah climbed back aboard the Jetstar to signal Dr. Spencer that everything was going smoothly when a girl in tattered clothes appeared at the bottom of the ramp. "Hello, bald lady," she said.

Mediah grabbed her weapon which she kept close by, but the girl didn't flinch or move.

"Go ahead, kill me. I'd rather be dead anyway."

"Why do you say that, girl? Don't I know you?" Mediah snapped her fingers. "Wild child! The one who drained my swimming pool. Now I remember! You look just as awful as you did then when you were with that boy. What was his name?"

Gelise shook her head and looked down. Mediah thought she was going to leave. "Wait, girl. Come aboard, but let me spray first."

Gelise gestured at the sleeping Grays. "Like you sprayed them?"

"No, just for germs. And odor. You smell like…I don't know. Like the earth or something." Mediah sprayed a perfumed mist from the console. "Now, that's better. Come up and sit there, girl." She pointed to a seat well away from her.

Gelise still hesitated. "Why? You ought to hate me for emptying your pool. And crashing your flying thing."

Mediah pointed to the sleeping Grays. A few were stirring groggily. "For one thing because those drumman dirtballs are waking up, and I'm going to blast them as soon as Val rescues the children. And for another, I want to find out why you say you wish you were dead. Two very good reasons. Now I don't have time for small talk. Either you get in or run for your life. Your choice."

Gelise climbed into the cabin of the Jetstar, although she was careful to sit just inside the door. "Smells like spring in here," she said.

Mediah looked up from the console where she was pushing a number of buttons. "What's spring?"

Gelise smiled, her white teeth shining in her dirty face. "It's when birds sit on their nest and everything starts making flowers. Bees start buzzing and fish start jumping. The whole world comes alive again." She looked down, suddenly shy. Mediah was looking at her critically.

"Sounds out of control to me," Mediah said, turning back to her console where buttons were flashing steadily.

"Oh, it is." Gelise burst into a giggle. "It's wild. Like me."

Mediah didn't smile, but now studied the girl beside her openly. "There aren't many wild things left and all there are stay here in Trezarium. Sargon wants to hunt them all down and kill them. My son Val loves a girl who stays here so I have to keep it safe for them. What about you and that boy you were with when Androz brought you to my place?"

"Thur?" Gelise shook her head. "He will never look at me that way again."

"But you like him. I could see it in your face. If you were cleaned up a bit. Do something with your hair…"

Gelise stood up, despair dripping from her like rain. "You don't understand," she said. "I'm dirt so I'll stay dirty."

Just then they were jolted as something hit the Jetstar. Turning on the surround cameras, Mediah found herself looking straight at a lazor cannon. Behind it were Sargon and a bunch of Grays.

"Hold on." she said. With the flick of a switch, the Jetstar lifted straight up, firing down at the attackers as it went. They were blasted into cinders.

Gelise whooped with delight. "You did it! You smoked them, bald lady!"

"My name is Mediah," Mediah said, as she circled field, picking off any Grays who lifted a weapon. "What's yours?"

"Gelise." The girl clapped her hands in delight. "There's another one about to fire. Can I have a go at that?"

Mediah patted the seat beside her. "Come on up, Gelise. Let's see what kind of a pilot you'd make. I could use one I could trust, not anyone like that reptile Androz would send me."

Mediah turned over the co-pilot's controls to Gelise and together they circled the field, shooting at any of Sargon's men who tried to interfere with Val and the others carrying the children back to the school building. Miri and Qin were running, behind the others, each carrying a child and holding the hand of another when a Gray got to his feet, lifting his weapon. But Gelise was too fast for him and zapped him before he could pull the trigger.

"Good shot!" Mediah looked at the girl beside her with new eyes. "I could turn you into a first class pilot in no time. You've got what it takes."

"If it means flying one of these, it beats swinging the Forever Road any day. Hey, there's another dirtball!" Gelise spotted a man in a gray hood running from a barn. She made the Jetstar turn at a sharp right angle and, suddenly, they were upside down in the skyflying along only a few feet above the ground, barely avoiding a sleeping cow.

Just as Mediah righted the Jetstar, a shadow passed over head. "What'd I do?" yelled the terrified girl. "What was that?"

"I forgot to warn you," Mediah said calmly. "It rolls over like that sometimes. Comes in handy when there is someone above you."

"I mean something flew overhead when we were upside down. Was it a Fluglitz?"

Mediah turned the plane around. Now the field was full of people running in all directions as wild-looking men on scooters flew through the air. Some had landed, doing combat with Sargon's men. "Holy slitz! Those are Jetsters! Looks like the warriors have arrived."

Gelise let out another earsplitting whoop . "It's Mako and his clan! Come to the rescue."

Mediah was less than pleased. "So I see. Some rescue. It looks more like a mob of angry bushes than a rescue."

When they had landed, Gelise leaned over and hugged Mediah. "Thank you for letting me fly your plane, Mediah. It was the mostest fun I ever had. Especially when we were upside down."

Mediah gave the girl an appraising look. "You weren't afraid when we rolled over?"

Gelise shook her head. "Not a bit. I thought it was cool."

"Then you can have the job of piloting for me. But you will have to come to the city. I can't be out here all the time. I have to be where everyone can see me. Besides, since Chief Mako is on the temporary council, I imagine he will need a pilot, too. He can't keep flying that outdated piece of junk around the city. Someone might mistake him for a Fluglitz and shoot him down."

Gelise rubbed her hand lovingly over the shiny console. "I don't know. Mako doesn't think girls can do much."

Making a sound of disgust, Mediah dismissed the comment. "What do you expect from a barbarian? We'll show him, won't we? Besides, there were plenty of witnesses today—"

They were startled by loud hammering on the door. Glancing at the side camera, Mediah saw Valerian carrying a girl and Miri behind him with the children. She pushed a button to raise the hatch and Val stuck his head in the doorway.

"That was some flying, Mother. Here take the children inside, will you? Qin's had a noseful of Mercator's pest spray and feeling sick. Miri will take care of the children." As Val helped the girls aboard, he saw Gelise beside Mediah. "Having fun riding with Mediah? She's quite a pilot, isn't she?"

He was gone before they could correct him. Telling Gelise to look after the children, Miri scrambled down from the Jetstar and ran after Val. "Where are you going? Wait for me!"

With his mask pulled up over his face, his voice came back muffled. "To find Zak, Miri. It's too dangerous for you . Go back, will you?"

"No, I won't, not when you've got that look on your face."

"You can't even see my face."

"Your voice, then. It's in your voice."

"Go back and wait in the school then. Only stay out of the way."

She kept following him as he strode across the field, skirting bodies of Grays, some moving and groaning. "What do you want with Zak? I think he was in the office when the Grays invaded."

"You think he was?" Val stopped and turned, pulling down his mask. "Are you defending him?"

Looking up at him, she could only remember the way she felt when he first kissed her. The memory was so vivid, so disconcerting that Miri struggled to regain her composure. "Only because you're so angry and might do something you're sorry for," she said in a softer, sweeter voice. "Tell me why are you so angry with Zak?"

If she hoped he would say because of Zak's obvious affection for her, she was disappointed. If that were the reason, Valerian wouldn't admit it, even to himself. "I'll tell you why. Because he and his father set up this whole thing with General Androzarian—the ambush, my kidnapping, the plan to takeover this place. It was all Sargon's plan and Zak went along with it."

"If Zak was in on this plot, what proof do you have, Val? I mean I know he's Sargon's son but he said he was through with Sargon's shady deals. You heard him yourself—"

His anger was like a freezing fire. "Oh, you believed that, did you? I haven't got time to stand around debating his innocence. Meanwhile he'll get away. I've got to go. Go back to the schoolhouse, Miri. At least there, you'll stay out of trouble."

As she watched him run back across the field, Miri

felt an emptiness in her chest, as though her heart had gone with him. She was too surprised to let anger fill the gap.

When he got back to the control room, Val found Zak was gone. In fact, no one had seen him since before Sargon and the Grays had invaded. "What do you want Zak for?" Pier asked him. "You think he was in on Sargon's plan?"

"I'd just like to ask him a few questions, that's all."

Rufus left the security cameras long enough to join them. "I'll see if I can answer for him," he said, "since I doubt you'll get the truth from young Zak. The apple don't fall far from the tree, or so they say."

"Did anything unusual happen yesterday or the day before? Anything that could have put the farm at risk?"

Pier and Rufus looked at each other and back at Val. "Yes, now that you mention it. The security cameras went off yesterday and were down for about two hours until Pier got them running again."

"That would give them enough time to move their men into position. Anything else?"

"There was the wedding dinner." Rufus looked embarrassed. "Everybody drank too much ."

Pier clapped his old friend on the back. "Including you."

"The groom had the perfect excuse to get drunk. You see, I and Miri's mother got hitched. That's why everybody was at the party. She'll be a perfect mother to my little Nadja and Dax will have two more sisters. Ain't that some kind of a deal now? Three for the price of one."

"They're not potatoes, Rufus." Pier could see Val was even grimmer than before.

"But you endangered the whole village by getting drunk. I suppose the security cameras were off while you carousing around."

Pier looked at Rufus and they both nodded. "But a man is entitled to marry, ain't he? A man needs a wife and a family, don't he?"

"Not if he puts them in danger he doesn't." Val turned on his heel and walked out of the Control Room, leaving Pier and Rufus staring after him.

"What do you expect from a Borgie? He's got no idea what I'm talking about."

So Miri had tried to cover him, saying she thought he was in the control room when the Grays invaded. Valerian tried to brush the thought from his mind like an annoying fly, but it just came back again.

As he crossed the field in the early morning sun, he saw a familiar figure coming toward him through the mist. As he got closer, he saw it was Dax, accompanied by a strange group. Behind him were Sargon and Zak, shuffling through the mud, their hands tied behind their backs. Behind them were Oti and Thur, each with their lazorizers pointed at the fugitives. Behind them, were assorted farmers and warriors from Mako's clan, all armed with pitchforks and clubs.

Behind them, following at a distance was Miri.

The two friends greeted each other with a clap on the shoulder. "We caught them running toward the river where they had a boat waiting." Dax nodded at the prisoners. "Zak swears he didn't know Androz was behind it all. Just that Sargon was going to steal some food. Naturally, the old man won't do anything but snarl. Anyway, I couldn't make it all out. Maybe you'll have better luck, Val."

"We'll take Sargon back to the city in Mediah's plane. These men can think of a fit punishment for Zak, can't you, men?" Val asked, addressing the farmers guarding the prisoners as though they would like to skewer them on the end of their pitchforks. Val grinned.

"I'll bet you will." Turning to Dax and Oti, he said, "We'd better get going. Mediah can only spend so much time surrounded by birds and trees. She says the tweeting gets on her nerves."

Dax shook his head. "I'm not going back to Megacity, Val. My father and little sister are here and a whole new family I didn't even know about until last night."

Miri stepped proudly forward to slip her arm through Dax's. "He means Qin and I are his new sisters since my mother married his father last night."

"In that case, I won't go back either," Oti said from behind Sargon, keeping his lazorizer trained on his captive. "I've got my eye on that ginger haired girl who's got all those books. May she can teach me to read."

"You're too dumb, Borgie," Sargon snarled. "I can read and look where it got me."

"Your evil ways got you what's coming to you, Father," Zak shouted as he was led away.

"If that's what you call a family," Sargon said, jerking his head in his son's direction, "I don't know why you'd even bother with one. Absolutely no use at all, if you ask me."

"I'll help you take Sargon back." Thur had been quietly watching as Miri wrapped her arm through Dax's and smiled up at him. "There's nothing to keep me here," he added bitterly.

"Remember what you said to me at the bridge?" Val avoided looking at Dax and Otie. "If we stick together we can do great things."

Thur nodded. "Let's go then."

Sargon piped up in a whining voice, "That's right, can't keep Mommy waiting, can we?"

"I hope there's enough of Mercator's sleeping gas to put you to sleep." Val spun Sargon around and began marching him back across the field to Mediah's Jetstar.

"Otherwise, I'll have to knock you out."

"Wait!" As they passed her, Miri said, "I'm coming with you." She slipped her arm from Dax's. "Is there room for one more? That thing looks awfully small," she said, pointing to the Jetstar.

"Only if you sit in my lap." Val smiled down at her, sending her heart spiraling out of control, rivaling the aerobatics of the Jetstar.

"Now, ain't that sweet?" Sargon said. "She can sit in my lap any day and—" He crumpled under a blow from Val's fist.

"At least he'll be quiet on the ride back to the city." Val slung the drumman over one shoulder and took Miri's hand. "Forgot to tell you, Thur. Gelise is piloting the Jetstar so get ready for the ride of your life."

"Gelise? I didn't know she could fly one of those things." A grin spread slowly across Thur's handsome face. "That girl is full of surprises," he said, shaking his head. Then he glanced at Miri holding Val's hand as if she would never let go. "But aren't they all?"

Val and Miri looked at each other with such love and laughter in their eyes that, in that look, a new age began to dawn.

❦❦

"How do I know all this, an old robot like me? You weren't there, you say, traipsing around the farm in the mud and cow poo. I'm very glad I wasn't, you rude little sprouts. But I heard it from the heroes themselves when they were at their ease, laughing and joking as friends will do. Yes, I knew them all well, from before you were born, you might say.

"Getting restless, are we, little Lord Valerian? You want to go find some cave lynx, you say? That better be all for now. Old Blu, the nanny, has to recharge his batteries to become Blu, the dishwasher and clothes dryer. A robot's work is never done.

"What are batteries, little Lady Galen? That was before your time, dear, as all this story was. In fact, it is your history as told by a grumpy old robot. Go along with all of you now and come back when you want to hear about the new age that was about to dawn. Yes, you're in the story, I promise."

About the Author

Even as a child, Trisha O'Keefe was impressed by the inherent power of alternative medicines. Indigenous healing practices are an ongoing theme in her novels. As a native Southerner, O'Keefe claims to have "a lot of red dirt" flowing in her veins. Growing up, she spent summers on her uncle's farm in South Georgia, "mainly getting into trouble." That trend has continued throughout her life. After traveling abroad for fourteen years, running into revolutions or governmental coups nearly everywhere she went—even Britain was in the midst of a labor strike when she moved there—she returned to the States. She is the daughter of Jimmy Jones, a well-known journalist for the Atlanta Constitution under Editor Ralph Magill.

One of her earliest memories was the sound of a typewriter rattling away in the middle of the night. You would think that would have cured her from ever putting two words together, let alone a book. Still, at age six, she co-wrote *Spot, The Dog* with her sister, followed a long time later by *Hanahatchee, Poseidon's Eye, Lovesong of the Chinaberry Man, The Magi's Well, The Mama Tree* and *Of Unknown Origin*. "I guess some things you can't cure," O'Keefe says. "You just have to go where they take you."